THE
GUIDANCE MANUAL
FOR THE
CHRISTIAN HOME SCHOOL

A Parent's Guide for Preparing
Home School Students for
College or Career

David and Laurie Callihan

CAREER
PRESS
Franklin Lakes, NJ

THE GUIDANCE MANUAL FOR THE CHRISTIAN HOME SCHOOL
Cover design by Foster & Foster
Printed in the U.S.A. by Book-mart Press

To order this title, please call toll-free 1-800-CAREER-1 (NJ and Canada: 201-848-0310) to order using VISA or MasterCard, or for further information on books from The Career Press.

The Career Press, Inc., 3 Tice Road, PO Box 687
Franklin Lakes, NJ 07417
www.careerpress.com

Library of Congress Cataloging-in-Publication Data

Callihan, David.
    The guidance manual for the Christian home school : a parent's guide to preparing home school students for college or career / by David and Laurie Callihan.
        p.   cm.
    Includes index.
    ISBN 1-56414-452-6 (paper)
    1. Home schooling—United States. 2. Christian education—United States. 3. Universities and colleges—United States—Entrance requirements. 4. Vocational guidance—United States. I. Callihan, Laurie. II. Title.

LC40 .C35 2000
371.04'2—dc21   00-036004

ACKNOWLEDGMENTS

This page is probably the hardest for us to write. There are so many people who have influenced our life's journey, and we know we will miss someone along the way. There is no significance to the order in which we thank people; we feel that all of you have been critical to our success.

To our parents, Gene and Alberta Callihan and Hazel Perryman: We want you to know that we love you and are grateful that you have been so supportive of us even when we have not taken the normal routes through life. We thank Laurie's late father, Donald Perryman, who passed on a love for creation and learning.

To our spiritual mentors: Art Rae, M.A. Butler, Dave Coke, Harry Conn, Larry Allen, the late Gordon Olsen, Esther Trice, and Dr. Charles Smith, we thank you for your examples of Christian love, integrity, and wisdom. You prepared us well for the battles of faith we have had to face, and we continue to look to your examples as we follow Christ.

We thank Alan Snyder and Don Manzullo, whose input to this book and our lives has been so valuable. We consider it a privilege to be your friends. Your contributions to this great country of ours deserve an eternal debt of gratitude.

We thank our siblings, who endured us while we were growing up. Don and Gail Perryman showed us it was possible to survive with more than two children. Art and Kris Perryman and Diana Taliaferro witnessed to Laurie, which lead to her commitment to Christ. Phil Taliaferro gave us encouragement and legal help with our book. Sue and Bob Fulmer were there for Laurie when David was gone and were still there for us as family, friends, advisers, and fellow Pitch lovers. Don and Howard Callihan and

Kathy Root put up with a lot when David was growing up, and Danny, David's twin, did so much to make those years memorable.

We thank our college mentors. Neil Frey taught us that there is both an absolute content and source of truth. Dr. Ken Cumming encouraged us and showed us that we could make it against the grain. Dr. Gary Parker still influences our thinking though we see him so rarely, and Dr. Steve Austin shared his knowledge of creation with us. The late Dr. Richard Bliss encouraged Laurie's writing and her love for learning and teaching science.

To our fellow homeschooling parents in the Sauquoit LEAH chapter, who have put up with us for these past five years as we have tried to work together in teaching our children: Without your questions, concerns, support, patience, and love, this book would never have become a reality.

To Paul and Lorraine Matte, who never let us get to sleep before 4 a.m. when they dropped by: We appreciate the conversations and know we have just begun to fight.

We thank Rod, Sharon, Adam, Noah, Caleb, Terry, Michelle, Mike, Jenny, Dave, Debbie, Ed, Karen, Steve, Loretta, Roe, Paul, Laurie, and all of those who were there for us during a very difficult time.

We thank Steve and Cheryl Douglass and their children, who are our forever family in the Lord, no matter how often we get together. We thank Cliff and Julie Normand, who have fought and won along with us so many times. To Randy and Kathy Keeley: Thank you for encouraging us during the hard days and giving our boy a home away from home.

We thank David and Jeanette Durey for encouraging us to set goals and work toward them. To Tom and Maggie Calder who were there at the beginning of our quest for the truth: Where are you guys?

We thank Ron Fry and the Career Press staff, who have taken the risk to go into this new adventure, and who have just begun to become our friends along the way.

Thank you for all being willing to intersect our lives.

And to our children—Jeremiah, Josiah, and Wesley, our boys, who continue to show us that life is an adventure and to make us proud, and Rebekah and Katie, our daughters, who always remind us that beauty is not just skin deep, but also a matter of character and intelligence—we love you very much. You make being parents worth every crazy moment!

Last, we give praise to our Lord and our God, Jesus Christ, who helps us each day to practice our faith and understand what a Christian home school really is.

CONTENTS

FOREWORD

by United States Congressman Donald A. Manzullo

I t is my pleasure to have known Dave and Laurie Callihan for many years. The Callihans have succeeded in addressing in one book why homeschooling is important, whether or not parents should pursue it, and how to do it. These seasoned practitioners discuss the complete spectrum of homeschooling, demonstrating how they decided to homeschool, how they have gone about it, and how they have dealt with the issue of community acceptance, especially regarding the questioned "sociability" of their children.

Not all parents are called to this tough task. My wife, Freda, and I have some close friends who tried it for less than a week, gave up, and enrolled their kids in school. For us and our three children, it has worked with our incredibly demanding congressional schedule, living as we do between homes in Illinois and Washington, D.C. The flexibility homeschooling offers—and Freda's seemingly endless patience—make it a viable option for us. In a sense, we are pioneers: It appears we are the first congressional family to homeschool its children while serving in office.

I have often wanted to put my thoughts on homeschooling down in print. I don't need to anymore, because the Callihans have covered everything in their book.

The Guidance Manual for the Christian Home School

A s parents of five children with an age span of only six years, we have found parenthood to be as inspiring, rewarding, and infuriating as any occupation we could imagine. When the children were ages zero to six, we experienced the most draining *physical* work we have ever encountered. Now that they range in age from 12 to 18, we find the experience incredibly demanding on our *mental* capacities.

The teen years in our household have stretched to the breaking point our abilities to organize, prioritize, reason, and cope. We would like to help other families by sharing our experiences and what we have learned along the way. It is our intent in this book to help other families coordinate all the preparations for the future of their children as painlessly as possible.

We have chosen to speak to Christian homeschoolers in particular, since that is where our heart and expertise lie. In our family, Christ is first. We want to offer options to other Christian families to help them teach their children godliness as they teach them academics and everyday living skills. We are sure that non-Christians will be able to make use of this book, but we do not apologize for our adherence to Scripture, as we understand it, in all areas, including science and philosophy.

The idea to write this book came to Laurie as she spent some time substitute teaching in public high schools. She saw that students were able to get information on colleges, careers, the military, standardized testing, and future planning from their one-stop shop, the school guidance counselor's office. In the many years we have homeschooled, we have found that for homeschoolers, finding this information can take a lot of time. It occurred to Laurie that a book that could serve as a "portable guidance counselor" would be of great value to every homeschooling family. And so this book was born as a one-stop resource for every Christian homeschooling family.

Clearly, homeschooling families tend to be nonconformists. In that spirit, this book will discuss nonstandard routes to higher education and careers, in addition to standard ones. It is our goal to present parents and students the many options available to them. For parents, we provide information and contacts, as well as a master plan for getting through the school years with confidence. Students will find a source of ideas and inspiration on the many options available to them, as well as specific information to help them meet their goals.

You will come to know our family quite well in the following pages, as we use stories of our experiences as inspiration (we hope) and examples for you. For now, let us give you a brief description of ourselves. We (David and Laurie) have been married for more than 20 years and have had the privilege of raising five wonderful children for the Lord. Jeremiah was born in 1981, graduated from our home school in 1999, and is currently accumulating college credits toward a degree in business (he thinks). Rebekah, born in 1982, also finished her high school curriculum in 1999. She plans to graduate this year in the New York State Loving Education At Home (LEAH) commencement in June. She is working on college credits toward a nursing degree. Katie was born in 1984 and finished her high school credits in 1999. She is working on undergraduate credits with eventual hopes of becoming a missionary, youth worker, or veterinarian. In 1985 Josiah was born. He is in our home high school. Josiah is probably headed toward some facet of engineering, science, guitar playing, or basketball (typical teenage boy). Wesley, born in 1987, is beginning home high school this year. Wesley is a gifted singer and actor. You will hear more about all of them in following pages.

Our conviction to homeschool our children actually began before we were married. At that time, homeschooling was not a known option and we had never heard of anyone doing it. However, God clearly revealed His desire to us that we train our children ourselves. We have been committed to homeschooling ever since. We spent a few years as Christian missionaries, during which Laurie taught in a small school with other families taking part. However, we have always remained the primary directors of our children's education. We see homeschooling as a right, responsibility, and privilege of Christian families.

We have been involved in the homeschool movement for 20 years, since before Jeremiah was born. We have been active in support groups for homeschooling families in Illinois, Iowa, Nebraska, New York, Pennsylvania, and Texas. We founded and led our local chapter of the New York State Loving Education at Home organization for almost five years. This is something we continue to do with great excitement because of the support that members provide one another as Christian parents raising our children to be all they can.

We both earned degrees from Christian Heritage College, El Cajon, California, in 1982 (Laurie in biology, David in geophysics). David also earned a degree in theology from San Diego Bible College at the same time. David has continued his education in the professional realm, first as a geophysicist and later as a computer technology specialist. Laurie is pursuing a master's degree in education, as the Lord permits, given her busy schedule as mother, teacher, author, and lecturer.

Before we get into the meat of this book, we want you to know why we think:

Homeschooling is a great learning choice

There are many reasons for homeschooling. We decided to homeschool before our children were even conceived as a result of our personal, spiritual convictions. But, when our children reached the upper grades, we became aware of some distinct advantages of homeschooling—beyond the spiritual realm. While the opportunity to influence your children's spiritual growth is the most important advantage of keeping them in the home, there are also academic and social advantages to doing so. It will be important to capitalize on these advantages as your children near adulthood.

What about socialization?

The most often-cited disadvantage of homeschooling is the supposed lack of socialization. However, we are prepared to attest that one of the most valuable advantages of homeschooling is...socialization! We feel that proper socialization takes place when children learn to relate to people of all ages and socioeconomic groups, as well as to both genders. It includes respect for siblings, parents, friends, and relatives. It means being able to communicate intelligently with adults as well as children.

To our way of thinking, traditional schools diminish proper socialization because they foster peer pressure and discourage cross-age relationships. Siblings are separated according to age and isolated from each other. Children are forced to ally with others of their own age and put their trust in a teacher who knows best how to provide educational material for their intellectual consumption. After six to eight hours in this environment, they are sent back home to live in an environment in the real world that rarely matches this artificial one.

Where in real life are people separated by age? It does not happen anywhere else in our society except in the institutional classroom. Our idea of socializing is spending time as a family with people of all ages. Homeschooling provides superior socialization skills, as children are exposed to real-life situations through family friendships, part-time jobs, and special learning opportunities (tutoring, clubs, organizations, etc.). As they venture out from the homeschool into college, industry, business, the military, or other areas of society, homeschooled children are well rounded and able to cope with real life because they have learned to communicate with others in diverse settings. Clearly, children are best socialized in the homeschool environment.

The power of commitment

We believe our convictions give our children stability in a very unstable world. Our children see the time, money, and energy we have invested in homeschooling, and thus they know they have great value to us. As a result, they have a positive sense of self-worth that contributes to their confidence and ability to succeed academically. Statistics in *Home Schooling Works Pass It On!*, by Lawrence M. Rudner, show that the average homeschooled student ranks in the 85th percentile on standardized tests, regardless of his parents' levels of education. The only public school students with the same level of achievement are those whose parents have a college education. While such consistent academic success may result partly from the tutorial method of teaching, we believe it is also the result of the profound commitment homeschooling parents make to their children.

Safety and school

The past decade has seen a significant deterioration of the institutional school environment. Many parents have been shocked by the tragic shootings at the Jonesboro and Columbine schools and elsewhere. They fear for the safety of their children, and rightly so.

While there are obviously many safe schools in America, the Littleton, Colorado story showed all of us that no one can guarantee a particular school's safety. When children feel safe, they can concentrate on learning, and where will they feel safer than in the home?

Our hope

Finally, if you are new to homeschooling, or just contemplating it at this point, we refer you to this book's Afterword, "Parents and Education: The Biblical Mandate," by Dr. K. Alan Snyder. After all, "Faith comes by hearing, and hearing by the Word of God. (Romans 10:5 [NKJV])" When you know it is God who has called you to direct your children's education, you will have faith to finish the task. And trust us—there will be times when you need all the faith you can get!

We hope you will find the information in this book to be valuable as you explore the possibilities awaiting your children, and as you help them meet their goals. Most of all, we pray that you will be inspired by the many options and opportunities awaiting your homeschooled students in their future.

CHAPTER 1

Inspiring Your Children to Love Learning

"Behold, God is exalted in His power; Who is a teacher like Him?"
–Job 36:22 (NASB)

We once spotted a bumper sticker that captured the essence of how our eldest son thought as a young teen. It read, "Hire a teenager...while he still knows everything." If you work with children, you will recognize a disturbing occupational hazard: When they turn 13, *your* IQ suddenly plummets! However, we propose several ways to avoid this attitude in the first place, and to work with those children who may have already reached this point.

When we decided to school our children at home, we wanted to teach them to love learning. Our number one educational goal (as opposed to spiritual goals) was to instill a desire to learn in each of them. Once the desire for learning was deeply felt, we knew our children would be able to determine their own directions in using it, with our guidance at first. We both have always had a great desire for learning, and we knew that if we could transfer this desire to our children, they would never lack for things to learn.

Our educational philosophy directly affected our everyday practices. Over the years, we have developed a style of learning within our home that has produced the results we desired. Each family will develop its own learning environment as the years pass. The following ideas can enrich that style and make your efforts more enjoyable and efficient.

The 4 "R"s of Elementary School

The goal of the elementary years must be to build a foundation of learning that will provide a firm basis for whatever direction the student takes in later years. You must include the three "R"s (reading, 'riting, and 'rithmetic), but there are really four necessities.

The fourth "R" that should be learned in elementary school is *research*. The child who knows how to research information is a child who can learn anything. We find it much more prudent to teach children to find information and use it properly than to have them memorize a plethora of facts.

The mechanics of research have changed immensely over the last 10 years, mostly due to the Internet. It is much easier to track down information today than it was when we were in school, yet this also means that employers and professors expect better, more accurate information. Thus it is imperative that all children in the elementary years have the opportunity to become proficient in computer skills (including keyboarding) and Internet research.

Each of our children learned to type correctly by using a typing tutor software program in early elementary school. We required that they spend a minimum of 20 minutes per day on their keyboarding skills before using the computer for schoolwork or games. Learning proper typing technique came easily to them at that early age. They did not have to undo bad habits and they now type faster than either of us! Jeremiah types 70 words per minute; David types 68.

Drawbacks of the Internet

Keep in mind, however, that with all the information on the Internet, a new problem occurs—validation. There are many sources of information on the Internet. Not all of them are accurate. Just because someone says that they have correct information does not mean that it is true. We must teach our children not to believe everything they read. We have the opportunity to instruct our children in discernment. Help them to scrutinize material. This will benefit them not only in research, but also in business and professional experiences.

Doing research electronically allows for incredible access. However, with ease of access also come new dangers. Profanity, obscenity, and pornography are out there. Investing in Internet screening software or services is essential. Companies like *crosswalk.com*, Prodigy Internet, and most, if not all, of the Internet Service Providers (ISPs), provide search-engine protection software to help keep unwanted information from penetrating your home. It is well worth the trouble, and many of these products are free.

You need to research and scrutinize your choice of ISP. One of the more popular ISPs, America Online, is not child-friendly. For this reason, many parents try to avoid the Internet altogether. This is a personal choice. As you decide on whether or not to provide Internet access to your family, realize the following: The Internet is here to stay. It is just as profound in its culture-changing influence as the printing press, television, and space exploration.

Do you pick and choose which books your child reads? Do you select the television shows your children can watch? Do you screen the radio stations they can listen to, which CDs they buy, and which magazines they read? Treat the Internet the same way.

It is right to protect our children. They should be sheltered from immoral and suggestive materials at all costs. During the adolescent years, they can learn to use computers to develop basic typing skills, study math, science, and history, communicate with other homeschool students, and, with help and guidance, search and research on the Internet. By giving them healthy experiences and teaching them properly in ways to avoid negative materials, we are preparing them for life beyond the home. By the time they enter high school, we have created a pattern to help them learn discernment. When they are old enough to move out on their own, we can hope they will continue to avoid vices and be productive champions of their world, living and learning in a Christian context.

Jesus Christ said to "be in the world but not of the world." We need to teach our children what this means. It is better to help them to scrutinize their environments while they are under your care and protection than to leave them to figure it out on their own later on. At the same time, you are teaching them to override evil passions by the truth of God's word and Christian principles.

"I am enough of an artist to draw freely upon my imagination. Imagination is more important than knowledge. Knowledge is limited. Imagination encircles the world."

—Albert Einstein

Once these precautions are taken, the opportunity for learning is endless. Microsoft's slogan, "Where do you want to go today?" says it all. History, music, science, maps, hobbies, economics, medicine—whatever you want to study, it is all available at the push of a button. The number of homeschool sites is growing daily. Web-based courses, online curricula, and hundreds of programs on virtually any subject are all available on the Internet. Even *Encyclopaedia Britannica*'s world-famous material is now available free of charge at *www.britannica.com*.

This does not mean that good old research techniques of finding books and articles in the library are passe. It is equally important that children know how to find and use other everyday sources. Newspapers, magazines, books, and journals are still important places to find information. Capitalizing on your children's individual interests will help develop a healthy curiosity. Children who research subjects they are curious about are much more likely to apply and retain the knowledge.

Making the basics fun

The family is God's perfect educational institution. You as parents provide the direction and the tools. Together with your young, impressionable students, you can have fun while learning.

Learning many elementary topics requires a certain amount of drudgery. Reading and phonics skills must be learned, multiplication tables memorized, and state capitals drilled. However, once your child has a firm grasp on basic math, language, and research skills, you can build creatively on that foundation through a variety of learning techniques. We have outlined for you some of the most effective teaching and learning ideas we have found in our homeschool experience. The following can help take the drudgery out of basic tasks while developing a sense of adventure in learning:

Educational games

Educational games are excellent for teaching basic conceptual facts while involving many ages at the same time. If older children are patient, playing games can also give the children a chance to interact with each other in learning, regardless of age level.

⅄ Spelling bees are a well-loved old standard with most children. Also, nothing beats a good game of *Scrabble* to teach spelling and vocabulary.

↟ The game of *Authors* was one we both played as children, and our offspring enjoy it just as much as we did. They now have variations of *Authors* for history, sports, music, presidents, and famous Americans, as well as many different types of literary figures.

↟ *Hail to the Chief* is a wonderful game that teaches the presidents and the presidential election process, including the electoral college system. Most states require a course in civics in elementary school. Playing this game teaches civics better than any other method we have encountered.

↟ *Flash cards* exist for geography, state capitals, presidents, basic math, and many other topics. Children learn well through the repetition process that playing with flash cards provides. They are easily used on car trips and during waiting time at the doctor's office. Metrics, measures, and multiplication tables can be learned with any number of games usually found on the box of flash cards.

↟ *Jigsaw puzzles* teach hand-eye coordination, classification skills (used in science), and logic. You can add to the learning value of puzzles by using those that have to do with geography or art.

↟ Financial games like *Monopoly* teach principles of finance, economics, and money-handling (making change). Our favorite is *Money Matters* (by Christian Financial Concepts, Norcross, Georgia) since it allows children to play roles with varying income and circumstances, while learning about tithing and meeting financial obligations. Another is *The Game of Life*.

↟ *Masterpiece* is a game that deals with famous works of art. Children can learn to recognize famous works of art and their styles simply by playing this board game a few times.

↟ A favorite in our home is *Jeopardy*—in any form. Though it is primarily a trivia game, we have found that playing *Jeopardy* as a family has increased our all-around knowledge and has given us an appreciation for learning new things at any age.

↟ *The Phonics Game* is useful for reinforcing and practicing basic reading skills. It can be used with elementary students to sharpen reading aloud and spelling skills as well. Why not allow older children to teach reading fundamentals to younger siblings with this game?

Educational games are available through catalogs and stores. Museum shops carry many types of learning cards and games, and you can find many more through curriculum and book distributors. You might guess that our closets are full of all sorts of games, and in fact, they are the items we are most tempted to buy at book sales and conventions. We have rarely regretted these purchases; game-playing has become a big part of our family's learning together. It also provides an opportunity to spend some time together.

Field trips

Field trips are great for homeschoolers because of the flexibility in schedules. Most homeschool support groups work together to arrange visits to interesting businesses, industries, cultural events, and places of historical interest. Field trips broaden the understanding provided in books as students see various disciplines applied in the real world.

Museums

Museums provide a huge array of support for school studies. Children may be exposed to art, local history, scientific exhibits, and historical artifacts when visiting a museum. One note of caution: Museum curators generally function under the current opinions held by scientists and anthropologists. (We do mean opinions.) Be sure that when you visit an exhibit of any sort that the students are aware that what is printed on the signs may or may not be accurate.

When we were first married, we used to spend many Saturdays visiting a well-known museum of natural history. One of their most popular exhibits showed the history of man through the ages. This anthropology exhibit contained busts of supposed prehistoric men, recreated from pieces of uncovered bones and other artifacts. It was intriguing to us at the time that such sophisticated models of prehistoric creatures could be reconstructed from things like a tooth and a jawbone! One of these exhibits was a reconstruction of a recognized hoax, Piltdown Man. It was recreated from a skullcap and what was proven to be an artificially aged jawbone. In other words, this "objective" scientific establishment failed to remove an exhibit even when it had been proven false.

Clearly, there is a need for discernment and scrutiny when we visit these institutions. We need to make sure we help our children understand how to differentiate between fact and fiction, especially within the supposedly objective halls of science like our natural history museums. The trick is not to avoid such places, but to go there with open minds and a willingness to question the information they contain.

Reading

Reading aloud is a nearly lost pastime in this country. Television and movies provide almost all entertainment and learning exposure in our homes. If you want your children to love learning, you must teach them to love reading. Start with reading the Bible. The Bible is not only inspirational, it is actually the most important textbook you have. [Author's note: This is one of the most basic reasons we believe public schools miss the mark. Our public schools for the most part have rejected the value of the Bible. In fact, there are public school libraries in this country that do not have even one copy of the Holy Bible on their shelves!] Read historical novels, quality fiction, and biographies. Everyone in the family will benefit from the time spent together while learning and being inspired to learn as well. Families that read together, learn together.

Favorite pick: Our family's all-time favorite read-aloud books are the *Chronicles of Narnia* by C.S. Lewis. Though written for children, these books are fascinating and inspiring at any age. The beautiful allegory contained in the *Chronicles* parallels the Christian life in so many ways.

Contests

Contests are a great way to motivate the young learner. Using competition, prizes, and rewards as motivators from time to time can be fun and inspiring. Competition against oneself, among siblings, or within a support group can drive students to reach beyond their comfort zones. There are also numerous state and national competitions in geography, spelling, and writing that can be wonderful learning experiences and great confidence boosters.

One component of our homeschool has been an annual summer reading contest. Points are earned for number of pages and variety of books read, and for writing book reports. (See Appendix F for summer reading contest rules.) Points can be exchanged for cash or other prizes. Our children enjoy the competition and read huge numbers of books during these contests. Their love for reading is bolstered and they generally continue to read more even after the competition ends.

Unit studies

Many homeschooling families use unit studies as their main curriculum structure. Even those who do not can use unit studies for a change of pace or for a special topic. You may incorporate all subjects into a unit study on a certain topic that is of interest to the child. For instance, a unit study about baseball could include math (calculating batting averages, player statistics, and game records), history (of the game), physics (velocity, gravity, parabolic motion, and physical forces), and language arts (reading biographies of famous players and writing an essay about the current state of the game). Moral issues such as the Pete Rose or John Rocker controversies could be studied by high school students as current events and discussed against the background of biblical principle. The home is the perfect place for these issues to be addressed. Unit studies are also wonderful for family learning, since the activities can be modified to fit any age.

Projects

Projects are another way for students to learn research skills, visual arts, and writing skills all at once. A project differs from a unit study in that it usually covers only one or two subject areas. Most students produce at least one science project in their elementary years, but they need not be limited to science. History, art, music, health, and even math projects can be great learning experiences. Projects provide an opportunity to integrate information from research into practical results. Projects can be designed by the parent or student, or they may be part of a curriculum. Many homeschooling support groups organize project fairs to allow students the chance to display their work and learn from projects of others. For more information on holding a project fair, see Appendix A.

Clubs

Clubs are a wonderful way to enhance home studies. Girl and Boy Scouts, Civil Air Patrol, 4-H, and various activity clubs (such as foreign language and chess) exist in most communities. We started our own clubs where none existed to meet the needs of our children.

Our family moved to the Utica, New York, area in 1995. We organized a local homeschooling 4-H club that provided our children with an avenue to learn numerous skills like cooking, tending animals, and building model rockets. Our daughters learned how to raise and care for goats, chickens, and rabbits. They also learned to sew aprons and pillows. Our sons spent most of their time on model rocket and cooking projects. They each entered their projects for judging at the county fair. They also had the opportunity to be elected as officers in the group. The leadership skills they gained through these efforts will last a lifetime.

Developing a learning lifestyle in the secondary school years

As a student progresses into the secondary years, the role of the parent shifts to that of a mentor. By this time, your children will have developed certain learning styles and interests that you can help them use to their advantage. It is important to speak to the individual in the students, to find what they love and what motivates them. If you can successfully identify your child's spiritual gifts and God-given talents, you will be likely to have success in guiding them toward a fulfilling and profitable future.

The high school years are suited for in-depth study. Your children may not have discovered their talents and may need opportunities to explore and try out different careers. Look for opportunities for them to learn all they can about any area they may want to pursue. Chapter 6 will provide more information on preparing for careers, including discussions of apprenticeships, part-time jobs, and club projects. Make the effort to seek out extra lessons in art, music, or even horseback riding. These may provide experiences that can persuade or discourage the young adult to pursue a particular vocation.

We made it a goal to encourage any reasonable vocational desire our children had that was within our means. This encouragement has taken many forms over the years. We purchased a quality telescope for the astronomer who eventually lost interest. For our hopeful veterinarian we started a dog-breeding business (we still have three dogs from this venture). We have bought and built hundreds of model rocket kits (for our budding engineer) and attended countless basketball games (for the NBA-bound student). We encouraged the entertainer in our family to participate in drama productions and singing competitions.

There are career events in most communities that provide opportunities for students to ask questions about professions in medical or other fields. It may also be possible to explore options by going to work with a friend or relative for a day.

Once you are confident that your children have mastered fundamental skills, you can develop their love for learning by continuing to immerse them in a learning environment. Provide varied experiences for your young adult. Surround them with books, educational videos, and opportunities to learn new things. Go beyond core subject requirements. Integrate subjects through unit studies. Take every opportunity to expose your children to adult life and work. The idea is to make a clear impression on your child that life is all about learning.

We school year-round in our home and never make a clear delineation between daily "school time" and "off time." We do not have vacations from school, though we do change what we are learning. For instance, we tend to suspend core subjects at holiday times and some parts of summer in favor of learning new crafts, customs, or cooking skills, or traveling. That does not mean we are on vacation from learning. On the contrary, these are the times when we focus on learning some very valuable skills. These skills will enhance the personal and family life of our children in the future. The bottom line: Make all time school time, and try to make it all as enjoyable as possible for the whole family.

Travel teaches

Many homeschooling families have the opportunity to travel because of the flexibility of the children's schedules. Exposure to various cultures, whether domestic or foreign, is always enlightening and enriching. Experiencing geography is much more valuable than only reading about it.

Our children have benefited greatly from visiting historic sites in New England during our study of the Revolutionary War, visiting relatives in various parts of the country, and living in several states. We have traveled to Mexico and to Indian reservations on mission trips. We have also had the opportunity to accompany Dad throughout the Northeast and Midwest on many of his business trips. Not only did this allow the children to see and learn new things, it also gave us the opportunity to be with Dad when he would otherwise be away.

Personalized lessons

One of our favorite things about homeschooling is the ability to allow our children to explore personal talents and interests. It has always been our goal to help them develop their own interests as much as we are able. Each child has definable interests that can be focused on in the homeschool environment. The home is a very efficient environment for learning. Homeschool students learn at their own pace, so core subjects can be completed in a few hours a day. The rest of the time can and should be used for developing interests. Our rule was that the children could usually do what they wanted beyond the basics as long as they used their time in some constructive pursuit.

Unrestrained enrichment

Enrichment through involvement in the arts is another valuable plus. Homeschool students are free to engage in music, art, and dance without straining their schedules. Lessons with professional artists and musicians are often more readily available in the daytime, when other students are in formal school. Many studios and art schools provide special programs for homeschooled students.

Those students who don't actually participate in the arts should at least be exposed to them on a regular basis. Take your children to the symphony, attend a drama, visit an art gallery. Exposure to the fine arts will enhance any curriculum.

Love for learning is inherited

Finally, if you value learning new things yourself, your children will notice and will make it a value and a habit of their own. In our home we are constantly reading, exploring new places, taking courses, researching topics, playing educational games, and anything else we can think of to enhance our understanding. It is a way of life for all of us. One of the most positive effects of homeschooling is that students do not view learning as something you do Monday through Friday from 8 a.m. to 3 p.m., September to June. Rather, learning becomes an all-the-time, whole-family, lifelong endeavor. Parents who make learning a natural part of life will have no difficulty preparing their students for anything the future may hold. Your ability to instill a love of learning is the ultimate educational tool you can give your children.

CHAPTER 2

Focusing on the Heart

"For what does it profit a man to gain the whole world, and forfeit his soul?"
—Mark 8:36 (NASB)

For those of us who believe spiritual instruction is to be dominant in our children's education, teaching about Scripture, Jesus Christ, and Christian principles must be a primary focus of our homeschool curriculum. In all of our homeschool efforts, it has always been our goal to guide our children on the path of light and life. It is possible for us to do a great job of training our kids to be successful people and yet avoid God's ways entirely. We have to make a determined effort to keep on the narrow path. This chapter offers practical ways of accomplishing our spiritual goals in the home school.

As children grow and learn, parents have the opportunity to train them in proper thinking and behavior. To us, education is more than teaching facts and figures. Unless we teach our children the proper use of knowledge (better known as wisdom) our training is not complete. The well-rounded student will be equipped in character as well as in academics. This is why we parents commit to making the sacrifice. We want to provide our children with every possibility to become the best they can be. We want them to experience the depth of spiritual development missing in other educational approaches.

Opportunities to teach through a godly example abound in the home school. As Christian parents, we need to keep this goal at the forefront of all we do in the home school and in our planning for the student's future.

Instilling good morals

As parents, we command the strongest level of sway in our children's lives. For this reason, it is critical that we live as consistently as possible with our children. We must live a holy, righteous life in front of them. We must be an example of good so that our children can experience a strong influence to develop their own internal moral compasses. Furthermore, we must recognize that our children need to be converted to Jesus Christ. They do not become Christians without an experience of new birth. Jesus Christ said it best when he said, "The Kingdom of God suffers violence, and violent men take it by force," and, "men are pressing their way into it." We must encourage our children that they too enter the Kingdom as children. God resists the proud but gives grace to the humble. All of this needs to be included in our instruction.

It is not a popular thing in our modern world to point out that there are absolutes, but there are. There are 10 Commandments. There is an abundance of teaching on how to live a right and proper life in the Scriptures. There is right, and there is wrong. We know that sometimes it is hard for us to tell the difference. However, if you teach your children using Jesus' exhortation of the fulfillment of the law (to love the Lord with all your heart, soul, mind, and strength, and your neighbor as yourself) you can't go wrong. The 10 Commandments are pertinent today; they are fulfilled and surpassed by loving God and others supremely in our daily life.

We must convey a respect and high view of Scripture if we are going to expect our children to take it seriously. Our respect for principles of faith will only make sense if we live them ourselves. Our children will see our hypocrisy as quickly as anyone. If we live a lie, they will know. We must be consistent if we are going to expect them to be.

Teaching about humility, repentance, compassion, grace, kindness, peace, gentleness, meekness, and tenderheartedness should be as integral to our homeschooling instruction as English, math, and history. Otherwise, our instruction is just academic.

Our children will love the things that we love. If our lives are absorbed with vices, evil thoughts, malicious behavior, bad company, and wrong actions, our children will have a harder time doing what is right and good. Evil and wrong will be that much more attractive. On the other hand, starting with repentant hearts, as we embrace the love of God, doing good works in the name of Jesus Christ, living a life of prayer, giving to others, showing compassion, being filled with grace, forgiving others, and worshipping our maker, we will speak volumes to our children. All these actions will influence our children to do likewise. In short, we must live a consistent Christian life before our children.

During the early years, we can instill in our children principles of Christian virtue that are imperative for incubating essential concepts in their formative minds and hearts. Here are some practical ways to do so:

Give your kids materials that reinforce a Christian world view (more on this in Chapter 3). Include Bible reading as a part of their curriculum on a daily basis. Read to them books by famous Christian authors. Obviously, going to church together and participating in Christian activities regularly is vital. Become involved in missions together. Take a mission trip as a family (we have done it twice).

While our children were growing up, we regularly read them books like C.S. Lewis's *Chronicles of Narnia*, Bunyan's *Pilgrim's Progress*, and Josh McDowell's *Don't Check Your Brains at the Door*, as well as regular readings of Scripture. Read together at the breakfast or dinner table.

Make sure to pray as a family. During times of personal or family crisis, make sure you include times of family prayer, asking God to bring relief and providence to your regular life situations. These will be tremendous reminders to them later of the power of God in our lives.

When our children were very young, we went through a household move due to David's layoff from Shell Oil Company. It was a difficult time. On one occasion, we had very little food. David was at work one day during lunch when Laurie instructed the children to pray to the Lord to provide our needs. As only children can do, Rebekah, Katie, and Jeremiah prayed to the Lord to provide. A couple of hours later, a lady we knew from church came to the door with three bags of groceries and a check for $250. We had seen God's providence in a way that our oldest children still remember to this day.

Sing together as a family. We still sing to tapes as we travel in the car. We sing together at church. We have gone caroling as a family on numerous Christmases. Fortunately, David has sung and played guitar since before we were married, so this was not unusual for us to do regularly. It will be easier for some than for others to make this a part of your home. The Scriptures admonish us to "speak to one another in psalms, hymns, and spiritual songs." Providing opportunities to impart truth within the context of music is a very powerful medium to instruct little minds. It is a habit that lasts a lifetime.

Our first priority, then, is to create an environment for our students that is conducive to learning right and wrong, good and evil. Show them the power of the right, while recognizing the debilitating strength of the wrong. Teach them the value of good over evil.

Dads, rethink your priorities so you can spend time with your children. The very last words of the Old Testament reflect the importance of this action. God instructs his people to turn "the hearts of the fathers...to their children, and the hearts of the children to their fathers, lest I come and strike the earth with a curse."

Fathers have the opportunity to instill spiritual values in their children even before they begin their formal education. In the very early primary years, we can give them numerous opportunities to learn about God, His beautiful and wonderful world, and their places in it.

If your child has a question about a math problem, do you find time to stop what you are doing to help him figure out the answer? Can you be flexible enough to be there when your child is under pressure, going through personal issues, or just needing Dad?

Do you give your children a positive example of a loving marriage? Are you faithful to your wife? Do you demand respect for your wife by each of your children? Do you teach your boys to treat girls as the Lord would demand? This lesson will last long after the boys leave home. In this day, when politically correct attitudes toward women contradict clear biblical standards, do you take a stand to make sure they know that you value womanhood?

What about your use of language? Do you control your tongue? What kind of words do your children hear from your mouth? When things go wrong, do you still find ways to speak with grace? What attitudes do you convey with your words? Do you praise your children even when they do not "produce"? Are you more concerned about your children's character than their performance?

Do you take the lead in the spiritual growth of your family? Do you lead in family devotions? Are you willing to step up and be there for your kids?

It is so important to make sure our children understand the difference between right and wrong both intellectually and experientially. Hebrews 6 indicates that a mature Christian is one who "has his senses trained to discern the difference between good and evil." It makes sense to begin this training by providing our young ones with a firm understanding of truth, right, good, virtue, etc. We live in a society that blurs the lines of morality continually, and it is your responsibility to teach your children that there is a right and wrong.

Children can learn right from wrong

Once we reach the secondary school grades, our children should have a clear picture that there is a right and wrong, good and evil, true and false; there are absolutes. Now, it is critical that your children not only know that there is a right and wrong, but to be able to discern which is which, and why.

Teaching our children discernment is never easy. As your child enters secondary school, it is even more difficult because of the additional influences that confront this age level. The effects of puberty are taking their toll. Hormones are engaging while we are trying to teach our young ones to become discerning. It is a double challenge. Learning wisdom in and of itself can be a challenge at any age, and even that much more when emotions get out of balance.

We have a real opportunity as parents to be involved with our teenagers as they learn how to discern things. On the other hand, anyone who has ever tried to motivate a teenager whose hormones are just starting to kick in knows it is a challenge. Teens can want to sleep until noon, become quite obnoxious on a regular basis, and develop hearing impairments (or at least they have a hard time listening to instructions even though we clearly know they heard them).

We have followed the advice of James Dobson, Ph.D., founder of Focus On The Family, who recommends taking each of your children away for an "adolescent trip" sometime between the ages of 11 and 18. We have done this with all five of our children. Mom accompanied each of the girls, and dad the boys. We do not regret spending one penny of the money or one second of the time invested in these trips. We took Dobson's *Preparing for Adolescence* tapes with us and listened to them during the trip. Each of our children chose his or her trip. Jeremiah went with David to Hawk Mountain in Pennsylvania and then to a Philadelphia Eagles game. Josiah went to visit two of his best friends in Philadelphia, after a nine-hole golf outing, followed by an Eagles game as well. Wesley chose to fly to St. Louis and joined David at a National Christian Businessman's Committee Conference. (Yes, that was Wesley's choice. He just wanted to go away on a trip somewhere with his father.) Rebekah chose a trip to Niagara

Falls, staying at a nice hotel and shopping at a mall there. Katie went to a dude ranch to spend time with Mom riding horses, swimming, and boating. The parent makes out better than the kids in some respects, as Laurie will attest. She had a great time with both daughters.

The greatest value in this sort of trip is the relationship it reinforces between the young person and the parent. It shows that we value our children. It gives us an opportunity for valuable one-on-one time. And we get to air out some significant issues, like puberty, sex, trust, peer pressure, and other issues of concern to adolescents. It has unquestionably been worth the cost to us.

We want our children to be active thinkers. How do we accomplish that? What are the tools we can use to teach discernment? A good place to start is the Bible. David said, "Thy Word have I hid in my heart that I might not sin against Thee." Times of memorization and meditation on Scriptures are very valuable. There are many good resources out in the homeschool marketplace that help with Scripture memorization and meditation.

A great book to begin with is Proverbs. These 31 chapters are filled with practical statements that any person, whether eight or 80, can use to learn how to live justly. Issues involving moral situations, handling pressures, financial decisions, areas of obedience, listening to parents, avoiding foolishness, and much more are covered in these pages. Study the teachings of Jesus, especially the Sermon on the Mount, the parables, and His many personal interactions with the disciples. No one is a better teacher for our children than our Lord. Additionally, many Old Testament situations involving David, Solomon, Samson, Samuel, Esther, Rebekah, Elijah, Jeremiah, and others lay the base for learning moral issues.

We also need to realize that the individualized, personal interaction with each child is the place where true homeschooling is confirmed. The difference between other forms of education and the home school is the opportunity to provide one-on-one education with our students. What this ultimately comes down to is time. It does not take rocket science to figure out that our time with our children is the main factor in giving them an advantage over those schooled outside the home.

For most of us, this is obvious, but it is still difficult to practice. As we previously stated, fathers find a real challenge juggling work responsibilities with instruction. Finding ways to be involved in your children's lives may take creativity. Evenings and weekends may demand sacrificing time with the guys to spend it with the kids. Fathers cannot cede their roles as the leaders of their homes. Fathers have unique opportunities to instruct their children in creative ways. They do not need to teach in a sterile, classroom setting. They can just be Dad. Go play ball with your kids at the YM-YWCA. Work together in the yard. Split wood together. Go to a concert together, or to a park. Spend time with your kids.

Overall, it will be in the crucible of daily life that our children will learn to discern truth. Hopefully we will be able to teach them valuable lessons while they are in our homes, so that when they are on their own later, they will not have to suffer through foolish choices. Out there in the real world, they will not have our protection from the consequences of their choices.

Developing godly character

As we teach our children to learn discernment, we are moving them toward self-government. Until we give our children the ability to control themselves in our absence, we are not done. Our goal is to make our children realize that not only is there a right and wrong, not only do they need to be able to discern between good and evil, but that they have a moral obligation to do what is right. Only when all three of these objectives are met, do we see the development of godly character. We have two decades to accomplish this with each child (give or take a few years), with the guidance of the Holy Spirit.

We have to obviously prepare our children for the future by giving them the information they need to learn in order to be productive members of the society they will be entering. But once again, we must keep in mind the primary purpose of education from a Christian perspective. The apostle Paul explains it in one of his letters, when he reminds Timothy that "the goal of our instruction is love out of a pure heart, a good conscience, and a sincere faith."

In practical terms, we are aiming to instill character in our children that will formulate and solidify over the years. In this sense, it is more than a "program." It is a process. It starts with instilling a love for learning, and then teaching by instruction and example, until our children, each through his own choices and motives, owns it. The goal is that as a result of our careful, methodical efforts, they are able to move into gainful employment, career success, solid citizenship in our great country, and, most importantly, to live uprightly before their God.

The goal of our instruction

We have taught our children a phrase to help them understand where character comes from. It goes like this: Our choices govern our actions, our actions grow into habits, our habits decide our nature, our nature becomes our character, and our character will determine our destiny. That wraps up what we have said in this chapter quite nicely.

Jesus Christ has the keys to heaven, and wants to provide them to anyone who believes in Him. He said, "I am the resurrection and the Life; He who believes in Me, even if he dies, yet shall he live." We make no apology that we want our children to gain this knowledge as their most important choice in life. To miss this would be to miss the whole point. It is the basis of everything else.

Our prayer is that the Lord will empower you and provide you with the grace to succeed. The rewards will be worth the costs. Your efforts will impact not only your children, but their children and grandchildren.

CHAPTER 3

Guiding Toward a Christian Worldview

"Sanctify Christ as Lord in your hearts, always being ready to make a defense to everyone who asks you to give an account for the hope that is in you, yet with gentleness and reverence."
I Peter 3:15 (NASB)

E very child will graduate home school with a particular philosophy that will affect his decisions and his future forever. Our goal as Christian parents is to be sure our children's outlook on life is founded in Christian principle. When children are young, it is appropriate to tell them what is right and wrong without much explanation. As they mature, however, if you do not teach them why things are right and wrong they will flounder on issues that have not been defined for them. Establishing a distinctly Christian worldview is not an easy task, but it will be one of the most important you will undertake.

We need to make very certain to teach our children discernment. We need to train our children to be careful about what they read, to discern truth and fact from opinion or bias. For very young children it is wise to totally avoid books with questionable content—like dinosaur books from the library or bookstore that assume the evolutionary worldview and time scales. We were careful to review all books for our young children. Because they did not yet have the reasoning capacity to discern, they assumed everything they heard and read was true.

Additionally, we are very careful to protect our children from exploitation by the new computer technologies, particularly the Internet. We want to make sure our children keep their innocence. We will guard them at all costs.

As our children grow older we need to teach them to discern on their own how to use God's word and their natural observations to determine what is true and reasonable. Out of this understanding, they will be able to make decisions that go beyond intellectual discernment to the moral level. This is a process that takes many years. When children reach the secondary home school, it is very important to let them think through their questions and obtain reasonable answers for themselves, using the Scripture as a foundation of absolute truth.

Where do we begin?

The world gives us a virtually infinite supply of material to move our children away from a Christian life perspective. For those of us who are old enough to remember the early days of television (or who watch "Nick At Nite"), you can see how much our culture has been affected by non-Christian sentiment in the media during the past 40 years. Can you remember the segment of *The Andy Griffith Show*, for example, where Andy and Barney sing "There Is a Fountain Filled with Blood" as the show ends? How far we have digressed! People today argue over whether or not America was founded as a Christian nation or not. It all is a sign of the deterioration of the Christian consensus and its replacement with a religious evolutionary humanism throughout our land.

Books, magazines, television programs, radio stations, public school textbooks, newspapers, movies, video games, computer software packages, and Internet Web pages all have the potential to draw our children away from the truth through enticingly slanted stories, misleading information, colorful fictional images, and other seducing means.

We have been given a divine commission by God to teach our children what we believe to be truth and falsehood. In giving us this calling, He has not left us alone. He has given us an absolute content of truth, the Bible, with which we can compare the multitude of materials our children are exposed to as they are learning and growing.

We are convinced that much of what passes as science is tainted by those who prepare it for public consumption. Much of the material in high school textbooks today is clearly biased toward an evolutionary worldview and is not backed by proper scientific proof.

We also live in the information age. It has been said that the total pool of knowledge is now doubling every seven years. Within the computer industry, "Internet years" are measured in weeks or months. We are seeing new information being created to replace prior sources in a fraction of the time it would take traditional media in the past. Our children have access to material on virtually any subject in almost limitless volumes.

But there is a real problem associated with such access. How do we validate this material? There is so much out there. How do we know what is correct and what is not? We need to protect our childrens' young minds from the influences set to distract them from true knowledge based on Jesus Christ (Christian truth).

The first step is to make sure our children's curriculum includes consistent and regular reading of Scripture. Give your child a Bible. It is the most important investment you can make in your child's education. Hundreds of years of testimonies by millions of people illustrate the value of the Bible as their most significant source of learning.

Make sure the Bible you provide is a readable version. Some parents think that any translation but the King James Version is suspect. We respectfully disagree. Not only are there translations that are easier to read, but many of the newer ones are more faithful to the original manuscripts. So the *New American Standard Bible*, *New Century Version*, *New King James Version*, or *New International Version* are good alternatives. There are others as well. (We suggest avoiding paraphrased versions like *The Living Bible* and *Good News For Modern Man* because they are not translations from the original languages, but rather are paraphrases of English bibles.) Rotating versions over time is another option.

Set up a daily reading schedule for each homeschooler. Have your child read portions from both the Old and New Testaments regularly. Help your children to learn to read with an attitude of prayer so that they are sensitive to the fact that God is speaking through His Word. This may seem obvious to you, but communicating it reinforces the fact that the Bible is more than just some old book being read as a religious exercise. It will affect their lives if they are allowed to willfully listen to the Holy Spirit as they read.

Obviously, you should read the Bible together as a family as your children are growing up. Times of family Bible reading are essential in order to give your children a respect for the Word of God as a part of your household. It sets the Bible up as a unique book among books. Make sure your children gain a high view of Scripture by reading with them from their earliest days and continuing this practice through the high school years.

There are also many daily Bible-reading programs available that enable the student to read through the entire Bible in one or two years. Our favorite, the daily reading plan from "Walk Through the Bible," takes portions from the Old and New Testaments, so that both are completed simultaneously at year's end. Also have your children study specific books from both Testaments for each book's specific value. All of this will give them a clear understanding of the truth of Scripture in its own words and let it speak for itself.

There are a number of tools available to help your students study the Bible. Make sure to have at least one of the titles from each of the following references:

- ▲ **Concordances** (these will help your student to understand specific words in context, their root origins, and varieties of meaning):
  - ▲ *Strong's Concordance.*
  - ▲ *Young's Concordance.*
  - ▲ *Cruden's Concordance.*

- ▲ **Bible Dictionaries** (these will help the student to understand unusual words, locations, and names that are unique to the Bible):
  - ▲ *Vines Bible Dictionary.*
  - ▲ *Halley's Bible Handbook.*
  - ▲ *Websters 1828 English Dictionary* (not a Bible dictionary per se, but filled with definitions that contain examples of Scripture in context) .

- ▲ **Topical References** (these break down Scripture references by topics and associations):
  - ▲ *Nave's Topical Bible.*
  - ▲ *Thompson Chain Reference Bible* (this is a Bible, but it has excellent reference notes, so we include it as a reference work).

Another valuable tool that our children have used over the years are the daily devotional diaries published by organizations like Youth With A Mission (*www.ywam.org*) and Word of Life Ministries (*www.wol.org*). You can order either of them at their online bookstores. These diaries allow our children to read daily passages, with time for personal prayer and devotional reading. The diaries allow students to write down their thoughts about what they have read, as well as spiritual insights they may want to record as they read. It also lets them record their prayer requests and answers.

One area of concern that we addressed early in our children's education is supporting material for their Bible reading. As your homeschooler reads the Bible, it will become necessary to augment the study with collateral resources that will reinforce the texts. For example, plenty of good information is available from the Institute for Creation Research (ICR), Santee, California (*www.icr.org*), to support the early chapters of Genesis consistently with Biblical context. Books like *The Genesis Record*, *Scientific Creationism*, and *The Genesis Flood* will help the secondary student reinforce his understanding of specific passages. Other books deal with the validity of Scripture and provide evidence of its authenticity. Josh McDowell's *Evidence That Demands a Verdict* (two volumes) and *More Than a Carpenter* are great for helping students gain confidence that the word of God is valid. *Many Infallible Proofs*, by Henry Morris, is another book that can give students a clear perspective on why the Bible is believable.

ICR also has a great free monthly newsletter called *Acts and Facts*. It can be downloaded from their Web site (*www.icr.org*); or you may contact them and ask to be added to their mailing list (see appendix for address and phone number).

If your child is not established in his faith at this time, it is important to provide resources for him to find answers to honest questions. There are many useful books available through such publishers as Master Books (*www.masterbooks.org*) for this purpose. We believe the creationist magazine *Ex Nihilo* is also a valuable learning tool (available through *www.answersingenesis.org*).

You believe what?

There are numerous opinions in the educational and scientific establishment as to what is true and false. Many people think that believing the Bible as the basis for truth is like believing the world is flat and that the earth is at the center of the universe. Many scholars believe we have evolved beyond this point (at least they are consistent). They think that the ancient idea of God creating an intelligent order to the universe in six literal days, then putting Adam and Eve into a beautiful garden to watch over it, name the animals, and live happily ever after, are wishful notions of a past culture whose time has long gone. (If you want to receive a real enlightenment, check out a copy of Humanist Manifesto I & II [*www.humanist.net/documents*] and spend an hour or so reading what men like John Dewey, Aldous Huxley, and others believed more than half a century ago. These are the ones who have framed modern thought.) The more "intelligent" position is that we evolved out of the primordial ooze and crawled onto land through stages of evolutionary development taking millions and millions (or billions and billions) of years. In other words, belief in a creationist view of the universe is considered religion, while the evolutionist's view is considered truth, science, fact, and reality.

We have to wake up and teach our children that a worldview is a religious view. Evolutionism is just as religious as creationism is, and vice versa. Both are models that explain the origin of things. Neither can be proven nor falsified. Both must be taken as a matter of faith. Both are equally religious. The problem is that evolutionists are not willing to admit this. We need to explain this to our children and instruct them in how to discern the difference between facts, theories, hypotheses, and models.

Educators have forgotten how to differentiate fact from theory. In actuality, concepts about origins are not true science because they fall out of the realm of the scientific method, unable to be observed, falsified, or verified. We can never prove how we originated using the tools of science directly, because we cannot recreate the environment, conditions, parameters, or other factors that make up the original events. On the other hand, the model that is purported to prove we evolved from lower forms of life has yet to show any evidence from the fossil record or any other venue to explain the vast gaps in the development from amoeba to man. Even noted scholars like Dr. Steven Jay Gould of Harvard University, an evolutionist and world-renowned paleontologist, believe there are significant gaps in the fossil record that Darwinistic evolution cannot account for. What we are left with is an ongoing debate, which we can allow our children to participate in without embarrassment, as we train them to learn how to think and look at all available information, using the Bible as a framework for learning.

This approach to education allows us to teach our children all points of view. The Christian worldview opens up the opportunity for learning. Those who are confident in their understanding and belief of the truths of the Bible can give their children a more rounded educational experience. They can learn about the models of evolution and creation. They can learn about world religions in the context of their own faith. They can be prepared for what will come in college as they are challenged to question their own beliefs. The home should be a safe haven in which children should be able to question hard things, knowing they have their parents to help them work through the issues. The better we can prepare them while they are at home, the less concern we will have when they leave and go out on their own into the world.

Think for yourself

One point that concerns many fathers is their role in the homeschool process. We, like many other families, have the problem of deciding what Dad can teach effectively as an evening educator. We feel that foundation material, such as the study of origins and theology, is primarily a father's job. (We acknowledge that there may be an exceptional mother who shines in these areas.) To us it is imperative that a father read up on the subject of creation science through ICR materials, Creation Research Society publications (*www.creationresearch.org*), or other sources. Even if his ability to input information is limited due to work pressures, there will be those times when his role as father and spiritual leader will allow for opportunities to teach critical concepts, especially as they relate to Genesis-based topics like sexuality, human origins, sin and suffering, and capital punishment. Those out in the world will not be shy about imposing their worldview on your children. Make sure that you clearly present your Biblical perspective to your children early and often (see Deuteronomy 6).

One other source of information that may be very useful is to have your family attend an Answers in Genesis seminar or an ICR Back to Genesis seminar. We have attended both and find the materials very good for giving to our children.

Older high school students may also want to read some of the works of the late Dr. Francis Schaeffer, whose work in the area of Christian presuppostional apologetics is classic. This material helps students understand why Christianity is true, versus other religions, and teaches them how to think as a Christian and love God with the mind as well as the heart, soul, and strength. Jeremiah has been reading Dr. Schaeffer's material recently and will verify that it is "deep." That is why we recommend it for the junior or senior who is looking for more serious material. The *How Should We Then Live* video series (and book) by Dr. Schaeffer is an excellent resource to help students think through various aspects of culture (such as art and music) and their relationship to the Bible and Christian life.

Another author we respect for his careful intellectual perspectives on the Bible is C.S. Lewis. *Mere Christianity* is a great overview of the reasons that Biblical Christianity is relevant. Other works, like *The Screwtape Letters*, show students that there is more to this world than what can be perceived with the five senses—that there is a spiritual dimension to the universe beyond the physical.

One other suggestion that will help prepare your high schooler for the outside world is to take advantage of the materials and events from Summit Ministries of Manitou Springs, Colorado (*www.christiananswers.net/ summit*). Summit's purpose, as stated on its Web site, is "equipping tomorrow's servant leaders to analyze competing worldviews and champion the Christian faith, inspiring each one to love God with his heart, soul, mind, and strength." The ministry strives to give Christian young people the tools they need to actively defend their faith and be a positive Christian influence as they enter college or embark on a career path.

Summit holds an entire summer of two-week-long leadership seminars for high school juniors and seniors at their Colorado campus and Bryan College in Dayton, Tennessee (the same city where the famous Scopes Trial took place in 1933). Our son Jeremiah attended the Summit at Bryan College in the summer of 1999. He says it was arguably one of the best experiences of his life. The intense two-week schedule included lectures by world-class professors on a variety of subjects, including thinking as a Christian, creation versus evolution, apologetics, ethics and morality, reliability of the Bible, economics and the Christian, and marriage and family.

Summit Ministries publishes a monthly newsletter called the *Summit Journal*, which we highly recommend. It includes very challenging articles, as well as information on Summit's work. You can order a subscription online (*info@summit.org*) or write them at Summit Journal, P.O. Box 207, Manitou Springs, CO 80829. They also have video lecture series available to homeschools. One of them, the *Worldviews in Focus: Thinking Like A Christian* series, is designed as a 12-week worldview curriculum for the high school student. For those who want to get in deeper, they offer the WorldView video curriculum, for teaching a Biblical worldview to both junior high and high school students. The courses are a bit pricey, but worth the cost if learned thoroughly.

Another option is WorldView Academy Leadership Camps (*www.worldview.org*). These camps provide week-long training in such Christian subjects as Introduction to Worldviews, The Roots of Order, Christianity and the Arts, and Servant Leadership. WorldView Academy has produced a video that teaches critical thinking and a book that compares and contrasts worldviews. You can check out their materials on their online catalog, write to them at WorldView Academy, P.O. Box 310106, New Braunfels, TX 78131, call (830) 620-5203, or e-mail them at *wvacad@juno.com*.

There is no excuse for being in the dark about the issues affecting our culture and our nation with this material from Summit and WorldView Academy. It is something every homeschool family should consider to prepare its students to win the battle for their minds.

The Walk Through The Bible (*www.walkthru.org*) seminar will help any homeschooler gain basic Biblical knowledge. These one-day seminars will help your young student learn the basic historical sequence of the events in the Bible. Our family attended one of these seminars some years ago, and we were amazed at how it helped us all put together the sequence of the Bible in our own minds. We highly recommend this as a family activity. Our ages ranged from eight to 40 when we attended, and all of us learned equally well. It is well worth the cost and time involved.

We strongly urge parents to be their children's teacher of doctrine and theology, as well as academics. Just as we have strong convictions about proper theology, we hope that many of our readers do as well. However, each parent and each family will have specific convictions about Christian doctrines like the virgin birth, the origin of sin and its characteristics, the atonement, the second coming of Jesus Christ, the Church, and so on. Some will be strongly Calvinist, others strongly Arminian. Some will be dispensational, others charismatic, some fundamentalist, and others evangelical. Whatever your beliefs, we encourage you to teach your children well. Be sure of what you believe and why. Challenge your children to think through their positions. Let them know there are questions to which you do not know the answers. Work with them on answering hard questions. Show them the love of God along with His justice, longsuffering, mercy, compassion, and holiness. Help them to learn about Jesus Christ and who He is as a man and as God. Help them to realize that the Bible is historically accurate but that it challenges our thinking in the area of faith and practice. Help them to develop a sound doctrine. Above all, remember that most theology is caught, not taught. It is what you practice that will probably form more of their views than what you instruct. So be consistent.

Get up and go

The other activity we highly recommend doing with your children as they enter the high school years is a mission trip. This experience will affect their lives forever. We have taken mission trips on several occasions. Putting together the logistics is usually very simple because most missionary organizations always need help. They will work with you. No matter what denomination you are a part of, or where you would like to go, there are many opportunities available. Here are a few suggestions:

Youth With A Mission (YWAM) is an interdenominational mission organization that has plenty of options available throughout the year. From summer outreaches literally anywhere in the world to one-week or two-week mission trips at a YWAM base or on a mercy ship, YWAM experiences will open the eyes of your teen to the spiritual, material, medical, and educational needs everywhere. YWAM's focus on "knowing God and making Him known" is a challenge to the teenager as well.

If you go as a family, there is usually no problem with taking along your younger children, as long as the parents are there. You should check with the YWAM coordinators to make sure this is the case for the specific outreach you plan to do. If you are sending your teenager alone, you will need to verify age requirements for the outreach as well. Some do not allow children under 18; others do.

YWAM also sponsors special Summer Of Service ministries. This is a great way to prepare your teen for future mission service. These six-to-12-week mission trips provide opportunities for instruction, evangelism, worship, and living by faith that will shape your child's life.

Teen Missions is another organization that sponsors short-term mission trips for young people. You might know of a mission outreach within your church or denomination, or with a specific missionary associated with your church. You might want to set up a mission trip with your homeschool support group.

Love the Lord with all your heart, soul, mind, and strength

Remember, a truly Christian worldview is one that will pervade everything your children do. We are compelled to teach our children to think as Christians. In our day, the word "Christian" has been compromised so completely that those who use this name can at the same time question the existence of God, the relevance of the cross of Jesus Christ, and a multitude of issues that used to be central to Christian faith. We must lead our children through the process of forming their own convictions to keep them from stumbling when confronted by the confusion and delusion of the world, especially as they meet up with secular professors, instructors, and even ministers.

By the time our children are ready for college or a job, they need to have a firm grasp of where they came from, why they are here, and what their ultimate purpose in life is. Make sure they are strong in the faith, ready for battle.

CHAPTER 4

Planning for Long-Range Goals

"Trust in the LORD with all your heart, and do not lean on your own understanding. In all your ways acknowledge Him, and He will make your paths straight."
—Proverbs 3:5-6 (NASB)

I n Chapter 1 we discussed some ideas to help your child love the learning process and to make learning a lifelong habit. In this chapter, we will outline our idea of a solid educational background, one that will allow your children to go on to whatever their futures might hold.

Keep in mind that a truly great education will ultimately be designed around the individual student. Still, every child should master the basics. The more skills the child has, the wider the array of options open to him or her in the future. Planning begun early in the child's educational life will be sure to pay off later. But while planning should start early, it may be your choice to delay formal learning until the child is older. Whatever your educational style, the goal should be the same, to prepare your children to meet their long-term goals.

We have designed a basic timeline with information on what you should be thinking about, planning, and accomplishing for your students at various ages. The timeline covers only basic requirements at each level; we then elaborate on specific preparations beyond the basics that will set the course for the future of each student.

The basic requirements timeline

By Ages 12-13 (Grades K-6)

- Master basic skills in language, math, research, and computing.
- Begin to uncover and develop spiritual gifts, interests, natural talents, and personal desires for the future.

Ages 12-14 (Grades 7-8)

- Review and practice basic skills, or start high school credit work, or
- A combination of review where necessary and high school work where ready.
- Exposure to and dabbling in various interests (parents facilitate learning by providing opportunities); trying out skills.
- Determine tentative plans for college, apprenticeship, or occupation.
- Plan high school studies.
- Begin to take part in extracurricular activities.

Ages 14-16 (Grades 9-10)

- Refine interests, continue extracurricular activities, add community service and leadership opportunities.
- Parents transfer majority of learning responsibility to student (let them own it).
- Complete 10 or more credits of college preparatory or basic high school curriculum.
- Keep accurate transcript records.
- Take vocational aptitude tests and/or PSAT.

Age 16-17 (Grade 11)

- Continue with above.
- Plan post high school direction—college, work, military, apprenticeship.
- Establish plan for remainder of high school in accordance with goals.
- Begin preparations if planning to attend college (take SAT or ACT, gather catalogs, research, and visit schools).

Age 17-18 (Grade 12)

- ▲ Continue with above.
- ▲ Dabble—get some college credits, do apprentice work.
- ▲ Finish coursework.
- ▲ If planning to attend college, complete and mail applications, apply for financial aid.

Now that we have outlined the basic timeline, let's consider the details.

Elementary foundations

The purpose of elementary school is to lay a foundation for more sophisticated study in the upper grades. In these first school years, the student should master all the basic skills needed for further study and for basic survival in society. We worked to be sure that our children were both literate and self-sufficient by the time they finished their elementary training. (By self-sufficient we mean that the children possessed the skills that would allow them to survive and prosper on their own if they were forced to do so. This includes the ability to work on their own, indicating they understand the concepts of initiative and industry. Clearly, we do not shove our children out into the world to fend for themselves at that point; however, they could survive if we did. We outline in Chapter 5 what is included in these skills.)

Now, what does "literate" mean? What are the basic skills needed before going on to secondary school? How much time do we need to spend "in the books"? How do we train children to be self-sufficient?

According to Webster's 1828 Dictionary, literate means learned, lettered, instructed in learning and science. According to the Merriam Webster 1999 Dictionary online, literate can mean: educated, cultured; able to read and write; lucid, polished; having knowledge or competence. Obviously, there is no clear standard of what literate means, yet everyone can recognize an illiterate person. We propose that by the end of elementary study the student should be competent in the following skills:

- ▲ Mathematics—adding, subtracting, multiplying, and dividing multi-digit numbers (such as 34,675 divided by 622), decimals, and fractions; calculations of area, perimeter, and volume for basic geometric shapes; measurement; percentages; ratios; graphs; and handling money.
- ▲ Reading—reading silently with good comprehension at a reasonable speed; reading aloud with correct pronunciation and inflection; ability to recognize the themes and structure in literature.

⅄ Writing—legible penmanship; using proper grammar and spelling in writing; ability to express themselves through creative writing; ability to clearly report on factual events and topics; keyboard and word-processing skills.

⅄ Speaking—presenting an oral report; using spoken grammar and good diction; reading aloud; and having confidence to present a topic before a group.

⅄ Research and logic—finding and organizing information on varied topics (as opposed to memorizing factual knowledge in science and history); constructing timelines; solving word problems; relating knowledge across disciplines.

⅄ General awareness of the world—familiarity with major historical events, awareness of differences in cultures, familiarity with world geography, understanding of the basic processes in nature (photosynthesis, animal life, etc.).

⅄ Keyboarding and computing—using a keyboard with ease; typing properly at least 25 words per minute; safely navigating the Internet; familiarity with computer components (hardware and software); using software programs for learning.

In addition to the above guidelines, we encourage you to start foreign language in elementary grades, if possible. It's easier for younger children to absorb foreign languages, and it will give more time for other studies during the high school years.

Secondary school studies

In our home school we did not have a junior high. We recognized two levels of study—elementary and secondary. However, even though we did not have a middle school in our home, you may want to. If so, our suggestion is to use this time (grades 7 and 8) to either review and enhance basic skills or to begin slowly working on high school skills. Generally, no

When Jeremiah was about to begin 7th grade, he developed an interest in attending Cornell University to study ornithology and economics. We called Cornell's admissions office to find out what they would require of a homeschooled student who wanted to gain admission. We were planning for the most demanding possibilities we could imagine him encountering. We then made plans for his high school years that would meet or exceed Cornell's standards. Though he has since chosen another path, our preparation for this challenging avenue gave him many options.

new material is presented in junior high curricula. In formal schools the material is essentially a reworking and enhancing of elementary concepts. In some cases, formal schools are encouraging their students to begin high school level work in 7th and 8th grades. Many students now start basic algebra, earth science, literature, or foreign languages at this level.

Our suggestion is to take time to be sure your student has fully mastered the elementary basics and is ready for secondary work. As we have said before, you may not need a full 7th or 8th grade curriculum; you can pick and choose activities that will give extra practice in areas your child may find difficult. Then, when you and the student feel confident, move on to high school work, being sure to record studies as high school credits. In areas where you feel review is not necessary, begin high school work right away. You may mix and match review courses and advanced courses to maximize the effectiveness of the middle school years. The advanced courses can also be taken at a very slow pace.

Once your student is ready for high school work, your planning will be a bit more complicated. You want to work with your children to plan secondary training that will result in their ultimate ability to pursue the opportunities of their choice. Here are our suggestions to help with the nuts and bolts of preparing your student for the future.

Book work

How much time do we spend on this book stuff anyway? We get asked that a lot. Well, it all depends. There are many ways to learn things. By the time they reach high school, students should be able to do a lot of work in textbooks and workbooks on their own. Difficult subjects may require one-on-one time with you, or even a special program with a tutor or video class. However, a homeschool student will rarely need to spend as much time per subject as students in traditional schools do. In elementary school, it is not uncommon for homeschool students to complete their lessons in a few hours per day. In high school, a good basic curriculum will usually require three to five hours of study per day. In Chapter 7 we outline the average college preparatory curriculum, so here we will focus on what is necessary for high school graduation if the student does not plan on college.

> One useful way to review math basics is to do a course in business math. If you downplay the use of a calculator, you can use this course to practice math functions while learning the new applications of keeping a checkbook, figuring sale prices, and more.

A basic high school course of study should include the following:

- ▲ 4 credits of English (composition and literature).
- ▲ 4 credits of history (American history, world history, economics, and government).
- ▲ 2 credits of mathematics.
- ▲ 2 credits of science.
- ▲ 1 credit of art or music.
- ▲ 3 credits of physical education and health (combined).
- ▲ 4 credits of electives (such as Bible, foreign language, home economics, etc.).

Each credit should roughly correspond to one year of work, or the completion of one high school textbook. (For specifics on Carnegie units, see Chapter 7.) Of course, homeschooling means you have flexibility in what texts to use and how to present courses. Some courses may not use a text at all, but depend on reading classic literature, or practicing skills in a learning environment. Book learning is an important part of education, but it is not the only form of education that is important. Consider the ideas in the remainder of this chapter to have equal significance in your students' well-rounded educational experience.

Keep in mind that state requirements may demand a certain course. For example, New York requires a course on the history of the state in 7th grade. Simply make that a part of the requirements for that year and adjust your curriculum and textbook reading accordingly. This should be easy to accomplish.

Reading and writing

The best way to help your children improve their basic English communication skills is to encourage them to read and read and read. Seeing words in context will reinforce their knowledge of vocabulary. Reading in a wide range of disciplines (science, history, technical information) and forms (nonfiction, novels, poetry, biographies) will raise their general knowledge and awareness level. Reading the Bible gives guidance for life. The Bible is an excellent reading text because of its breadth of literary styles (narrative, poetry, prose, etc.). Reading is also the single most important builder of writing skills. Having a pen pal or missionary to write to regularly can also help develop good writing skills.

Extracurricular activities

Many organizations can help your secondary school child with basic skills. 4-H clubs are a great place to learn concepts like measurement (cooking, sewing), biology (gardening, animal husbandry), economics (business skills), and public speaking (through their presentation program). Scouting and Civil Air Patrol teach leadership skills as well as specific, task-oriented information (first aid, aeronautics). Church activities can provide opportunities for the whole family to learn about music, missions, Bible study, or ministry. Obviously there are many other organizations that can provide added knowledge and skill for homeschoolers.

Sports can be an important addition to the homeschool experience. Contrary to popular opinion, there is a wide array of sports options available to homeschoolers. Nearly every community has a Little League baseball program for both boys and girls from ages five to 15.

Gymnastics and martial arts programs are available from private studios. Local YMCAs offer swim teams, basketball leagues, and lessons of all sorts. Many areas have homeschool teams for softball, basketball, and even archery! Contact your local support group to find sports teams in your area.

Homeschooling is an all-around education

To homeschoolers, all of life is school. Going to the store, vacations, working with Dad in the shop, doing craft projects with Mom—everything is an educational opportunity for your kids. Take advantage of every chance to find the instructional value to your child.

Community service

Want to give your kids a valuable experience they will not soon forget? Spearhead a community service project. Pull together a group of homeschooling families and clean up a park, offer to do a repair project for a retirement home, or work at a local rescue mission. Many public schools are now requiring that high school students spend a certain number of hours in community service per year. Churches normally reach out to those in need on a regular basis. Finding ways to include community service in the home school is fairly simple. Take advantage of service experiences for the benefit of your child and those whom they serve. Making service to the community and Christian family a part of your family's learning activities will benefit everyone involved.

Foreign language

As we said before, start your child early in foreign language and allow it to become a part of daily conversation. As Americans, we tend to minimize the value of foreign language study. Encourage your children to study a language and give high school credit for any work done in the secondary school program. It is an enriching experience to be able to communicate with others in a language that is not your native tongue.

Spiritual gifts

As Christians, we know that God has equipped each of our children with spiritual gifts. These gifts manifest themselves in part through our children's personalities and through the abilities they have to meet the needs within the church. While spiritual gifts are specifically meant for the edification of the body of Christ (the church), these same gifts determine in large part what types of activities and work we enjoy and prosper in. For this reason, we suggest you study the lists of spiritual gifts identified in Romans 12, I Corinthians 12, Ephesians 4, and I Peter 4:10-11. Help your children understand spiritual gifts, discern what their gifts are, and work out their gifts diligently in ministering to fellow Christians. God gives gifts for the edification of the church but don't forget that your family is just as much a manifestation of the church (or should be) as is your community fellowship.

Motivation

We provided motivation for our children through an educational program that allowed them to go at their own pace and explore their own interests. We believe that the most important thing to teach our children is to love to learn. Once that is done, motivating them to complete their education is a matter of setting proper goals for them to achieve individually.

Each child develops differently. One of the most important lessons we must learn as parents is knowing when to push our children because they are lagging behind their ability, and when to let them experiment with their own pace. By the time your students are in their high school years, you should be spending less time directly instructing them and more time coaching their efforts and directions. The more clearly you can get your students to plan toward their ultimate goals, the more motivated they will be. If they have a long-range goal in mind, one that they are anxious to fulfill, you will probably have a hard time keeping them from it. As long as the goal is honorable and God-directed, you can be sure your young person is on the right track.

When our middle daughter, Katie, was in 7th grade, she determined to complete her high school education before she was in 10th grade. She took her first college class at the age of 14. Our younger boy, Josiah, was not ready for high school studies at 13, as his interests lie outside the realm of book work.

CHAPTER 5

Basic Training

"Make it your ambition to lead a quiet life and attend to your own business and work with your hands."
—I Thessalonians 4:11 (NASB)

T he number of high school graduates who enter adult life without the ability to do a load of laundry today is amazing! Most homeschooled children will not have this problem, because laundry is usually an essential part of the curriculum. However, we would feel remiss if we did not include a brief chapter on how to prepare your students for the challenges and necessities of everyday life—laundry included.

As we have previously stated, we wanted our children to be considered self-sufficient early in their high school educations. To this end, we took steps to be sure each of our children was competent in basic life skills. This is not accomplished in every home, since it is usually easier for Mom and Dad to just do the work themselves—or at least it seems so at first. However, there are many benefits to training children to take on responsibilities within the home.

Skills for self-sufficiency

The alarm clock rings at 6 a.m. Your 7th grader rises immediately, takes a shower, gets his own breakfast, sits down at the dining room table, and spends the next five hours working through his math, English, general science, history, and creative writing courses. He then cleans his room, takes his clothes down to the basement, and does his own laundry. By 3 p.m., he is ready to go outside and mow the yard, or he asks you what he can do to help you clean the house. "Am I dreaming?" you wonder. Of course you are!

Most parents realize that adolescents do not normally take responsibility for their lives as described in the above scenario. Nevertheless, we believe there is an extent to which even 12, 13, and 14 year olds can be called upon to be responsible and motivated to help around the house.

Beyond the training in righteousness, character, and moral responsibility that we strive to give our children in a homeschooling environment, we need to help them learn skills that are appropriate for becoming useful, capable, and industrious adults. And the sooner, the better.

Rebekah and Katie took the attitude that anything Mom can do, they could do too. They proceeded to become expert pie makers (Mom's specialty) and to cook and bake anything they could think of. They then began to sew and do various crafts. They decorated and painted their living areas and they put wallpaper up at friends' homes. Katie has recently taken up knitting, even sitting down with Grandma and Aunt Sue to learn their techniques.

Jeremiah, Josiah, and Wesley split and stacked (with Katie's help) nearly all the wood used to heat our home when we lived on a farm.

They all learned to work with their hands and be productive. These habits have persisted into high school.

When our children were in upper elementary school, it became our habit to assign a week's worth of book work at a time. Once they finished with that, the children had free time. Since they often finished in record time, we would allow them to spend their free time on what we defined to be constructive activities. In other words, they were not allowed to play video games for hours on end simply because they finished their book work. We encouraged them to experiment with hobbies and crafts, since we consider these constructive. Jeremiah began to really enjoy cooking. He started out with simple menu items, but soon progressed to planning and making gourmet meals for our family and even guests. His culinary skills have blessed us now for years.

Cooking

Even if you are a parent who loves to cook, and who takes pride in feeding your family, you must give up some of your own comfort to have your children take over some of the cooking responsibilities. In our home, Laurie used to cook and bake every day. The kitchen was always spotless, since she would always clean as she went. Everything was in its place. Today, our children have a rotating schedule and are usually responsible for two meals a week. (Two meals times five children is 10 weekday meals. Lunches and weekends are make-it-yourself or are taken care of by Mom or Dad.)

Yes, we have actually arrived at the point where neither one of us ever has to cook. We do cook, though, often just to treat the kids to a Mom meal or a Dad breakfast. Is the kitchen still spotless with everything in its place? Yeah, right. It is basically clean and orderly...usually. Certainly it is not the way it used to be. But it is definitely worth it. Every one of our children is good at cooking the basics, and some are even aspiring gourmets. Mom and Dad have time to manage the home, teach the children, and write books!

Teach your children by your side in the young years, and, as they grow, challenge them to take on new duties. Help them to enjoy cooking by making them responsible for planning and serving entire meals. This will allow them to gain the recognition for the event and encourage them to do it again.

One thing to keep in mind, though, is to implement these ideas incrementally. It might also seem at first glance that Mom can create a vacation-like environment in her home if she can get little Susie and Johnny doing the housework and cooking every day. Wrong. Although we are now at the place that our children can manage the kitchen very well (Rebekah just recently offered to do the grocery shopping and all the cooking in order to help Laurie get this book done), they still fight about who is supposed to clean up the dishes. Our children are still children, even if they are teens who are gaining in maturity. Parents still have to oversee the cleaning, the cooking, and the complaining. (Remember, the spirit wars against the flesh and the flesh against the spirit, even in families committed to the Lord.)

Caring for the home

If you are a fussy housekeeper, it may be difficult to put up with a toilet cleaned by a 7 year old and to patiently train that child to do a good job. It takes time. It takes patience. And it is as much a part of school as learning to add and subtract.

Begin by assigning such simple tasks as setting the table or sorting socks. Laundry can be handled in large part by a responsible 10 year old. The truth is, Laurie gave up laundry years ago! Many parents feel that children cannot properly care for the machines or learn to sort and treat clothes. We have found that with minimal training our children can do an excellent job with the laundry.

It is also good to teach children basic home-repair skills, such as unclogging a pipe, changing a tire, painting a room, and driving a nail to hang a picture. Most people never think about training students to do these basics things, but if you simply remember to allow them to work beside you as you go about your weekend repairs, they will learn.

Although parents have many important roles in the home, being the maid is not one of them. You will not be doing your children (or their future mates) any good if you constantly clean up their messes. Train them to do the dishes, mop the floors, dust, sort and organize, and scrub bathrooms. You are to manage the home, not do all the work.

For a number of years, we lived in a rural home with a wood/oil-burning furnace. In order to save money, we made it a regular chore to cut and split wood. This was a season (or two)-long activity of cutting, hauling, splitting, and stacking that allowed for dad and boys to have hours of "male bonding" time. Most Saturdays, David, Jeremiah, Josiah, and Wesley would go to their favorite woods a couple of miles from home and cut up the felled trees. The first year, Dad did most of the cutting with the chain saw. Jeremiah was just 14, and it took Dad some time to convince himself that Miah (as we call him) was mature enough to handle this dangerous power tool. However, there came the day when father and son went alone to the woods and son took his first shot at handling the powerful wood-cutter. Visions of Tim Allen-like testosterone aside, it was a moment that indicated a sense of accomplishment in the life of a father and son. The same kind of success can be accomplished at different ages with other children by allowing them to use the weed-wacker, the mower, or even a vacuum cleaner. The point here is that our children need to work along-side us so that they learn the skills (and safety precautions) they will need the rest of their lives.

Managing money

Of all the areas of our lives as parents, this has been the most diffi-cult for us personally. We admit it, managing our money is our "thorn in the flesh." However, we have made it our goal to be sure that our children are much more prepared in this area than we were.

It is very important that students be capable of managing their money before they go on to higher education. College students today are actually targeted by credit card companies. They can usually obtain a MasterCard or Visa before they earn a dime! Forewarned is forearmed, as they say. Make sure you teach your students real-life financial accountability before they leave home. They should know how to create, and live within, a budget. They should be aware of the basic costs of living. They should know the relationship between diligent work and earning wages. And, of course, they should know how to start and maintain a bank account, write checks, make deposits, and balance accounts.

It is also important for our children to clearly outline their expectations and goals for their financial futures. Young women who plan on marrying and having a family should be challenged to think through whether they plan to commit to staying home. They need to consider how they will deal with financial pressures that may arise. Women also need to have a plan for self-support if they don't marry. Allow them to learn how to manage household expenses.

Young men need to know all the same basics, but they should also have a plan for how to support a family, should the desire and occasion arise. The more our young men appreciate the importance of having a financial plan, the more likely they will be to withstand emotional pressures to marry on a whim. Before they find wives and begin families, they

---

When Jeremiah was 14, he wanted to get an allowance that he could use to purchase his own clothes and necessities. We told him to make a budget for himself for a year, allowing for every type of expenditure. We had him include savings and tithe, as well as clothing, entertainment, and gifts. He then determined the yearly and monthly amounts he needed for each category in his budget. We reviewed it and found it reasonable. We gave him his allowance (1/26 of the yearly amount every two weeks) on our payday. He was then responsible for purchasing his own clothing and needs. Suddenly, he realized that he really did not need those $135 basketball shoes, but could start his own trend with his $30 pair. At the time, Air Jordans were in, so he named his choice Air Miahs. Soon all his friends were copying him! He learned to tithe and save, and how to plan and spend wisely. He also learned to do extra work when he needed to supplement his budget.

should understand the profound responsibility of caring for a wife and children. Young men must understand what supporting a family entails and be ready to provide that support. Our society would be experiencing much less debt, and marriages would be much less stressful, if every young man owned a house and had the financial means to meet family needs before he proposed.

Driving

Many parents are terrified to teach their children to drive! It really is not that difficult, though. Take your time and allow a child with a permit to practice for quite a while before actually taking a road test. Most states require some form of driver education course, so your child will have the opportunity to review the basic rules and dangers of the road. Teaching your children to be safe, responsible drivers is an important part of their education.

Decorating

Young women will benefit from some experience in decorating. (Not to say that boys cannot learn from this too.) When you are redecorating a room, allow them to help plan. Teach them about color schemes and how to make a living space warm, comfortable, and inviting. When it comes time to paint and wallpaper, the more hands the better, so involve the boys. Keep teenagers busy with making crafts and sewing for the home. Allow them to decorate their own rooms. These everyday experiences are not available in traditional schools. The opportunity to contribute to the family's comfort by designing and decorating will allow your children to prepare for one day keeping a home of their own.

Health, first aid, and CPR

We recommend that your high school health curriculum include two parts. First, we suggest a weekend away to listen to the "Preparing for Adolescence" tape series by Dr. James Dobson. Each child should spend the weekend away with a parent (girls with Mom, boys with Dad, if possible) to listen to the tapes and talk through the issues they raise. This will provide understanding of what you can each expect from the coming teen years. It is usually best to take this trip when the child is 12 to 14. The weekend away provides a time to focus and have private discussions about dating, sex, marriage, and other issues your teen will face. This opens a line of communication that is a lifeline throughout the adolescent years.

Even if you are a parent who is making a decision to homeschool a teen for the first time at age 15, 16, or 17, this series is still an excellent investment. The weekend away may be even more relevant to allow for you to restore your relationship with your child and rebuild trust that may have been lost earlier in adolescence. Make sure to give your teen the choice of where to get away to. It may be the best money you ever spend.

Second, have the student take a first aid and CPR course, available nationwide through the American Red Cross. These courses will inspire confidence during a crisis situation, and may even prove life-saving to someone in your family.

Hospitality (and being a good guest)

The best way to teach hospitality is to practice it in your home. The truth is, when you are homeschooling a family, having guests may not be easy. However, the Scriptures command us to practice hospitality (Romans 12:13), so we are never off the hook. Look for opportunities to have singles join your family for dinner or a holiday. Sponsor an exchange student. Hold holiday gatherings in your home where you can celebrate in a manner that will give glory to the Lord. Have another family over for games and snacks. House traveling missionaries or evangelists. All of these opportunities will expand the minds of your children while giving them practice in serving. Allow them to participate in planning, preparing, and serving meals, cleaning the house, and entertaining.

We often overlook teaching our children how to be good guests. Train your children to offer to help with meal preparations or cleanup while visiting friends. Make sure they know how to practice good manners when in someone else's home. We are always pleased when parents who have hosted our children seek us out to tell us what a blessing our children were in their home.

Leadership skills for a Christian home

Most parents spend much more time, effort, and money preparing their children for college and the working world than training them for marriage and family. Many homes today do not even provide a good example to children of godly and healthy family relationships. Yet family relationships have eternal impact. It should be a goal during the high school years to train our children to understand what the Bible says about marriage and raising young ones.

To date or not to date

One of the potentially difficult topics to get through with 21st-century teenagers is dating. Think about all of the pressures on children to start dating in the early teens. The divorce rate is higher than 50 percent in both the churched and unchurched communities. We have been through at least three generations where dating has been accepted as a healthy, normal part of teen life by the majority of Americans. And why not? Isn't it healthy for boys and girls to spend time together in pre-marriage relationships going to the movies, studying together, watching TV in the den with Dad and Mom upstairs? What could possibly be wrong with this basic American tradition? Plenty.

Our culture says it is a good idea to try out all sorts of relationships in order to see what is right for you. We disagree, because our goal is to train our children according to Biblical principle. Neither of us was raised with such a conservative view, so it has been through study and experience that we have come to our conclusions. When young people engage in the dating lifestyle, in an effort to "learn about relationships," they actually learn how to begin and end emotional ties on frivolous grounds. Rather than learning that God intended a man and woman to have a relationship based on commitment and unselfish love, they learn how to get what they want out of the agreement or move on. This by itself is a destructive lesson, before you even get to the obvious problems of premarital sex and emotional attachment.

It is quite possible to learn about the opposite sex through group events and interaction. In fact, we suggest it be a family habit to socialize with other families together, rather than having the teens pair up and go out by themselves. Granted, our opinions are idealistic; they are based on Scriptural principle. Still, even the Scriptures are not as specific as we have been. In our family, we have made it a goal to communicate with our children and to have some flexibility. We have given our older teens some leeway in determining their own views on the subject, and we have not been disappointed.

Our oldest three have asked to attend a few special occasions with a date and we allowed them to. When Jeremiah was nearly 18, he wanted to pursue what he called a "special friendship" with a young lady from our church. We let him know that because he was nearly 18, he would need to make his own choices, but that we would always be there to offer guidance when asked. He has developed this friendship while being careful to keep communication open with us and to keep the relationship pure and proper.

We are really not intending to write the definitive opinion on dating, but rather to encourage parents to think about the standards they want to set in their home. As we were writing this our son Wesley asked if he could share his thoughts on this topic. We found that he actually expresses our thoughts quite well (see box).

We recently shared with some close friends that our two daughters, Rebekah and Katie, who are very bright, talented, and beautiful young ladies, have never seriously dated, do not have boyfriends, and do not want boyfriends. David comically points out that if he can figure out how this happened, he could make millions teaching other fathers how he has gotten his daughters to think that way. And although protecting his girls from the "bad boys" until Mr. Right comes along is David's goal, it is really Rebekah and Katie's own conviction (which we hope we have helped them to form) to put off dating until they are ready for marriage.

Our children were blessed to take part in a "Someday a Marriage Without Regrets" Bible study, developed by Precept Ministries. We highly recommend this wonderful Bible study about all aspects of marriage. (You can find the contact information for Precept Ministries in Appendix C.)

We need to make it clear to our young adults that if they are not ready to lead a family, they are not ready for marriage. If they are not ready for marriage, there is no reason to date. Obviously, they do not have to be perfect before they wed; none of us is. But they do need to be mature enough to know their dependence must be on God.

I think that people should wait until they are mature enough to take full responsibility for a family and are ready to provide money and shelter for a family to even think about dating or courting. If you think that you have met the right person to spend your life with, then I think you can wait until you are old enough to take care of that person, to prove that you really love that person. I also think that your parents should try to be the ones to tell them the "goods and bads" of dating, if you know what I mean. I may only be 12 years old, but I do know more about this than most kids my age; my parents love me and thought enough about me to teach me the good things I need to know for life's little fastballs. I should mention that the age range I think you should allow your kids to even think of dating would have to be 17 or 18 (depending on your view of their maturity).

–Wesley Callihan

When the young man or woman is ready for marriage, it is wise for them to allow the parents some oversight of the process. By this time, they will be adults, and may not even be living at home. If you have succeeded in helping your children through the difficult teen years and have given wise, gracious, and understanding counsel to them, they should be anxious for your input as they seek mates and prepare for marriage.

Preparing for parenthood

Dare we say that young women and young men should not necessarily receive the exact same training in the high school years? Absolutely. That is not to imply that God says women are automatically meant to do all the housework—we made sure *all* our children know how to perform household chores. However, the Biblical roles of the husband and wife are not the same. The role of the husband/father is to provide for his family. That is his primary role. The mother then is free to concentrate on the nurturing and training of the children. There are many variations on how this can look, so let us give you some examples from our very varied past.

When we were first married, both of us held down full-time jobs. We then attended college together, during which time David also worked full-time and Laurie part-time. After graduation, David continued to work full-time, and Laurie stayed home with our two small children. David still had home responsibilities, but Laurie was free to concentrate on the home and children because David was providing for the family financially.

When David was laid off several years later, Laurie went to work as a teacher, while David stayed home with the small children. We then devoted some years to missionary training and service as a family, during which we were supported financially by churches and individuals. David supplemented our income with part-time jobs. For the past few years, David has worked out of an office in our home. Though this has its downside (like the kids yelling or dogs barking in the background while David is on the phone to a client), we have found it works well for us as a family. David also travels, but when he is not on the road he is always nearby.

Now that the children are teenagers, David works as a consultant, as well as with Laurie in a home-based business. Laurie also works with the children on their schooling and on her own as a writer. The children take care of the housework and some of them also have outside jobs.

Obviously, there have been a lot of changes in our situation over the years, but we have always made it a priority to have one of us (at least) providing the care and teaching of the children at home. We have had difficulties and made sacrifices along the way, but they have been worth it. We have found that Laurie is best suited to caring for the children in the home, and David is best suited to the marketplace. This is the Biblical pattern, though it is not the absolute.

There are some who will read our thoughts in this section and will characterize us as old-fashioned, bigoted, or worse. How dare we believe that the father is the breadwinner and the mother is to stay home and raise the children and take care of the house! That idea went out with Ozzie and Harriet! We live in the new millennium now. How can anyone think that the nuclear family has any legitimacy these days?

Well, maybe it is time that someone started to shout from the rooftops that God intended for men to take responsibility for being fathers, and for women to be mothers. What are we willing to sacrifice to see that our children are raised in a loving, godly home where they know the value of hard work, caring relationships, and loving commitment? We need to dedicate ourselves to raising disciplined children with values that are based on right and wrong, where good and evil are clearly defined and taught day after day. Each of our sons needs to realize that sometime in the near future he will be responsible for caring for a woman and being a father who is an example to his children. Our daughters need to be aware of the realities of caring for children and being loving and supportive wives.

The virtue of wisdom is characterized in Proverbs as a female. This is no accident. There is a legitimate place for female virtue in our culture today. Young women need to stand up and say they believe that remaining virgin until marriage is right. They need to be respected for wanting to have one husband whom they faithfully "love, honor, and obey" until death. We need a change of thinking in America and it may take a grassroots movement like homeschooling to effect that change.

One of the biggest lies that has been perpetuated in modern society is that for a woman to be free and fulfilled she must have a career. In actuality, the fact that the husband commits to provide materially for the family is the source of true liberation for women. In this family form, the woman may have a business (see Proverbs 31) or not, she can concentrate on her children and her husband, and she can store up wisdom to share with younger women in days to come. What a wonderful esteem God has for women, to put them in charge of the most daunting challenge of all—raising wonderful, godly children. ("Her children arise and call her blessed; her husband also, and he praises her. [Proverbs 31:28]")

If men and women are designed to perform different roles as adult members of a family, is it not reasonable to train them differently in preparation for those roles? That is not to say that women should not prepare for college or learn skills that will enable them to succeed in careers. It is wise, though, to encourage young women to pursue opportunities that will help them assume the roles of wife and mother in the future, should God call them to this high vocation. Since they will probably be the keeper of the home, it is important for them to have skills in cooking, child care, and home management.

Conversely, because the husband is generally to be the provider in the family, boys must focus on preparing to enter a vocation that will provide financially for themselves and their future families.

Ready or not, here they come

Sometime in the not-too-distant future, you will be releasing your children into the world to make lives for themselves. While those who went to public school are calling home to ask mom how to get their clothes clean, your student will be ready to focus on college or career (and cooking for their roommates). More than this, they will have a realistic understanding of what adult life entails. Give your students a head start by training them in the basics of life while they are being schooled at home.

CHAPTER 6

Looking Ahead to a Successful and Fulfilling Career

"Six days you shall labor and do all your work..."
–Exodus 20:9 (NASB)

W e found that our children developed tendencies toward certain vocational interests at early ages. When Josiah was two years old, David was insulating our house by blowing cellulite into the walls. Josiah joined his father, sitting on the floor playing with Dad's tools. He sat for hours, taking the sockets out of the toolbox and meticulously lining them up from smallest to largest. It was amazing to us that he showed the ability to select and organize at such an early age. We took that observation of Josiah and used it to give him opportunities to develop skills in mechanics and engineering, such as rocket-building, as he grew up. He definitely has a God-given mechanical aptitude that has developed over the years. Though Josiah could end up as a musician (he also plays guitar), instead of a scientist or engineer, we wanted to provide as many positive experiences as possible to prepare him for a future career that will be fulfilling for him.

Finding a niche

As you attempt to discern your child's natural abilities, talents, and spiritual gifts, you will need to do some learning of your own. Spend some time studying your child. As your children's mentor, you will naturally observe their interests, likes and dislikes, and areas of giftedness. As you learn about your children, use your discernment and experience to help direct them in their search for a place in the world. There are four areas to carefully assess and keep in mind as you guide your student toward a career.

Natural abilities

Natural abilities are usually pretty easy to spot, but parents don't always help children develop them. It is also true that natural abilities don't always come with the desire to pursue them. For instance, Laurie found out through aptitude testing that she has a natural ability to understand mechanical information. However, she is not at all interested in being a car mechanic or an engineer. Her gifts, talents, and temperament have led her in other directions, and her calling to be a wife and mother has taken precedence over even those directions.

Everyone has natural abilities. They are a part of our human makeup. They may include mechanical aptitude, mathematical ability, ability to work with the hands, problem-solving skills, aptitude for language, etc. These sorts of skills can usually be uncovered by taking an aptitude test (see Chapter 11), or they may be quite obvious. While people may choose not to use one of their natural abilities, if they do not have some natural ability in their chosen occupation, they will not be very successful. Most people have more than one natural ability. Be on the lookout for the abilities your child displays, as these will give clues for future job options.

When we refer to God-given talents, we mean those traits that we possess that are exceptional. For instance, a person may have an aptitude for music without being gifted. However, the musically gifted person will be able to sing or play an instrument with minimal effort. Almost every student can participate in sports, but a few are so gifted athletically that it becomes obvious. Talented people cannot take credit for their ability because it is purely a gift from God. However, they can choose to either develop or squander their talents, and they will be responsible to God for what they do with them.

Not all students have obvious profound talents, and those who do may still choose not to make their vocation in that area. We have known very talented individuals who have enjoyed their abilities as a hobby or with the church, but who have pursued paying occupations in other fields. However, a talent can also lead to a wonderful, fulfilling career. Keep options open by providing opportunities to refine and develop talents in every child.

Temperament

It's also important that your child understand his own temperament and keep it in mind when considering careers. Temperament includes personality traits that differ with each person. Some people are naturally melancholy, others are upbeat; one may be outgoing and another introverted; some are quick-tempered and others hard to rattle. People with outgoing personalities who love to be involved with others will probably not enjoy being cooped up in a solitary office day in and day out working as an accountant. On the other hand, a very introverted person will probably be uncomfortable in a job that requires constant people skills, such as pastoring. Careers should be chosen to complement personality traits.

There are personality profile tests available to help with discerning how your students' temperament will affect their careers. The *Life Pathways Personality I.D.* is a self-scoring assessment tool for determining personality characteristics and how they can affect relationships and career. This book is available from Christian Financial Concepts, P.O. Box 2377, Gainesville, GA 30503-2377, *www.cfcministry.org*. There is also a free abbreviated version of the Personality I.D. available online at the Web site. The Life Pathways ministry of Christian Financial Concepts provides several other resources for determining career directions. There are also online personality tests available for free at many sites, including *www.ansir.com* and *www.keirsey.com*.

Spiritual gifts

Spiritual gifts are those special abilities given by God to every Christian for the purpose of building up one another and contributing to the church body. If you are a believer, God has given you His spirit. Along with His spirit come spiritual gifts. Understanding spiritual gifts will allow students to gain clarity in their value not only to the Church, but in determining their life direction. It will help them to bring together the spiritual with the practical (since the two concepts don't need to be in conflict).

Because spiritual gifts are meant to edify the church, you might wonder what they have to do with preparing for college and career. We believe that God should be in control of every aspect of a Christian's life. A spiritual gift can be applied to one's career choice as much as it can be applied to serving in the Church. It is found in I Peter 4:10, where it says, "As each one has received a gift, minister it to one another, as good stewards of the manifold grace of God." The late Dr. Francis Schaeffer once said, "To the Christian, no area of one's life is autonomous." In other words, in Christian life, there is no line that separates the sacred from the secular. Jesus Christ is Lord of all, if He is Lord at all. So the spiritual gift is used to minister in the secular setting just as much as it ministers in the spiritual setting.

As a Christian you are called to live in such a way that "Whether you eat or drink, or whatever you do, [you] do all to the glory of God" (I Corinthians 10:31). Paul, the apostle, said that "None of us lives to himself, and no one dies to himself. For if we live we live to the Lord, and if we die, we die to the Lord. Therefore, whether we live or die, we are the Lord's" (Romans 14:7-8). In other words, all that we do, either in this life or the next, is unto God. We need to help our children understand this, so that as they determine a career direction, they see it in light of the eternal.

So how do we help our homeschoolers clarify which spiritual gifts they have been given? First, find a resource through your local church or favorite Bible study source and have them study the issue as part of their homeschool curriculum. There are four sections in the Bible that define this subject: I Corinthians 12-14, sections of Romans 12 (1-8), Ephesians 4 (1-16), and I Peter 4 (10-11). We would also suggest the use of one or more of the following resources:

Spiritual Gifts, Kay Arthur, Precept Ministries, P.O. Box 182218, Chattanooga, TN 38422; 1-800-763-1990 (order line); *www.precept.org*. This is a 13-week Bible study workbook usually done in a small group with a trained Precept Ministries Bible Study leader. However, you may be able to call and get a copy of the study at a minimal charge. It is an excellent Bible study that will help your homeschooler get a good handle on the subject. Once the study is done, one of the following tools can be used for further study, as well as to assess what your homeschooler's spiritual gifts are.

Your Spiritual Gifts Can Help Your Church Grow, C. Peter Wagner, Gospel Light/Regal Books, 1997, ISBN: 0830716815. According to the review on Amazon.com's Web site, "There are five steps to help you use your spiritual gifts to build God's kingdom....This book...features a spiritual gifts questionnaire to help you determine your gifts. It also includes the latest information on gift-based ministries in today's Church. Drawing on nearly 30 years of experience in studying and teaching on spiritual gifts, Dr. C. Peter Wagner has written a thorough, easy-to-understand book that identifies and discusses 27 spiritual gifts, tells you how to find your gifts, and how to use them effectively."

For those who have access to the Internet, there is a great piece of shareware out of New Zealand that is as good as anything we have seen.

It is called GiftMaid by MAIDinNZ. You can download the software by connecting to *www.maidinnz.com/gifts.htm*. Because it is shareware, you can evaluate the software before you decide to buy it for $19.95. According to their Web site, "GiftMaid uses a multiple-choice quiz format to evaluate your spiritual gifts. Select one of four possible responses to over 130 statements, such as, 'With God's enabling I can reveal what will happen in the future' and 'I find the spiritual welfare of a Christian group an enjoyable responsibility.' At the end of the questionnaire, the results are tallied and presented in an attractive report, complete with graphs. You can print a blank questionnaire on paper for use in classroom or seminar settings. Results can then be punched back into GiftMaid for saving and printing. In addition, the program can be run in preset mode, where evaluation parameters, previous evaluation results, and system settings are hidden from the respondent."

One word of caution is in order for those who come from more conservative Christian perspectives. GiftMaid software assumes that you

---

Our daughter Rebekah has always been extremely sensitive to the needs of others. She displayed her mercy towards others from a very young age. We remember fondly how, at nine months of age, she ministered to an 80-year-old member of our church. One Sunday morning after the service, while we were greeting friends after church, David was holding Rebekah as an older lady walked by. We knew that she was a lonely woman with no children of her own, and with no particular outward affection toward children. However, as she walked by, Rebekah reached out, grabbed her around the neck, and gave her a big, spontaneous hug while patting her on the back. The older lady was shocked at first, then embraced our daughter back with tears running down her cheeks. She told us that children didn't usually like her. Rebekah ministered to this woman's needs with no prompting from us. Their friendship continued for months, until we moved out of state.

As Rebekah has matured, it has become clear that she has the gift of mercy. She intends to pursue a degree in nursing, a great choice for someone who wants to minister to others. She is also involved with mission work and has been on two mission trips to northern Wisconsin to minister to Native Americans. She especially loves working with the children there. Whatever God eventually brings into Rebekah's life, we are sure it will involve her ministering mercy to the body of Christ and the unsaved.

hold to the Pentecostal viewpoint of speaking in tongues and interpretation of tongues, so be prepared to answer questions about this when your child takes the test. We think the software is very good overall.

Finally, we recommend an online spiritual gift assessment, such as the one at *www.lhbc.com/gifts/Serv/gift.html*. This assessment "will help you to determine your spiritual gifts. It is composed of 133 statements and will take about 15-30 minutes to complete. To evaluate your spiritual gifts simply indicate the degree to which each statement reflects your usual tendencies by clicking on the dot next to the appropriate response." (Copyright 1998 Lake Highland Baptist Church and New Life Bible Church.)

Once the assessment is completed, it gives a list of each spiritual gift (e.g., teaching, exhortation, evangelism, etc.) and a relative scoring of the self-assessment. You can then click on each word for a definition of the term and how the individual exhibits that gift in daily life. Each spiritual gift also lists associated ministries and Christian worker careers tied to the gift. The nice thing about this assessment, found on the Web site of the Lake Highland Baptist Church of Dallas, is that it is free and simple to do with an Internet browser. It will give as good an evaluation as most students will need.

All of these suggestions are just that—suggestions. Each has its pros and cons. Once the spiritual-gift research is done, you will still have to interpret the gift or gifts in light of a specific career direction. This is a bit more complicated. One way you might be able to make sense of this information is to graph the results, either on graph paper or with a spreadsheet program like Microsoft Excel or Lotus 1-2-3. List each of the scores for your student's self-evaluation. Then create a graph with the gifts along the X-axis and a scale along the Y-axis that is marked from zero to the highest value on the list. Break the scale into even units and chart the scores from the self-evaluation. Connect the dots or draw bars and what you will see is a graphic representation of the gifts that are most prominent in your student. Most probably, one, two, or three of these gifts will stick out above the rest. Have your student think through the kinds of jobs that would be associated with these gifts. For example, if the high scores were to align with administration, evangelism, and mercy, your child may consider sales management in the medical industry, or a job as a clerk in a retail business where serving the customer will be a key component. Some tools, like those on *www.lhbc.com*, help determine Christian vocations. Using these as a guideline, you can piece together some possible career options for your homeschooler. It will take work, but you have some options to work from.

Calling

Calling will affect the Christian's career choices as well. No matter what your child pursues as a career, God may call in another direction. Or God may call to a specific manifestation of the careers they have chosen. Receiving a calling from God need not be a mystical experience. God calls us all to live holy lives, full of the fruit of the Spirit. He calls every husband and wife to be faithful to each other. He calls all parents to raise their children in a godly home and to teach them God's Word and ways. In our home, our calling to parenthood (which happened at the conception of our first child) meant that we would be the caretakers and educators of our offspring. We would not relinquish these responsibilities to others. Most often it is the mother who is called to stay at home and care for the children. This is the highest calling that anyone could have; after all, the hand that rocks the cradle truly does rule the world.

One more point is relevant here: Your child may get a calling from God, just as any Christian could, to a specific ministry or mission. God may call your child to do foreign work for a short time, or even to give her life to spread the Gospel in a desolate place. Be prepared. It will tear at your soul to see your baby go, especially when all of your goals and plans for that perfect career may go up in smoke. Will you be able to accept that? (For more on this topic, see Chapter 12.)

Resources for assessing possible career pathways

There are several notable resources for helping to determine a career direction. Life Pathways, a ministry of Christian Financial Concepts, provides the following tools, all of which have a Christian viewpoint:

- ▲ *Your Career in Changing Times*, a career textbook for Biblical planning.
- ▲ *Finding the Career That Fits You*, a career self-assessment workbook.
- ▲ *The Pathfinder*, a career decision resource book.
- ▲ *Guide to College Majors and Career Choices*, a reference for higher education.
- ▲ Career Direct—YES!, an interactive survey for children ages 13-16.
- ▲ *Personality I.D.*, a self-scoring personality profile booklet.

▲ Career Direct Guidance System, which includes a paper or CD-ROM assessment that produces about 30 pages of individualized reports, audio teaching tapes, a choice of *The Pathfinder* or *Guide to College Majors and Career Choices* book, an action plan, and a job sampler, all for $89-$106.

The American College Testing service (*www.act.org*) provides the DISCOVER program (software) that creates a personal profile assessing personal interests, abilities, and job values. An online demo is available at the Web site, but the program is only available through schools and libraries at this point, although it will be available online in the future. However, ACT also produces the Realizing the Dream program, which offers parents and students the resources to work through the career planning process together. The Family Edition of the program, which is $19, includes:

▲ A brief guide written to relieve doubts you might have about how to get started with the process of advising your children about their career futures.
▲ An eight-minute video.
▲ *Realizing the Dream for Parents*, a booklet that includes specific and easy-to-follow strategies, activities, and suggestions to make you a more effective career advisor for your child.
▲ *Realizing the Dream for Students*, which contains activities and information to help your child make successful educational and career decisions.

(Taken from the *www.act.org* Web site.)

Those who enjoy their work tend to be the most successful. Those who find work that fits their abilities, temperament, gifts, and calling will enjoy it. The more we are able to think through and understand what our traits are, the more we will be able to find those career options that fit us best. This will be the most likely route to a satisfying career, and give others the benefit of our best efforts and capabilities. It creates a natural win-win situation.

Preparing to enter the world of work

Homeschool parents have a unique chance to observe talents, gifts, and tendencies in their children. These traits are good indicators of what type of job will provide fulfilling employment in the future. Use that knowledge about your child's interests and gifts to help him choose from the following opportunities for finding a vocational calling.

Exploring spiritual gifts through work in the local church fellowship

The local church is a microcosm of society in many ways, and as such can be a great place for your children to try out their spiritual gifts. Most churches would love to have a few new volunteers. Think of the variety of interests to explore—working with children in the nursery, teaching Sunday school, cooking for special events, visiting the sick in the hospital (a great way to get a look at medical and service jobs), helping out with a new addition (carpentry skills), taking care of an elderly person's yard (landscaping), accounting, janitorial work, graphic art and Web design using church computers, running the sound system, and administrative duties as a receptionist or office worker. Your local church is definitely one place where young people can learn their value through the use of their talents.

Providing lessons and tools in areas of interest

Once there has been some sense of direction in determining your child's potential career direction, you will want to think through options for his or her preparation. Depending on the extent of the educational requirements, there may be the need to plan lessons and provide tools to help in the process from outside the home.

Finding outside activities such as participation in church, civic groups, clubs, and extracurricular functions may be all that is needed to solidify your child's skills. Some organizations have guilds that may be of help for the child who wants to pursue a craft. Be creative in your quest. It may involve extensive travel or financial investment. Try to join forces with other homeschool parents who are looking for similar resources for their children.

One of the advantages of the Internet is that there are many new ways to access information that until now was hard to find. CD-ROMs are also available for many subjects. It is important to find materials that fit the specific needs of the student and allow for comprehensive coverage of the material.

Apprenticeship in fields of interest

Homeschooling is perfect for vocations that involve apprenticeships. Homeschool students are not restricted in their schedules like school students, and it is amazing how willing professionals are to work with homeschoolers to provide apprenticeship opportunities. Homeschoolers are usually more responsible, conscientious, mature, and punctual than their counterparts in traditional schools. Having an apprenticeship can help your child determine whether a field is worth pursuing before investing time and money in an expensive educational path that may not be as enticing as first anticipated. The financial benefits to catching this early are clear.

Clubs

There are two clubs that are very helpful in preparing homeschoolers for future careers: 4-H and Junior Achievement. These two organizations are very good for teaching children how to lead and become industrious, productive citizens.

A 4-H Club is a great way to teach young people basic home economics, agriculture, citizenship, business, conservation, and public health. Many homeschool groups have formed their own clubs. This works very well because they can schedule meetings during the regular school day. The homeschool mothers serve as the adult leaders and work with their children to run the club meetings. We have found that 4-H agents love homeschool clubs because of the huge amount of parental involvement. They are very impressed with our commitment to our children.

According to the 4-H Web site, *www.4-h.org,* "The 4-H Program was founded sometime between 1900 and 1910 to provide local educational clubs for rural youth from ages nine to 19. It was designed to teach better home economics and agricultural techniques and to foster character development and good citizenship. The program, administered by the Cooperative Extension Service of the U.S. Department of Agriculture, state land-grant universities, and county governments, emphasizes projects that improve the four Hs: head, heart, hand, and health."

Members work on such individual projects as model rockets and bird houses, participate in public speaking events centered around science or cooking, and make everything from baked goods to sewing projects. They learn to grow fruits and vegetables, raise farm animals, and display them at county and state fairs. The 4-H slogan teaches young people to serve their country, live a clean life, be loyal to their communities, and keep a proper attitude in heart and mind.

As for Junior Achievement, according to their Web site, *www.jaintl.com*, the organization's "programs teach students to understand and appreciate free enterprise. In the process, JA programs promote entrepreneurism and economic self-determination while giving young people the skills they need to play an active role in our global economy." The only possible negative for homeschool parents may be the "global" emphasis. However, as we have noted before, we can control what our children are exposed to. We feel it is better to be there with our children as they confront these issues.

JA's approach is to educate young people through partnerships established between business and education. They use programs to increase understanding in six key areas:

▲ The Importance of Market-Driven Economies.

▲ The Role of Business in a Global Economy.

▲ The Commitment of Business to Environmental and Social Issues.

▲ The Commitment of Business to Operate in an Ethical Manner.

▲ The Relevance of Education in the Workplace.

▲ The Impact of Economics on Their Future.

JA wants to teach young people to value the free enterprise system, business, and economics, so that they will continue to work to improve the quality of life in their communities and their world. Programs are available in three levels: K-6, junior high, and high school. The focus is on encouraging young people to complete their high school educations, appreciate lifelong learning, build positive work habits in a diverse culture, and create business and educational partnerships in an academic setting to prepare for the workplace. It can fit in well with a homeschool environment, and it teaches children how to prepare for work in the business world.

Unit studies and projects

By focusing on the specific interests of our children, we can help them to prepare for the future. Unit studies allow students to focus on a particular interest while developing multiple academic skills. For example, suppose you have a son who is tremendously interested in rocketry. This one subject lends itself to the study of the history of rockets and the politics involved, such as the race to the moon between the United States and the Soviet Union. Your son can study the science of trajectory,

Newton's laws, and such physical concepts as velocity and the parabolic motion of a Mercury launch. He can learn about economics as it relates to the cost of a rocket launch. Mathematics can be used to calculate various aspects of the science of flight. Business administration can be addressed by doing research on commercial satellite enterprises. Physical education could be accomplished through learning and practicing the United States Air Force's physical fitness program, and so on.

There are almost an infinite number of unit study topics for a homeschool. These studies provide an eclectic curriculum for a student who has mastered the basics but who is not yet prepared for college. Studying an area of possible career interest may also make sense for your homeschooler.

You can also assign additional projects in specific subjects—such as science or math—to supplement your textbooks. This may become necessary for specific children who need additional work or who are preparing for college and the SAT or ACT.

Getting a job

There are some basic things you can do to help your child prepare for work. According to professional employment advisors Kenneth Hitchner and Anne Tifft-Hitchner, authors of *Counseling Today's Secondary Student*, future job success will demand certain broad skills, including:

1. Self-analysis: Being able to objectively analyze personal strengths and weaknesses and to make the necessary effort to enhance both areas.
2. Cooperative learning: This promises to be more than a passing fancy at elementary and secondary educational levels. (Homeschoolers practice this virtually every day.)
3. Global thought capability. (Jesus says to be in the world and preach the gospel to every nation; it is an essential part of our Christianity.)
4. Conflict resolution. (We have been given the ministry of reconciliation.)
5. Passion for performing well. (Do all things to the glory of God.)
6. Willingness to change and to accept change. (Repentance is a cornerstone of the gospel.)
7. A keenness toward networking. (Homeschoolers do this every day as well.)

8. Optimism in the face of uncertainty. (Faith is the substance of things hoped for, the evidence of things not seen.)
9. Facility with oral and written communication.
10. Openness to criticism. (As it says in Proverbs 12:1, "He who hates rebuke is stupid.")

With the increased competitiveness of the job market, the ability to communicate effectively both orally and in writing is even more important to prospective employers than one's grade point average. Character, integrity, a positive, industrious attitude, honesty, and diligence are all qualities that employers want to see.

According to a Census Bureau survey of 3,000 nationwide employers conducted in 1994, the most important qualities considered in hiring of new non-supervisory or production employees are, in order of importance: attitude, communication skills, previous work experience, recommendations from current employers, recommendations from previous employers, industry-based credentials certifying skills, and years of schooling completed. Of far less importance to these hiring managers are scores on tests administered as part of the interview, academic performance, reputation of the applicant's school, and, last in importance, a teacher's recommendation.

Employers looking to hire a new employee want a positive attitude about oneself, work in general, the company, and the particular job. They want the employee to exhibit enthusiasm, a cheerful demeanor, interest in the company based on some knowledge of its products or services, and eagerness to learn more about the company and the job. They should listen well and have good English oral and written skills and an organized thought process. Employers want to hire people who have integrity and honesty and a sense of self-worth. They want employees who have computer literacy, which includes keyboard skills and knowledge of basic terminology and the principal ways systems are used in the company.

Worth the effort

Just as there are no two people who are completely the same, there are no two people with exactly the same vocational skills and academic interests. Helping your child find his way to a career that will honor God, provide financially, and be rewarding is a complex process. Don't be fooled. It will demand hard work. Make sure your children know this is true.

Parents have a unique perspective of their own children. When combined with a firm grasp on reality and a big dose of faith, this perspective can produce an ability to counsel them like no one else. Parents see the abilities and idiosyncrasies of each child; they know their children—and their faults and talents—better than anyone. Combining this knowledge of your child with research of the many available options will help pave the way to a secure and fulfilling future.

CHAPTER 7

Steering Toward College

"Be diligent to present yourself approved to God as a workman who does not need to be ashamed, handling accurately the word of truth."
II Timothy 2:15 (NASB)

I f your homeschool students have any desire to pursue a college degree, you will want to prepare them thoroughly. If they change their mind later, the preparation described below will certainly not hurt them, and in fact will be useful to almost any vocation. So, if in doubt, prepare!

Course of study

The college-bound student will need to have an accumulation of credits in high school that will both prepare him for college-level study and allow him entrance into the school of his choice. Each traditional high school develops its own standards for students, according to state standards and the resources of the school. In the homeschool situation, you establish your own criteria for graduation, and your transcript and diploma will be the records you need for college entrance. It is wise to adhere to a basic college preparatory program if your student intends to pursue higher education.

A good all-around education is the most important criterion in college preparation. The abundance of homeschoolers seeking college entrance in the past few years has driven colleges to determine their own standards for acceptance. If your child wants to attend a particular college, it may be prudent for you to investigate what that college requires before the student begins high-school work.

In general, our investigations of college entrance requirements have disclosed that there are really two necessities—SAT or ACT scores and a transcript (see Chapter 13 for tips on keeping a transcript) reflecting a basic college preparatory accumulation of credits. So, what does that accumulation of credits look like? Of course, there is room for individuality; however, it is wise to cover the basics.

Junior high (grades 7-8)

For the junior-high student, make sure all the basics in math, reading, writing, and study skills are mastered. If your child is behind in any of these basic skills, you should take the time in junior high to remedy the problem. You can do this within the definition of junior high without making the student think he or she is behind.

> When Jeremiah was 13 he was very interested in both ornithology and economics. He was 7th-grade age, but was ready both academically and emotionally to begin his high school studies. We lived in upstate New York at the time, and Jeremiah thought he might eventually want to attend Cornell University. We did not want to begin his high school work and find out later that he needed to change course. We knew that if he met the admission requirements for Cornell, he would likely be able to attend any school he eventually chose. So we launched an investigation of Cornell's prerequisites.
>
> David made a call to the Cornell admissions office and personally spoke to an admissions counselor. After explaining that we homeschooled, he asked what the specific requirements for Cornell entrance would be. We were delighted to find that Cornell would consider Jeremiah upon completion of high school, presuming he had an acceptable SAT score and a transcript of his course work prepared by us. Cornell has already admitted homeschoolers using SAT scores, transcripts, and the standard application process. Jeremiah would compete with other applicants based on SAT scores and the grades he earned in our homeschool.
>
> Jeremiah has now completed high school and has plans other than attending Cornell, but the process was useful in providing us with the confidence to proceed.

Generally, in traditional schools (and therefore traditional curricula) for junior high there is very little new information presented. Grades 7 and 8 are spent reviewing and practicing elementary skills, allowing time for the student to mature. Topics first encountered in elementary school are handled a little more deeply, and students are asked to interact with the material a bit more (that is, more writing assignments, thinking through topics, etc.). If the student has mastered the basics of the elementary grades, he can go on to high school work without skipping a beat. With this secret of junior high exposed, you should feel free to pursue the following options: review basics with mastery as your goal, and/or begin high school work (at a slower pace if necessary).

It is not necessary for students to complete courses at a particular age. It is perfectly acceptable to record any high school-level work on the

In our homeschool, we dealt with each child individually when it came to starting high school work. Jeremiah, Rebekah, and Katie began high school work directly after completing 6th grade. Jeremiah was strong in history and language and took advanced courses in these areas early. Math was a bit more of a challenge for him, and it took him more than two years to complete Algebra I. Since he started algebra at 12, he actually finished it at the same time as his contemporaries in traditional schools. Rebekah was the opposite—a whiz at math. By 16, she had completed four years' worth of high school-level math along with her other subjects. Katie is a diligent worker and highly motivated, so even though she is three years younger than Jeremiah, she never likes to be behind her older siblings. She finished 6th grade a year early and high school before she was 15. The three of them took their first college course last year at our local community college at ages 14, 16, and 17.

Fourth and fifth in line are Josiah and Wesley. Josiah finished his 6th grade work at the normal age, and though he also could have handled high school-level academics, we knew he was not as motivated or as mature as his older siblings had been. We did not want to push him to the point of disliking his work. So we took a more relaxed route through junior high, working on his writing skills and keeping sharp in math. He is the engineering type and has spent a good deal of time working on model rocketry and experimenting with machines. He will be starting high school work at the normal age of 14. Wesley began junior high (review) work last year, after finishing 6th grade early, and he will slowly begin high school work this year with Josiah.

high school transcript, regardless of when it is completed. For instance, if French I is taken in 7th grade, record it as high school credit—it is a high school-level course. It is also not necessary to complete the whole course in one year. As long as all of the required work is done, record the credits when they are completed.

In junior high you can also mix and match. For instance, if your child is a bit shaky in basic math skills, take time to work on that. However, the same child may be an avid reader and writer, allowing him or her to take high school-level courses in literature or writing. The secret is to allow the child to work at his or her level of competence in each subject.

High school (grades 9-12)

The basics

In the home school it is not necessary to specifically differentiate 9th grade from 10th, or 10th from 12th for that matter, except as necessary in relating to the rest of the world (Sunday school, etc). Rather, be sure that courses follow in logical progression (i.e., do not start advanced math before Algebra I).

A minimum outline of college preparatory work will look like this:

- **English**—4 credits (must include composition and literature; recommended to include research and public speaking).
- **Social Studies**—4 credits (must include world history, U.S. history; recommended to include government/civics and economics).
- **Mathematics**—2 credits (must include algebra I and II, or algebra I and geometry; recommended to include additional 2 credits in trigonometry and advanced math).
- **Science**—2 credits (must include physical science and biology; recommended to include additional 2 credits in chemistry and physics with labs; see following discussion).
- **Fine or Practical Arts**—1 credit (music, visual arts, home economics, etc.).
- **Physical Education/Health**—2 credits.
- **Foreign Language**—2 credits.
- **Electives**—3 credits.

One credit in high school is traditionally accepted to be one year of a subject, working 40 minutes per day for 180 days (or 120 hours), plus homework. In the home school, students do not waste the huge amount of time that is wasted in the classroom, so your student may take much less time to do the same amount of work. College-bound students should have a minimum of 20 credits, being sure to cover all required subjects.

You will want to tailor work in the later phases of high school to fit the college study goals your child anticipates. For instance, if he or she wants to study in a field of science, another two years of math and science are recommended. In choosing electives, you can use Bible or another subject of interest. Be sure to keep your child's uniqueness in mind when you design his or her course of study.

There are various ways to tackle the job of making sure high school credit requirements are met. When our oldest was in 6th grade, we developed an outline of all the courses we would require for graduation from our home school. It was actually quite ambitious and went beyond what any traditional curriculum would cover. It included requirements in character development, Bible study, and Christian service. We knew when we wrote it that it was a template, an ideal, and that we would probably need to update it as we actually experienced these years with our children. However, it provided a source of motivation and direction. We encouraged our 7th graders to begin on it as they were motivated and ready.

Our oldest three have now completed our program (at ages 14, 16, and 17). Though we did make some changes, we stayed surprisingly close to the model. Each of them has earned quite a few credits beyond the requirements of a traditional school.

Difficult areas

Some areas of the high school curriculum are difficult to handle in the home. With a little resourcefulness, you can succeed at providing your children with the experiences they need.

Laboratory sciences are a very important part of college preparation. In addition to their science content, laboratory experiences provide problem-solving and practical skills that will be necessary in college work. Many see the difficulty of experiencing labs as one of the biggest problems for homeschooling. Because our background is in science, and specifically in teaching science for Laurie, this has been less of a problem for us than for some. We have organized and taught group lessons for lab work in general science, biology, chemistry, and physics. Other families we know of have used video labs. There are even laboratory experiences, such as frog dissection, available on the Internet (though it just doesn't smell the same). Another option would be to take the upper-level science courses at a community college for high school and college credit simultaneously (see Chapter 12). If you are adventurous and resourceful, you can also do many labs at home with some basic equipment. Some support groups might consider purchasing equipment cooperatively and having a lab equipment library.

What about courses you really cannot handle, such as foreign languages, advanced math, and music theory? Most of us are not proficient in every subject area, and some parents have little experience in any. The truth is, having a graduate degree in every subject area is not necessary. In the upper grades, it can be of great benefit to hire a tutor for difficult subjects (you would not hesitate to hire a piano teacher, so why not a chemistry tutor?). Other subjects are available in video or satellite form. Distance courses over the Internet and software are abundant on any imaginable topic. The key is to be open-minded when looking for options. At this point, there are resources available to help homeschoolers with everything from American Sign Language to driver's education. Be willing to get help in areas where you do not feel proficient.

Tests, tests, and more tests

Several tests should usually be taken by students who expect to go on to higher education. These include the PSAT, SAT I, SAT II, and the ACT. It is not necessary for any student to take them all, but choose the

---

Part of the reason Jeremiah spent nearly three years studying algebra was that we could not hit on the right way to teach it to him, according to his learning style. We were entering a state of desperation when Jeremiah told us he would like to take a video course. Because we are both quite capable in math, we had never thought we would use video classes, but by then we were willing to try anything. As it turned out, the video presentations were just what he needed. He enjoyed having a teacher other than his parents at that point, and he had the freedom to go at his own pace. He caught on quickly and advanced well, taking the tests and excelling at them. We thought we would never need to resort to video classes in our homeschool, but being open to whatever might work for him turned out to be a big blessing and relief.

most pertinent to their needs. Please see Chapter 11 for a thorough discussion of these exams. One special note for the college bound: It may not be necessary to take any of these tests if the student accumulates college credit in high school, as in this case the student is judged based on actual course grades.

What else do they need?

Great study skills

It is crucial for any student to learn good study skills. This will prove valuable even if college is not the end goal. For instance, in the business world, new applications for computers are constantly emerging. It will be necessary for a successful businessperson to be able to evaluate new systems, which will require research and study.

The following is a list of study skills that students must have in order to excel in college:

- **Reading Comprehension**—College students are required to cover and absorb large amounts of reading material on a strict time schedule. The better your child's skills for taking in reading material, the better he or she will cope with college work.
- **Outlining**—The ability to condense reading or course material into outline form is a skill that will enhance the college student's test-taking ability. College courses offer large amounts of information in various formats, and outlining can bring things into focus.
- **Note taking**—In the home school most students never have to take notes on a lecture, since there usually aren't any! It will be important for the college-bound student to have some experience in taking down what is being said. (Taking notes on church sermons or on video classes can be good practice.)
- **Listening**—The greatest of skills. Though we hope our students have learned this skill well in our homeschools, some may need a tune-up. In college courses, listening implies paying attention to subtleties (like what the instructor thinks is important) as well as details (following directions).
- **Discerning**—This is a crucial college skill, since professors are not likely to spell out every detail of what they expect to the student. In college, it is important for the student to be able to

determine what information instructors want for exams or projects, and how they want things done.

▲ **Researching**—Frequent visits to the library and familiarity with Internet research capabilities will sharpen the skills that will be required of students in college. It will be important for students to know their way around the library and to be comfortable asking questions.

▲ **Reviewing**—College-level courses will require retention of a large amount of knowledge for a long time. The student who has skills in reviewing (note cards, notes, etc.) will do well in higher-level studies.

▲ **Test taking**—Whole books are available on this topic. Suffice it to say here that test-taking skills alone can make a letter grade difference in college. It would be worth the time to get a book on this subject and review the skills suggested.

▲ **Applying**—You will not see many people include this on a list of study skills, but we feel it is crucial. If you cannot apply what you have studied, you have not learned it, and if you do not apply it, you will forget it! So, try to find a way to work new vocabulary into your conversation, practice a newly learned skill, or discuss course topics in your everyday life.

When Jeremiah was 14, David encouraged him to learn a programming language. We got him a self-study course in Visual Basic. Jeremiah read the book and put together his first computer program. He was very excited as he shared it with us. But that is as far as it went. David tried to encourage Jeremiah to keep going, but to no avail. We could have pushed our son to learn this technology when his interest waned, but instead we decided to back off. We felt that pushing Jeremiah into programming could stifle any future interest in computers. So we let him go into other areas of interest. Occasionally, David would ask him if he was doing anything with programming on his computer.

About six months ago, Jeremiah decided to buy his own computer. He wanted it mostly to e-mail his friends. To our amazement, he began to get interested in creating Web pages. He has since gone out and purchased a number of books and magazines on the subject. He is currently working on building our business Web site. So we may have done the right thing by not pressuring our son into computer technology when he wasn't interested.

We recommend including in your high school repertoire a short course (available in book, cassette, and video form, or in group lessons with other homeschoolers) on study skills.

More than computer literacy

There is quite a push these days to get our kids to be computer literate. (This is a task that we have found to be about the easiest in homeschooling! We do not need to work to get our kids to use the computer!) It is essential, of course, that our students can operate a keyboard, navigate the Internet, and run software. A basic understanding of computer hardware would be a great asset as well.

Our children were required to spend half an hour a day on typing software before they could play on the computer. They all learned proper keyboard skills before they were in 5th grade, which saved a lot of re-learning later. Each of them now types much faster than either of us— and we are pretty fast!

We have titled this section "More Than Computer Literacy," however, because in this new millennium people who *understand* computers will be most prepared. It is one thing to be able to run software and another to know why and how it works. In our home, our six computers take turns breaking down. As annoying as it is, we have learned to appreciate the ability to troubleshoot and repair minor difficulties. We would highly recommend a course or two in computer theory and programming (we use the *For Dummies* series) to acquaint your student with the unseen aspects of the computer world.

Remember, our children are probably more exposed to computers than most public school students are. Homeschool research indicates that the majority of homeschools have at least one personal computer in their home, versus less than 50 percent of public school homes. As we are giving our children access to computers through curriculum and electronic correspondence, they are becoming computer literate. Taking them to the next level, learning how to use the computer vocationally, will depend on factors such as temperament, academic preferences, skill sets, and personal desires. Anything beyond the basics will give them the edge in college preparation.

Extracurricular activities

In Chapter 4, we outlined many of the specific extracurricular activities that are available to secondary homeschoolers. We wanted to include a section here as a reminder of how important these activities are on the transcript or resume of the college-bound student. Colleges and universities are not solely interested in grades and SAT scores. They want to know that the students they accept have had experiences that have prepared them for higher education and that will help them contribute to the student body of their school.

The more activities the student has that are pertinent to the proposed field of study the better, but diversity is also important.

Crossing over (double crediting high school and college)

This topic is covered in detail in Chapter 12, but a short explanation here is warranted. When your student is in the upper high school grades, it may be wise to consider having him or her take some courses at a local college instead of at home. For instance, beginning chemistry is offered at most community colleges. Having your student take chemistry in that venue will be advantageous in several ways. It will provide college experience, allowing the student to gain confidence in the college setting; it will eliminate the need to find laboratory options at home; and it can be used for both high school and college credit.

Another option to consider is Internet or distance learning. Internet courses are available in almost any subject area, and they too can be double credited.

The practice of double crediting high school and college courses is neither new nor unusual. Simply enter the credits on the high school transcript with a note that they are college courses. The college will

---

Our daughter Katie has been interested in animals since she was very young. She has wanted to pursue a career in veterinary science since elementary school. We actually bought a farm at one point to give her an opportunity to raise animals and care for them. She operated her own kennel, breeding English Springer Spaniels, and she cared for horses, goats, chickens, rabbits, and cats. We also started a homeschool 4-H group, where she could learn skills related to raising and showing animals. She has also been involved in sports and other activities, but her 4-H experience will be important to her should she continue to pursue a career in veterinary science.

maintain a transcript as well for credit that can then be transferred to another school later. This college credit option may also allow your student to matriculate to college without the hassles of explaining your homeschool credentials. Once the student has completed college-level courses, a college transcript may be all that is necessary for transfer enrollment, with no need at all for a high school transcript. The secret is for the student to do well on the college course, so start out with courses that are not too difficult.

Just do it

Taking on the college preparation of your homeschool student can be rewarding when kept in perspective. As a homeschool parent, you have probably not taken the traditional path on many issues. So finding your way through to college entrance for your child can be an adventurous journey, free from status quo expectations. When you keep your goals in mind and keep the spiritual education of your children as the priority, you can and will succeed in providing the best higher education options available.

When Laurie attended public high school in New York in the 1970s, she took her entire senior course load at the local community college. She received credit for her high school diploma as well as college credit she transferred to another institution later as a sophomore.

Our daughter Rebekah will be pursuing a similar course. She accumulated enough credits for high school graduation by age 16, but has not taken some of the courses she needs to pursue the nursing degree she desires. She began last year by taking a course at our community college and will continue this year adding credits (to both her high school and college transcript) through the CLEP program (see Chapter 12). She did not want to officially graduate until 2000, as scheduled, so she will continue to accrue credits until then. When she graduates from high school, however, she will be able to transfer into college, probably as a second-semester sophomore or a junior.

CHAPTER 8

Ready for Anything

*"But the goal of our instruction is love from a pure heart
and a good conscience and a sincere faith."*
—I Timothy 1:5 (NASB)

I t's a familiar scenario: When Johnny was 13, he was sure he would go into the military after graduation. At 15, he said he was definitely going to apprentice as an electrician, and at 17 he decides he wants to apply to an Ivy League university! No matter how well we plan, we are sometimes blindsided. What to do? Don't panic.

Keep your options open

The best way to be ready for a change in plans is to make sure every curriculum includes all the basics, and that your children complete courses at their highest level of potential. For instance, early on it may seem that your child will never need algebra. After all, who needs algebra to run a retail dry cleaner? Still, if your child is capable of learning algebra, the better plan is to include it. If you are avoiding the subject because you can't teach it yourself, get a video program, take an online course, pay a tutor, trade babysitting time for tutoring by another parent who knows the subject, organize group lessons, or just learn it together. Your personal comfort with the subject should never be the determining factor. There are many options for a high school student to learn difficult subjects at home.

Now, of course, we have just used algebra as an example. In actuality, we recommend that you stick very closely to a college preparatory curriculum in high school, no matter what the student has planned. Since the college preparatory route is the highest academic option, it will prepare him whether he decides to be a farmer or a cardiologist. That way, you won't have to scramble in the last semester of high school when your potential carpenter decides to go into a pre-law program.

Get practical

One method you might use to monitor how well-rounded your course of study is (and how well-prepared your students are for any possible direction) is to evaluate your program regularly. We did this at least twice a year in our home school, though we never had an official evaluation form. We regularly looked at our children's progress, their goals, how the methods we were using were working, and how our home school was functioning as a whole. We were never afraid to ditch a whole system or curriculum whenever we felt the need. There was even a year when, in March, we determined nothing was working, and we dropped everything. We were under a tremendous amount of family stress related to jobs and moving, and quite frankly, we couldn't handle anything more than the basics of life. One day, we sat down and announced that all scheduled book work was off for the rest of the year, and we did what is known as unschooling. The children read, did crafts and cooking, watched educational programming on television, played games, and helped out with the farm and housework. It was the break everyone needed and it did not slow their eventual progress one bit. Other times we have just needed to switch a math course for one child. That's the beauty of the home school. You are free to be flexible and pragmatic, as you only need to ensure that your own children learn, not a classroom of 30.

It might be useful for you to have some measurement tool to determine your overall progress toward the end goal of college and career. To that end, we offer a set of surveys for self-evaluation at different levels. The intent is to check yourself to be sure that if your children announce a drastic change in plans at some later date, your program will have been well-rounded enough to support their choices. We suggest you fill out these surveys yourself, though you may obtain information from the student. Then file the form in the child's file, look at it again in six months or a year, and file another updated form with it. Feel free to reproduce these pages as needed.

Use the forms on pages 102-104 to focus your attention on areas that are progressing well and those that need attention. Make adjustments in curriculum and subjects as the need arises. You may find a pattern emerge after filling out several of these forms over a period of time—we suggest at least twice a year—which can help you and your child determine a good route for the future.

Change in plans

It looks like it's too late. Your educational plan has been aimed at training your son to take over your hardware store, and now he wants to get an engineering degree. How will you make up for lost time? Rather than starting from scratch and working through college preparatory subjects, try using CLEP (College Level Examination Program) exams, community college courses, or distance learning courses that can be double credited for both high school and college. These types of courses not only provide the opportunity to learn the material, but they look great on transcripts for the college bound. In most cases, students will do fine with these types of courses or tests even if they are new to the material (that is, they haven't taken a high school-level course in the subject). Check out Chapter 13 for information about CLEP, community colleges, and distance learning options.

Keep your perspective

You have planned, worked, and prayed toward one goal, and then, just like that, your child chooses to dump the whole idea. Take a deep breath. Remember the goal: "Love from a pure heart and a good conscience and a sincere faith. (I Timothy 1:5)" If you have focused on what really matters—the heart—and have provided a good, basic, all-around education, your homeschooler will be just fine.

As parents, and especially as homeschoolers, you have so many different things to keep in mind. You purposely focus on the spiritual aspects of your children's development, then wake up one day in a panic that they don't know enough math. We know. Now is the time to review your perspective. You can be confident that the Lord will be faithful to complete in you and in your students what He has begun. You must be faithful to seek His guidance, and diligent to do as He directs. Take a fresh look at the totality of your homeschool life, make changes where necessary, and trust God for the outcome.

Ages 8-11

Child's name _____ Date: _____

Spiritual growth

We are satisfied/unsatisfied that he/she is desiring to follow God. _____

We see the following fruit of the Spirit emerging (Gal 5:22): _____
_____

We need to work on the following disciplines: _____
_____

We have encouraged the following service opportunities: _____
_____

Our spiritual goals for the following few months are: _____
_____

To accomplish our goals we need to focus on: _____

To accomplish our goals we need to change how we: _____

Special thoughts or comments: _____

Educational growth

What subjects or activities does this child especially enjoy? _____
_____

What subjects or activities are especially troublesome? _____
_____

What was the highlight of the past few months for this child (in school or otherwise)?
_____

Have any new interests surfaced? If so, what? _____

We were so proud of our child's accomplishment in the area of: _____
_____

We wish he/she would work harder at: _____

Are math skills on target for his/her age? _____

Are writing (composition) skills are on target for his/her age? _____

He/she would _____ all day if we let him/her.

How does he/she feel about reading? _____
_____

He/she would like to be a _____ when grown up.

We recently participated in the following activities with others: _____
_____

Our educational goals for the following few months are: _____
_____

To accomplish our goals we need to focus on: _____

To accomplish our goals we need to change how we: _____

Special thoughts or comments: _____
_____

Ages 12-14

Child's name_____ Date: _____

Spiritual growth

We are satisfied/unsatisfied that he/she is committed to Christ. _____

We see the following fruit of the Spirit emerging (Gal 5:22): _____
_____

We need to work on the following spiritual disciplines: _____
_____

We have noticed a spiritual gift of (see I Cor 12-14, Romans 12:1-8, Eph 4:1-16, and I Peter 4:10-11): _____

What Christian service opportunities have we encouraged? _____

Our spiritual goals for the following few months are: _____
_____

To accomplish our goals we need to focus on: _____

To accomplish our goals we need to change how we: _____

Special thoughts or comments: _____
_____

Educational growth

What subjects or activities does this child especially enjoy? _____
_____

What subjects or activities are especially troublesome? _____

Have any new interests surfaced? If so, what? _____

We were so proud of our child's accomplishment in the area of: _____

We wish he/she would work harder at: _____

He/she would like to _____ after graduating from high school.

He/she is involved in the following extracurricular activities (clubs, sports, music, work, etc.):
_____

We know he/she is ready for high school because (check those that apply):

_____ There is evidence of mastery of arithmetic and prealgebra.

_____ There is evidence of mastery of writing (composition, research, and report) skills.

_____ He/she is able to research a topic and record the findings in a written report.

_____ He/she comprehends silent reading well and reads aloud fluently.

Or:

_____ He/she is not ready for high school-level work in all subjects yet.

_____ He/she is working on the high school-level only in (name subject):

Our educational goals for the following few months are: _____
_____

To accomplish our goals we need to focus on: _____

To accomplish our goals we need to change how we: _____

Special thoughts or comments: _____
_____

Ages 15-18

Child's name _____ Date _____

Spiritual growth

We are satisfied/unsatisfied that he/she is committed to Christ. _____

We see the following fruit of the Spirit emerging (Gal 5:22): _____
_____

We need to encourage him/her to work on the following disciplines: _____
_____

We see him/her beginning to be a part of the Body of Christ by exhibiting the following spiritual gifts (see I Cor 12-14, Romans 12:1-8, Eph 4:1-16, I Peter 4:10-11): _____
_____

What Christian service opportunities has the student taken part in? _____
_____

What commitments to purity has this child made in character, relationships (dating, etc.), convictions: _____

Our spiritual goals for the following few months are: _____
_____

To accomplish our goals we need to focus on: _____

To accomplish our goals we need to change how we: _____

Special thoughts or comments: _____
_____

Educational growth

What subjects or activities does this young person especially enjoy? _____
_____

What subjects or activities are especially troublesome? _____

Have any new interests surfaced? If so, what? _____

He/she is planning to _____ after graduating from high school.

He/she is involved in the following extracurricular activities (clubs, sports, music, work, etc.):
_____

He/she has demonstrated mastery of the following basic self-sufficiency skills (cooking, laundry, working, communicating with adults, etc.): _____

He/she has earned the following awards or achieved the following accomplishments: _____
_____

We know he/she is ready/is not ready for adult life because: _____
_____

How many more credits, and in what subjects, does this young person need for graduation?
_____

Our educational goals for the following few months are: _____
_____

To accomplish our goals we need to focus on: _____

To accomplish our goals we need to change how we: _____

Special thoughts or comments: _____
_____

How often do you need to reassess? That depends. We would suggest reviewing your progress with each homeschool student at least every six months, just to make sure things are on track and nothing is slipping through the cracks. If adjustment is needed, this will allow you to regroup and correct without too much stress to either student or parent. In actuality, the adjustments are usually much harder for the parents than the kids. We need to relax and take it easy. Our children usually have no problem.

What if

What if they never settle on a plan? At 12, there were just too many possibilities to choose from. At 14, only basketball mattered. At 16, they were sure they could not succeed at anything since they had been home-schooled. Now, your child's 18th birthday has come and gone, and yet, when you ask what he has planned, he says, "I don't know." You make suggestions. You cajole. You nag, but to no avail.

What do you do when your supposedly maturing high school senior or recent graduate doesn't know what he wants to do next? First, you pray for wisdom, both for you and your child. God has promised to give it, and we need to believe that first. Next, we give our child some slack. If we have done our job during the last decade-plus in raising our child to be a responsible member of society, then this is the time when we should see signs of accountability, responsibility, and initiative come to the surface. But don't expect it to jump forth all at once. Sometimes, depending on your child's temperament, you might have to be patient while he organizes his thoughts and makes plans.

If you are in between the high school and college period because your senior wants to stay home for another year before hitting college, use this time to solidify your adult relationship with that child. It won't be long before he will spread his wings and fly away.

There are some who advocate having your children live with you until they get married. At the other extreme, some parents are pushing the child out the door before the ink is dry on the high school diploma! We think there are arguments for keeping them at home as long as possible, in order to see the maturity level rise as high as possible. However, our true position is that decisions of this nature must be made on a child-by-child basis. Some are mature enough to handle life beyond the home; others are not. Individual circumstances will dictate how to approach each situation. What is important is that you and your child come to a reasonable, objective decision about the best course of action *before* they are packed and ready to go. Take the time and know what you think is reasonable before it escalates into a last-minute fiasco. You will all be more sane for it.

Maturity in your high schooler will definitely vary child by child, and also by gender. It's no secret why it used to be that girls became adults at 18 and boys weren't able to get married without parental consent until they were 21. We can definitely see the difference in maturity between our two daughters and three sons. This has nothing to do with their training, that's for sure. One thing we learned by having our five children in six years is that personalities and temperamental differences are real. The point here is that you must be the final decision-maker. Keeping that child in your home until he is ready to make adult decisions will be critical to his success in adult life. Keep that in mind as you direct each one.

Guiding your student to adulthood promises to be an adventurous journey. Few parents will escape the ups and downs completely. We hope that you will prepare with flexibility, because nothing is as sure as change. As a poster we once read states, "Blessed are the flexible, for they shall not break." We think that's a great motto for parents of young people!

CHAPTER 9

Giving Special Students Appropriate Opportunities

Those who wait for the Lord will gain new strength; they will mount up with wings like eagles, they will run and not get tired, they will walk and not become weary."
–Isaiah 40:31 (NASB)

The reality is that no child is "average" in every way. Our children are individuals, each with unique strengths and weaknesses. But the struggles faced by families with one or more learning challenged or disabled children are unique. However, there are many resources available these days to help families with disabilities guide their students into adulthood and achieve their highest potential. We hope to provide some special ideas to help guide challenged students on to a fulfilled future.

A great blessing of homeschooling is that every child can be treated uniquely. The home school is built around the principle that each child is special, created in the image of God, no matter what his specific difficulties or abilities. But is homeschooling best for special-needs children? Here is what Robert J. Doman Jr., of the National Academy for Child Development, has to say on the issue: "If you take your child with special needs to a public school and ask the 'experts' to describe the best possible learning environment for your child, they will probably tell you that your child needs to be in the least restrictive environment, to have lots of one-on-one time, to have peers that are outstanding role models, and to have a program designed to meet his or her individual needs. And they are right! Furthermore, what they have described is the home."

We have very dear friends who have homeschooled their daughter Rachel throughout her life. Rachel is autistic, though high functioning. We thought it would be helpful to include some comments from Rachel's mother about their journey.

The first thing you need to know is...it is not easy. The second thing is...it is one of the best decisions I have made for Rachel. You need to make sure you have a clear conviction as to why you want to homeschool your special-needs child. The road will be rocky sometimes, but your convictions will give you the determination you need to stay the course. You will get through the rough spots. As your child grows, his or her needs will change and you will have to make the necessary curricular adjustments. Adjustments are good; it means there is growth!

Many children in the school systems are labeled "special ed." However, I believe many of them do not have learning disabilities, but have different learning styles. If the child does not learn the way the teacher teaches then they are labeled. One of the benefits of homeschooling is that you can find out what way your child learns. Do they like hands-on? Do they like one-on-one instruction, or do they like to grab their books and go on their own? Do they benefit from the stimulation a computer program can offer? There are a multitude of ways to teach your special-needs child. It just takes time and research. Allow for trial and error until you find what works. I found it may take a year or even two of trying out different methods before you find your comfort zone.

I have gone through many curriculum changes over the years. Some...have stayed the same, but I'm always adding to provide variety and challenge. The Web has wonderful resources and ideas for special ed. programs. I have found what has worked best for me on most subjects is Alpha Omega. They break up the lessons into smaller sections, it is easy for my child to go back to find the answers, and there are small paragraphs with a few questions to follow, which makes retention easier.

I also love a computer curriculum to break up a day. It is fun and stimulating. There are some very good computer resources out there. I always focus on what my child gets right versus what she did that was incorrect. I have found a positive approach is the best. I let her do open-book tests. This helps with her research skills, she gets more correct, and it is more rewarding for her. My main goal for my child is to prepare her for life. So my program centers around life skills, like how to do the everyday things such as cooking, cleaning, and sewing.

Another aspect that is important is teaching Rachel how to interact with other people in a proper manner. This takes a lot of effort, as you know. Some of these skills are difficult for special-needs children. They need a lot of love and patience and a few good friends who understand their needs and are willing to be friends in spite of some quirky behavior. I have prayed and asked God to help lead us to some friends for our child, and he has given this to her. Some are long distance and some in the neighborhood. We have been very fortunate.

This leads me to a major misconception that society has about homeschooling. You know what it is already: "What about socialization?" I often wonder how our country ever survived before public schools! The center of socialization was your family and the church and maybe a barn dance once a month, where people would gather to see each other. Other than that, it was chores and playing with your siblings. And we wonder what's wrong with our kids today. If you ask me, it is too much socialization!

I have very carefully sought out different community organizations that I felt would benefit my child. We took it one at a time. It is very important to get to know your leaders or instructors and stay very tuned in to what is going on. For example, our child belongs to a horse club; she loves this. One aspect is the 4-H and the other is a camp where she goes during the summer two days a week. She had an actual paying job at the horse barn, which was wonderful for her.

She also belongs to the Girl Scouts. She has a wonderful troop leader who loves her and works hard to incorporate her into all the activities. She has been camping with her group and to many other neat places. This has been a wonderful opportunity and is helping her develop a much-needed sense of independence. Every group is different in your community; some things may work, some may not. We tried the YMCA program, but for us it did not work—it was too big and [there was] not enough structure and my child did not feel secure in this situation. I could tell she didn't like it so we stopped and found other things that worked for her. Once or twice a week she has a community event. We also have our church group, where she has friends. This is ample for her, for now. As she matures, we will look for other things that she can handle.

The most wonderful benefit of homeschooling for us has been our ability to nurture our daughter in a controlled setting. This has produced self-esteem in her and an understanding of her value as a child of God. I think the main destructive force in a public school setting is the constant negative atmosphere. You see, our daughter knows she has a disability; she likens it to a cousin of hers who has diabetes. She knows she has certain limitations just like her cousin and she is fine with that. She doesn't see herself as being abnormal or disabled, she has never been subjected to ridicule, she has never been called dumb or stupid or laughed at to the point where her self-image was destroyed.

Our daughter is one of the most self-confident outgoing kids I know. She jumps right in (usually too much!), and she has very supportive brothers and a wonderful sister who have nurtured her with love and acceptance for who she is. In almost every form you fill out for evaluating whether your child has special needs or not they ask "does your child have low self-esteem?" The reason they ask this is because, as difficult as this truth may be, children can be mean and they usually take it out on the weaker ones in a school setting. If you allow your child to be subjected to ridicule daily, this will be the end result. For this reason alone I have felt that our decision to homeschool our special-needs child has far outweighed any objection the most well-intentioned person could have.

I have had many a special ed. school teacher come up to me at a homeschool convention and whisper in my ear that my decision to homeschool my daughter was the best, and that they see special-needs children fall through the cracks of the system. There are school systems that have good special ed. programs, but they are few and far between. A wonderful resource is the NATHHAN newsletter. This is a national organization (actually, a family with several handicapped children started it) that has wonderful ideas and resources to help you find what you need to homeschool. They also match families up who have children with similar disabilities so they can share ideas with each other. They openly talk about the pros and cons of teaching at home.

I am in the process of developing a path for Rachel that will be a transition from homeschooling to some classes in a Vo-Tech situation. I have had professional evaluations along the way, and the "pros" have always given me rave reviews for Rachel's progress—not only in academics, but as a stable, well-mannered, well-adjusted young lady. They would actually say they could not believe how well I knew my daughter and how happy she seemed!

No matter what the challenge

This chapter is not meant to provide information on the symptoms of different disabilities, nor is it intended to specifically address curricula or programs for challenged homeschoolers (though we will include curriculum, resource, and Web site information). Instead, we want to focus on how you can find the information and uncover the avenues that will help your special student tackle adult life.

Guiding the special needs child toward college

Currently, about 9 percent of college freshmen report that they have some form of disability. Obviously, these students have found their way through the maze of college admissions and have taken their place in higher education. Disability awareness is at an all-time high and special services for special needs are readily available. The Americans with Disabilities Act of 1990 has compelled public institutions to make their premises accessible to handicapped individuals. The Internet provides a medium for learning, and even working, that poses few boundaries. The times are favorable for all those who are mentally able, though physically challenged, to achieve their academic goals. There is also a greater understanding of learning disabilities, which has fostered environments that help students compensate for their special challenges.

Of course, "disability" is a very broad term. Those students with disabilities who enter college will be of basically two groups—the physically challenged (hearing-, visually-, and mobility-impaired) and the learning disabled (dyslexic, suffering from ADD or ADHD, etc.) When considering a particular college, you will need to focus on the different services and facilities it provides. Those who are learning disabled, who do not find difficulty with the physical components of going to college, will want to know about programs that will help them succeed at academics. The physically disabled will want to know how accessible the college facilities are and if special services are available that will allow them to learn effectively.

It is possible that in the homeschool situation your child may not have been officially labeled or his disability categorized. You may have specifically avoided labeling for good reason. When it is time to consider college, you should reevaluate whether having the student's disability officially categorized will be beneficial or not. If the student wants or needs special accommodations in College Board testing (such as extended time limits or large print tests) and college academics, evaluation is required.

Provisions have been made to provide those with disabilities the highest chance of success in college, but they must be officially tested and categorized to receive such help. If you and your student do not need or want special accommodations (for instance, in the case of a mild disability), official evaluation is not necessary.

There are several extra steps beyond the normal admissions process that your learning-disabled students should take. The extra considerations in the college admissions process for the disabled that we list below are in addition to the college admission requirements listed in Chapter 17:

- ⋏ Consider having a professional evaluation, or, if you already have one, consider updating it. You can find more information on disabilities and higher education from the Educational Testing Service (*www.ets.org*).
- ⋏ Both the SAT and ACT College Board exams have special testing procedures for students with documented disabilities. Visit the SAT page at *www.collegeboard.com* or the ACT assessment page at *www.act.org*, for details on how to take advantage of special testing accommodations.
- ⋏ If your student has an Individualized Educational Program (IEP), it is important that all meeting and program requirements are kept in the senior year of high school.
- ⋏ Investigate the list of colleges that accept students with disabilities through one of the following books:
    - ⋏ *The College Guide for Students with Learning Disabilities*, Laurel Publication, Miller Place, NY, 11764, (516) 474-1023.
    - ⋏ *Lovejoy's College Guide for the Learning Disabled*, Monarch Press, 15
      Columbus Circle, New York, NY, 10023.
    - ⋏ *Peterson's Colleges with Programs for the Learning Disabled*, Peterson's Guides, Princeton, NJ, 08540, (800) 338-3282.
- ⋏ Make sure you visit the campus of your school choices and arrange interviews. In the interview be sure to:
    - ⋏ Ask extra questions, such as:
        - ⋏ Are there special admissions requirements for LD students?
        - ⋏ Can LD students maintain a reduced course load?
        - ⋏ What support services are offered?
        - ⋏ Are there additional charges for support services?
        - ⋏ Is the campus reasonably barrier-free?
        - ⋏ Are special housing arrangements available for the physically disabled?
    - ⋏ Advocate for yourself by:
        - ⋏ being honest in your evaluation of your own strengths and weaknesses,

▲ providing a portfolio of your progress, special work, and documentation of your disability.

▲ Investigate financial aid options. You can obtain a listing of financial aid for disabled individuals from the Heath resource center (see contact information at the end of this chapter).

▲ Once accepted, familiarize yourself with the disabilities support service staff. Be willing to ask questions. Be sure your professors are aware of your status and any special needs you may have.

Distance learning

Students with physical handicaps may find distance learning to be their best option. There are degree programs available online from many major universities, and in nearly every field of study. The Internet is truly without barriers to those who have the ability to operate a computer. This option can make earning a degree as accessible to the disabled as to any other student.

▲ ▲ ▲

With the proper motivation, attitude, and preparation, there is no reason that students with disabilities cannot gain college admission and succeed in college.

"Under the Americans with Disabilities Act (ADA) and Section 504 of the Rehabilitation Act of 1973, individuals with learning disabilities are guaranteed certain protections and rights to equal access to programs and services. In order to access these rights, an individual must present documentation indicating that the disability substantially limits some major life activity, including learning. The following documentation requirements are provided in the interest of assuring that LD documentation is appropriate to verify eligibility and to support requests for accommodations, academic adjustments, and/or auxiliary aids. Requirements for documentation are presented in four important areas: (1) qualifications of the evaluator; (2) recency of documentation; (3) appropriate clinical documentation to substantiate the disability; and (4) evidence to establish a rationale supporting the need for accommodations."

—From: *www.ets.org/disability.html*

Guiding the special needs child to employment

If your special student is not interested in attending college (or is unable to do so), but is able to work, you will want to investigate opportunities to gain employable skills. As with any student, it is prudent to discern the student's special interests, desires, and abilities. Armed with some ideas, try out various skills related to the field the student may want to enter. Apprenticeship opportunities are again a great idea. Starting a business may be a great opportunity. Though these young people have some limitations, the same principles of preparing for a career enumerated in Chapter 6 will apply.

There are many organizations that help disabled individuals find work and deal with special problems in the workplace. The issues for disabled workers are many and varied, and it is beyond the scope of this book to try to address them here. You should be able to find ample information to help you from these sources and the links they may provide.

- ▲ *Alternative Work Concepts* is a nonprofit employment agency for persons who experience physical and multiple disabilities. They also provide families with help achieving vocational goals. Contact: P.O. Box 11452, Eugene, OR, 97440; (541) 345-3043; *www.teleport.com/~awc*; e-mail: *awc@teleport.com*.

- ▲ *Careers On-line* provides job search and employment information to people with disabilities. Contact: University of Minnesota Disability Services, 12 Johnston Hall, 101 Pleasant St. S.E., Minneapolis, MN, 55455; voice/TTY: (612) 626-9649; e-mail: *careers@disserv.stu.umn.edu*.

- ▲ *Cornucopia of Disability Information* has a wide array of links and information on all sorts of disabilities. Contact: *codi.buffalo.edu*.

- ▲ *www.familyvillage.wisc.edu*: "A community of Disability-Related Resources."

- ▲ *www.disserv.stu.umn.edu/TC/Grants/COL/listing/disemp/* has employment resources for people with disabilities. This site has many links for actual jobs, other organizations, and information.

Telecommuting

As with distance learning, the opportunity to telecommute (perform work for a company from home using a computer and phone) may be just the ticket for many disabled individuals. Since your home will already be suited to your special needs, finding work that can be done from home will level the playing field between the disabled and the general population of job seekers. Many companies encourage telecommuting because it lowers their costs (facilities, absenteeism, etc.) and maximizes work time. You can find information about possible telecommuting jobs from an online search or from an online employment agency.

Gifted and talented

Gifted and talented children do not suffer from a disability, yet they do not always fit into the normal educational framework. The gifted child may quickly progress through academic work and be ready for college-level work at a much younger age than the norm. While it is possible to gain regular college admission for children who are underage yet academically prepared, we suggest you investigate options that allow for advanced study but keep the child in the home. Gifted children in higher education often develop social and spiritual problems because their intellect gets ahead of their maturity level. There are so many options (see "Taking on Advanced Studies," Chapter 13) for distance and nonconventional study these days. Therefore, keeping the advanced child at home while providing challenging educational opportunities should not be difficult.

The gifted child, one who is exceptionally talented in one or more areas, can be a bit more of a challenge. If you live in a city, it may be possible to find lessons and special programs for such a student. If you live in a more remote area, you may need to make some concessions to provide opportunities for your child. Summer camps are available in performing and visual arts as well as athletics of all sorts. Many colleges offer lessons, summer camps, and clubs for the same sort of activities. You will need to do your homework to check out the options in your area.

The reward

Every child is a gift from God. Our Lord is keenly aware of the struggles faced by those families of children with handicaps. He considers your love for your child a wonderful manifestation of His love, for many of you parents have indeed laid down your lives for your children. Your commitment to homeschool your special children will no doubt contribute to their ability to reach their highest potential in every area of life. What greater reward could you receive?

We have friends in their early 70s who have raised their Down's Syndrome child into her 40s. They have essentially homeschooled this child since birth, and continue to do so. These dear people were, without knowing it, pioneers in the homeschool movement. Their daughter is a sweet, loving young lady who loves Jesus and goes to work each day at a local community center. She is a productive member of society who contributes to the happiness of others because her parents loved her from the day she was born and gave her the chance to become everything she was capable of being. May we learn from this example of parental love!

More resources

- ▲ Ability OnLine calls itself "an electronic mail system that connects young people with disabilities or chronic illness to disabled and non-disabled peers and mentors...Ability OnLine is also a valuable resource for families and friends anxious to know more about an illness and help manage it." Contact: *www.ablelink.org/public/default.htm.*

- ▲ American Hyperlexia Association, 479 Spring Road, Elmhurst, IL 60126; (708) 530-8551.

- ▲ Association on Higher Education and Disability lists disablility offices at major universities, general information, and links to other organizations. Contact: University of Massachusetts, Boston, 100 Morrisey Blvd., Boston, MA 02125-3393; (617) 287-3880; *www.ahead.org.*

- ▲ Children and Adults with ADD (CH.A.D.D), 8181 Professional Place, Ste. 201, Landover, MD 20785; (301) 306-7070.

- ▲ Cornucopia of Disability Information offers a wide array of links and information on all sorts of disabilities. Contact: *codi.buffalo.edu.*

- ▲ Council for Exceptional Children (CEC), Division of Learning Disabilities (DLD), 1920 Association Drive, Reston, VA 22091-1589; (800) 328-0272 or (703) 620-3660.

- ▲ Council for Learning Disabilities (CLD), P.O. Box 40303, Overland Park, KS 62204; (913) 492-8755.

- ▲ The Essential Learning Institute provides testing for learning disabilities at home by parents, computer-based sensory integration therapy (SIT), academic evaluation and placement, and individually prescribed curricula. Contact: 334 Second Street Catasauqua, PA 18032; (800) 285-9089; e-mail: *eli@fast.net*; Web site: *rsts.net/home/index2.html.*

▲ *www.familyvillage.com* calls itself "A Global Community of Disability-Related Resources" and has links for kids and teens with disabilities, information for families of the disabled, information on employment and college, and more.

▲ Heath Resource Center is a national clearinghouse on higher education for people with disabilities. Contact: Suite 800, One Dupont Circle, NW, Washington, D.C. 20036; (800) 544-3284; *www.acenet.edu/about/programs/access&equity/heath/home.html.*

▲ International Dyslexia Association, Chester Building, 8600 LaSalle Road, Suite 382, Baltimore, MD 21286-2044; (410) 296-0232.

▲ National Academy for Child Development, NACD National Headquarters, P.O. Box 380, Huntsville, UT 84317; (801) 621-8606; e-mail: *info@nacd.org.*

If our youngest child, Wesley, were in a traditional school situation, he would surely be labeled both gifted and talented and ADHD (attention deficit hyperactivity disorder). We consider what others would label ADHD to be part of Wesley's individual makeup as a child of God. While he can certainly tire and exasperate us, we attempt to slowly but surely help him gain the fruit of the Spirit—self-control. We have had to take our focus off what others expect from a young child's behavior and put it on what God expects. God expects our child to be a child. He is patient with His children. Even God Himself could not force His children to behave properly at all times, and we do not expect to outdo God! We have needed to lose the condemnation and promote a life of grace and truth. In the home, we are free to do this.

The bigger challenge is to provide the opportunities he needs for developing his profound talents. Wesley is extremely talented in performing arts. In 4-H, he found a forum for his talents at a young age. At age 10, he was able to compete at the county fair, where his singing performance of "God Bless the USA," by Lee Greenwood, won him first place in the talent contest. This opened up opportunities for singing on the radio, at church, and at local Christian coffee houses. We enrolled him in a class at a community college to learn how to obtain acting jobs. We are in the process of finding classes, lessons, and clubs for him to join that will help develop his talent. We are committed to finding opportunities for Wes to use his God-given talents for the glory of God.

- ⋏ National Center for Learning Disabilities (NCLD), 381 Park Avenue South, Suite 1401, New York, NY 10016; (212) 545-7510.
- ⋏ NATHHAN (NATional cHallenged Homeschoolers Associated Network), P.O. Box 39, Porthill, ID 83853; (208) 267-6246; *www.nathhan.org*; e-mail: *nathanews@aol.com.*
- ⋏ Schwab Foundation for Learning, 1650 South Amphlett Boulevard, Suite 300, San Mateo, CA 94402; (800) 230-0988.

Curricula

- ⋏ Able Net provides creative solutions for teaching students with severe disabilities. Contact: 1081 Tenth Ave. S.E., Minneapolis, MN 55414-1312; (800) 322-0956.
- ⋏ Don Johnston, Inc., provides curricula, software, and solutions for students with disabilities. Contact: P.O. Box 639, Wauconda, IL 60084-0639; (800) 999-4660, *www.donjohnston.com.*
- ⋏ R.J. Cooper and Associates provides computer resources for disabled children. Contact: 24843 Del Prado #283, Dana Point, CA 92629; (800) RJ-COOPER; (949) 661-6904; *www.rjcooper.com*; e-mail: *info@rjcooper.com.*
- ⋏ The Homeschool Internet Resource Center has a learning disabilities section. Contact: *rsts.net.*
- ⋏ Joyce Herzog's Simplified Learning Products offers resources for the learning disabled, gifted, and those who learn differently. Contact: P.O. Box 45387, Rio Rancho, NM 87174-5387; (800) 745-8212; *www.joyceherzog.com.*

CHAPTER 10

Working During the High School Years

*"Prepare your work outside, and make it ready for yourself in the field;
afterwards, then, build your house."*
—Proverbs 24:27 (NASB)

S tudents who decide to take on a job while in high school will benefit in many ways. No amount of book learning can replace the experience that holding down a job can bring. However, some students will be distracted by the change in schedules and priorities that working causes. At this point in life it should be the parents' goal to guide their child toward the future by providing work experiences if they will enhance, not hinder, the overall spiritual, emotional, and intellectual growth of the individual. Remember that every young person has a special set of needs, abilities, and circumstances. Keep these unique traits in mind as you work with your child to determine whether entering the work world is the right choice.

Why send them to work?

Consider the following advantages:

⋏ Working can inspire confidence in a young person. Reporting to an employer and being responsible to complete appointed tasks allows the student to learn confidence in his own abilities. It may also supply a chance to practice humility, a trait often lacking in the teen years!

⋏ The experience gained in working will greatly enhance a resume by adding references and employable skills to the homeschooler's repertoire. References from employers and supervisors can make a positive impact in college admissions and future job interviews.

⋏ The homeschool schedule allows older students to be available for apprenticeships in a particular trade or skill. In apprenticing, the student gets paid to try out a job while learning skills and business practices.

⋏ The student who works gets a chance to develop interpersonal skills when dealing with customers and within the hierarchy of the business. He will become familiar with relating to a supervisor. He will learn what type of demeanor is expected in the work setting. He is forced to learn respect. Some may advance and have the responsibility for supervising others. Also, learning to always treat customers with respect will be valuable practice for future endeavors.

⋏ One advantage that is usually overlooked in our materialistic society is the fact that the employee furnishes a service to the community by contributing to the work force. Every business has work to be done; without good employees, businesses cannot survive. Without businesses, families and communities will suffer lack, no matter how wealthy they may be. All jobs can be service jobs if considered in this light. For instance, we all like to visit a local restaurant on occasion. If there are no people available to serve the food, it would not be a very enjoyable experience. Be sure to include instruction in your homeschool curriculum that explains the function of the worker in the business world.

⋏ Of course, the most obvious advantage to young people's working is earning money to save for the future or contribute to family

The day that Jeremiah was offered his first paying job was akin to a national holiday in our home. It signaled the end of one era and the beginning of a new one. Together, we had evaluated the pros and cons before deciding it was right for him, so were overjoyed when he had the opportunity to get a paying job. He was offered a job at a local bagel shop owned by a Christian family. It was Jeremiah's first experience of being completely independent of his parents and responsible to a boss. He excelled and he loved the chance to learn new skills and earn money. All in all, it was a very positive experience that led him to new opportunities.

financial needs. Since the students live at home, they have few expenses and can save or invest most of their earnings for college or for the future. For young men who do not intend to go on to college, it may be wise for them to save for a home so that they will be prepared when the time arises to provide for a wife and family. If your family has financial need, it may be necessary and beneficial for the child to contribute earnings to the family budget. The student can learn much from the responsibility of helping his own family. Even using a portion of the student's earnings to pay for clothes, entertainment, and personal expenses can be a great help in lifting the financial burden of a family with limited resources.

⋏ Many families that homeschool also maintain family businesses. In these cases, it usually is a natural progression for the children to become contributors to the work force. Children in this situation have the chance to make a real difference in the stability of the family business. Current tax laws allow for children to work for their parents in a family business as early as age seven.

⋏ If you have a home-based business, you can teach your children many valuable lessons in industry, work ethic, economics, technical skills, and more. It's one of the best real-life experiences we can give our children. The young worker will be a first-hand observer and participant, gaining valuable knowledge of business practices. The knowledge gained from being part of a business can replace years of book learning about businesses.

⋏ Exploring possible career directions is another benefit of working while in school. Teens have the freedom to try out different types of work while they are still living at home. If the student is unsure about a particular vocation, it can be very helpful to him to have the opportunity to take on temporary employment in that area to see how he likes it.

From their early teens, Rebekah and Katie took babysitting jobs to enhance their own clothing and personal budgets. They enjoyed being with youngsters and having a little pocket money besides. When they were older, they took on the responsibility of watching a young child in our home a few days a week. This gave them the opportunity to learn about early child development and care, while easing the financial burden on our family.

⋏ Some students become business owners on their own. There are many opportunities for ambitious teens to become entrepreneurs. Many families make business practice part of their curricula. The state of our economy and technology make possible small, personally owned businesses. There is nothing to stop a young entrepreneur from pursuing his own business dreams.

Or not...

On the other hand, working can be a detriment to some students. Consider these disadvantages:

⋏ Taking on an outside job can distract the student from his normal studies. Some students will have difficulty focusing their efforts on schoolwork when they are working part time.

⋏ A job will also consume a significant portion of the young person's time. Depending on the type of work and the schedule, it may interfere with family activities, studies, church activities, sports participation, and social engagements. Be sure to carefully consider the number of hours your child should make available for work. Some jobs take very little time and are quite flexible, while others can become very demanding. Make sure the job won't tie up the family car for other activities. Decide ahead of time guidelines for how much work time is reasonable for your individual student. Let the prospective employer know the time limitations you will be upholding so he does not expect to increase hours without consulting you.

⋏ A problem that few parents consider is the possibility of promoting premature independence. If the young person is not stable in his commitment to Christ and obedient to the authority over him in the home, it may be unwise to hurry exposure to the outside work world. In this case, the student may wrongly transfer his loyalty and respect to an employer. He may also use his new income to partake in activities that are not in his best interest. If your child is not submissive to the authority of you as his parents, it would be wise to keep him at home while you have the legal authority to do so.

⋏ Finally, if the student takes on a job in a secular business, he will certainly be exposed to ungodly, negative influences. It simply may not be worth it. Again, be sure to take into account the individuality of each child. Some young people are quite ready to deal with the outside world while maintaining their Christian testimony; others would be better off staying within the home setting until they have strengthened their convictions.

Getting and maintaining a job

For those who decide to pursue a part-time job, we offer these following suggestions:

⋏ First, decide with your child on the type of job to look for. Obtaining work relating to an area the student may want to pursue as an adult career is always wise. Apprenticeship positions are available in many types of work, from government and political offices to dental labs. In an apprenticeship, the worker agrees to do whatever work (sweeping, delivery, etc.) the employer needs done in exchange for the opportunity to learn about the profession from the inside. The employer pays the apprentice a fair wage for entry-level work, and the apprentice usually agrees to work for a specific period of time. It is not always possible to get work in the exact field desired, so be ready to be flexible. Apprenticeships are often available in congressional offices. Having your child work for government officials offers the added advantage of allowing the officials to see first-hand the quality of education homeschooled students receive.

For students who want to learn skilled trades, such as auto mechanics, printing, cooking, or computer programming, offering to work for low pay may provide an opportunity that would not be available otherwise. Once a worker proves his diligence, character, and enthusiasm, the employer is likely to want to keep him and thus be willing to pay more generously. Also, candy striping or orderly work at the local hospital as a volunteer is a way for your child to see if he would enjoy a medical career.

⋏ In most states it is necessary to obtain a working permit for minors. Permits are generally available from the local school district. The potential employer can give you more information about what is required for working in your state. In New York, for example, children ages 14 and 15 may work a maximum of three hours per day on school days, and up to six hours on Saturdays. It is important to follow state laws even though our children are not subject to the same schedules as students in the public schools. In fact, employers will require the same paperwork for their files.

⋏ Normally it should be easy to find good references for your children because of the relationships they have outside the home at church, community activities, and group lessons. A pastoral recommendation is usually a good consistent one. Any opportunities you have to allow your child to work for neighbors and friends doing landscaping, mowing, babysitting, or cleaning will benefit the potential employee when he applies for a more "official" job. Even working for relatives can provide experience and references.

⋏ Finding work might be the biggest difficulty of all. Word-of-mouth opportunities can be prospected at official or unofficial homeschool events. Letting your homeschool friends know that you are looking for work for your child gets the word out on the network. Sometimes a friend or acquaintance on the other side of town will be all that is necessary to get the ball rolling. Advertisements in the local paper are the obvious second option. Let students search on their own. Give them a chance to look through the want ad section to decide what might be attractive. However, keep in mind that most employers who put an ad in a local employment section are looking for workers who are of age and available at their schedule. As parents, you may have to

---

After working in the bagel business for a year, Jeremiah found that he desired a more flexible schedule. He enjoyed working outdoors at our small farm, so when he was offered some small landscaping jobs by friends and acquaintances, he jumped at the chance. He loved the work, and it turned out that he was quite talented in it. One of his regular customers was a woman who patiently taught him how to trim her many bushes and tend to her flowers and yard. Jeremiah is now a very capable landscaper and does freelance work as he is able.

He also did yard work for a small local printing business with a teen friend. The owners observed Jeremiah's diligence and desire to learn and soon offered him a permanent apprentice position in their print shop. Not only has he learned mechanical, business, and printing skills from the experience, but he has also gained a terrific reference. He is going on to college but he knows he always has an open door with these employers.

be prepared to explain your unique situation and sell them on the idea of giving your child a chance. Do not get discouraged. Businesspeople are usually open to taking risks when it makes business sense. Your ability to show your child's qualities may be enough to persuade them to give it a shot. We also believe that you should allow your child to communicate with the business owner directly. This experience is in and of itself a homeschooling opportunity that many students do not get until later in life. Helping your children through their first few employment searches will help them gain confidence and deal with rejection.

⅃ Applying for a job for the first time can be a challenge. It is important that the young person take the initiative to speak to the potential employer on his or her own. If the student is mature enough to work, it will be demonstrated by a measure of independence in the job-seeking process. The goal of the application is to gain an interview. It may take many contacts to reach this goal, so again, do not be discouraged.

⅃ Interviewing can be tough for anyone, let alone a young student. In some cases, it may be appropriate to join your child at the interview. Be available to answer questions. However, sit in the background and resist the temptation to take charge. This can be a tremendous learning experience for your child. If the employer is serious, your child should do well. The odds are good that your homeschooled child's maturity and brightness will come through in the interview.

⅃ Once your child has won the job, you will need to communicate clearly about your expectations. Working for an employer outside the homeschool environment is going to be different. It will be a new, exciting experience. It will also have numerous challenges. Issues like transportation, schedule conflicts, and personality conflicts may occur. You as a parent will need to work through these issues as they occur. There are many unforeseen situations that you will have to monitor.

Finding their way

The more opportunities our children have to acquire different skills, the better they will be able to mold themselves into the calling God has for them. A diverse background will help our children prepare for the real world and their roles in it.

CHAPTER 11

Testing, Testing, 1-2-3

"Please test your servants for ten days, and let us be given some veg-etables to eat and water to drink. Then let our appearance be observed in your presence, and the appearance of the youths who are eating the king's choice food; and deal with your servants according to what you see. So he listened to them in this matter and tested them for ten days. And at the end of ten days their appearance seemed better and they were fatter than all the youths who had been eating the king's choice food."

Daniel 1:12-15 (NASB)

Some of the most frequently asked questions in our homeschooling support group meetings are about testing. Parents always want to know what tests their children need, where to get them, how to give them, and when to give them. This chapter is meant to outline the tests recommended at various levels of schooling and to give ideas on how to obtain them, give them, and evaluate their results.

Here are some testing do's and don'ts:

⊿ Do not fall into the trap of "teaching to the test." Homeschooled students generally perform 10 to 30 points above average on standardized tests, as Brian Ray notes in *Homeschooling on the Threshold*. One reason for this is their all-around, practical knowledge of subjects, which comes from not being taught specifically for a test.

⊿ Do not overemphasize the importance of tests, particularly in the lower grades. These types of assessments have their place, but their usefulness is limited. It is counterproductive to base our evaluation of our children's education solely on a highly specific "snapshot" examination, after we spend every day teaching them to learn through experience and interaction, in addition to study.

⬥ Try to ease any test anxiety. Give the practice and actual tests at home, if possible. Even the test publishers suggest that they be given in the normal learning environment, which for you is in the home. If you do not have this option, choose a safe, familiar environment. It is important that you oversee the testing process very carefully if you are not administering the tests yourself. Bright, normal children who are very competent in their studies can test very poorly under the wrong circumstances. Treat exam days as a normal part of the yearly schedule. Reward effort and downplay shortcomings. You have taken the responsibility to home educate your children; do not forfeit it when it comes to testing. Also, minimize the tendency to view these tests as a measure of your ability to homeschool.

We have to admit that our children are a bit abnormal when it comes to tests. They have picked up their parents' attitude of loving the challenge and the opportunity to perform (not to mention a bit of competitive spirit). They each relish the opportunity to show off their knowledge, and generally viewed major test days more like vacation than trial. We have not found this a normal response, though, even amongst homeschoolers. Laurie is a certified examiner for the most commonly used standardized tests in elementary and high school, and as such has had the opportunity to observe a wide range of children. Many students are simply mortified by the appearance of a blank answer sheet that they have to complete. Others are anxious for a chance to prove themselves. Reactions will even differ among siblings. The parents' goal should be to make testing a normal and uneventful part of the education process. If a child has anxiety, do whatever is necessary to minimize it.

Which tests do you need?

So exactly which tests will the homeschooling family encounter through the years? This chapter will list the most common types and specific tests from which to choose. Choosing the correct assessment for your children is essential to their success and progress toward their goals. Be sure to carefully consider when and if a particular test should be included in each child's educational process.

Don't give up your parental right and authority to direct your child's education in this area. Do not have your student take a test simply because it is suggested by the school district. You should only submit to specific demands for testing to comply with state law. Even then, you are usually allowed to choose which test you want to give and where you will give it. Our goal is to give you the information you need to make those informed decisions.

State-required testing

Currently, nine states (Ark., Ga., Minn., N.C., N.M., Ore., S. Dak., Tenn., and N.Y.) have homeschool laws that require standardized testing at certain grade levels. Fifteen more (Colo., Conn., Fla., Iowa, La., Hawaii, Maine, Mass., N.H., Ohio, Pa., Vt., Va., Wash., and W.Va.) require testing or another form of evaluation (portfolio, narrative, evaluation by a teacher, etc.). States that require testing usually require one of the achievement tests listed below, but specific rules for administration differ from state to state. States usually only require tests in language and math skills. Be sure to check the legislation for your state before you administer an exam that you expect to use for official evaluation. Parents may also administer tests at their discretion aside from those required by the state; they are not required to report these scores.

Achievement tests

Achievement tests are designed to measure how much knowledge the student has accumulated at a given point in his schooling. All achievement tests cover math and language skills; some also cover science, social studies, and such skills as using maps, graphs, dictionaries, and encyclopedias. There are numerous achievement tests available to homeschoolers. We will list those commonly available, with their basic format, any peculiarities or advantages, and information on how to obtain them and who may administer them. Please note that any prices quoted are subject to change. One other note—these tests are rented; they must be returned to the publisher for reuse and for scoring. Reports are then issued to the parents, including scoring and norm information.

California Achievement Tests (CAT) are published by CTB/ McGraw Hill. This test series measures achievement in basic skills for grades K-12. Subject areas include reading, language, spelling, mathematics, study skills, science, and social studies. Parents may administer this test. The CAT requires little parental involvement for grades 4-12. Each level uses the same instructions, allowing children at different grade levels to take the test together. The kindergarten level is a preinstructional test in reading and mathematics. First grade includes word analysis, vocabulary, reading comprehension, language mechanics and expression, math computation, math concepts and application, science, and social studies. Grades 2-3 are the same, with the addition of spelling, but grades 4-12 drop word analysis and add study skills. Available from:

- Bayside School Services, P.O. Box 250, Kill Devil Hills, NC 27948; (800) 723-3057. Version 5 costs $25.
- Family Learning Organization, P.O. Box 7247, Spokane, WA 99207-0247; (800) 405-8378; Web site: *www.familylearning.org*; e-mail: *kathleenm@familylearning.org*.
- Thurber's Educational Assessments, (919) 967-5282. Version 5 costs $20-25.
- Christian Liberty Academy, 502 W. Euclid Avenue, Arlington Heights, IL 60004-5495; (800) 348–0899. Costs $20.

The **Comprehensive Test of Basic Skills (CTBS)** is designed to measure basic skills commonly found in state and school district curricula. It also tests cognitive processes, including recall, explicit information skills, and inferential reasoning. It is published by CTB/MacMillan/McGraw Hill and available for K-12. It is available from:

- Seton School, 1350 Progress Drive, Front Royal, VA 22630; (540) 636-9990; e-mail *testing@setonhome.org*. The 4th edition costs $20.
- Sycamore Tree, 2179 Mayer Place, Costa Mesa, CA 92627. Costs $50 per test plus shipping and handling.

The **Iowa Test of Basic Skills (ITBS)** is for grades K-8 and the **Test of Achievement and Proficiency (TAP)** is for grades 9-12. We have used the Iowa tests because they are good comprehensive tests of general knowledge, and the results give information on specific skills. They may be given by a parent in most cases. With the ITBS you can administer the complete battery, which contains 11 tests (vocabulary, word analysis, reading, listening, language, mathematics concepts, mathematics problems, mathematics computation, social studies, science, and sources of information), or just the core battery (vocabulary, reading, listening, word analysis, language, mathematics concepts, mathematics problems, and mathematics computation).

The TAP tests come in two forms. The survey battery includes short tests in reading comprehension, vocabulary, written expression, mathematical concepts and problem solving, and an optional test in math computation; the complete battery also includes tests in social studies, science, and information processing. Test questions are derived from an analysis of state and local curricula. Iowa tests are available from:

⅄ Family Learning Organization, P.O. Box 7247, Spokane, WA 99207-0247; (800) 405-8378; Web site: *www.familylearning.org*; e-mail: *kathleenm@familylearning.org*.

Metropolitan Achievement Tests (MAT) assess vocabulary, word recognition (primary levels only), reading comprehension, math concepts, math problem-solving and computation, language, science, and social studies. The MAT is the least time-consuming test that still includes a broad range of materials. These tests are published by the Psychological Corporation and are available for grades K-12. Available from:

⅄ Family Learning Organization, P.O. Box 7247, Spokane, WA 99207-0247; (800) 405-8378; Web site: *www.familylearning.org*; e-mail: *kathleenm@familylearning.org*.

Personalized Achievement Summary System (PASS) tests are norm-referenced tests, specifically developed for homeschoolers in grades 3-8, administered by a parent at home. The key advantage to the PASS is that it is untimed. The publishers recommend (and provide) a placement test to determine what level of test to use. The test covers reading, math, and language. Results show both overall achievement and performance in each of the three subject areas. The publishers recommend testing twice a year to obtain a more accurate measure of achievement. The tests cover reading, mathematics, and language usage; they are linked to Metropolitan Achievement Tests in order to provide national norms. Norms specially developed by the Hewitt Research Foundation, which publishes the tests, compare the child to other homeschooled students. Tests may be administered by a parent or other responsible person. Not all states recognize the PASS as acceptable for homeschooled children; be sure to check your state regulations. Available from:

⅄ Hewitt Research Foundation, P.O. Box 9, Washougal, WA, 98671-0009; (360) 835-8708. Costs $25.

Stanford Achievement Tests (SAT) should not be confused with the **College Board Scholastic Achievement Test (SAT)**. Stanford tests are published by the Psychological Corporation. The SAT is available for grades K-13. Test material is aligned with national standards. The multiple-choice tests cover reading, mathematics, language, spelling, study skills, listening, science, and social science. The administration requirements (who can give the test) are stringent for this test; not all parents will meet requirements.

Tester beware

It is important that you discern what achievement tests can accurately measure and what they cannot. Achievement tests are graded and scaled using one of two methods: norm-referencing or criterion-referencing.

A norm-referenced exam evaluates the student by comparing him to a standardized set of test takers. The norm group is a group of students who take the test before it is published. The same group is used for several years. In other words, if your student ranks at the 62nd percentile, he scored better than 62 percent of the norm group of testers. Note that the highest percentile possible is 99 because the child cannot do better than 100 percent of testers (including himself). Studies show that homeschooled children on average rank at higher percentiles than the norm groups.

Make sure not to confuse percentile ranking with percentage scores. A percentage score (getting a 95 percent on a spelling test) is a direct measure of how many questions are answered correctly. Percentile rankings only tell how well your student compared to the group of public school students used for the norm.

On the other hand, criterion-referenced test scores are based on which questions are answered correctly in certain areas. Specific skills or knowledge can be tested and test reports can show exactly what areas need work. However, in order for these tests to be accurate, the questions must be directly based on the curriculum that student has been taught, or on a specific set of skills designated as appropriate to that age. Neither of these is relevant for most homeschool students, since they will usually not be learning material at the same time or with the same curriculum as other students. In order to do well on published, standardized, criterion-referenced tests, it is usually necessary to "teach to the test."

Certain norm-referenced tests can be graded in such a way as to reveal some criterion-referenced information, such as the Iowa Test of Basic Skills. You can get a score report from the ITBS that lists the specific skills each question on the test was designed to test, and how your student scored. This information can help parents design their curriculum around what the student still needs to learn. Unfortunately, these are not completely accurate either, since the student may guess on answers. Furthermore, the questions on the science and social studies portions of the test are only accurate in measuring the curriculum used. Much of the emphasis in public school science and social studies curricula these days is on evolutionary theory and multiculturalism and is skewed in favor of anti-Christian philosophies, so the Christian homeschool student may do quite poorly on these tests. (You may be glad he did!)

Most standardized tests will give results in a variety of formats besides the percentile ranking. You should be aware of how to interpret these results. The raw score tells how many questions were answered correctly out of the total number of questions (that is, 32/45). A stanine (short for standard nine) is a score between one and nine that divides scores into nine equal groups. Stanines four to six represent average scores, one to three below average, and seven to nine above average. The stanine is the most reliable score to use in comparing test scores from one year to another. Just be sure that no matter what type of result you are using, you are comparing results from the same test (that is, Iowa tests with Iowa tests, Stanfords with Stanfords, etc.). Grade equivalent scores can be very deceptive. A grade equivalent score is not meant for placement and does not indicate the grade level of work your child should be doing. If a 9th grade student receives a grade equivalent score of 11.7 it only means that he did as well on the 9th-grade test as an 11th grade 7th-month student would do on the same test. It does not mean the student can do 11th-grade work.

Aptitude, cognitive ability, and IQ tests

Aptitude tests are very different from achievement tests. Aptitude tests are used to determine the student's ability to learn a particular skill. There are many types of aptitude tests, meant to measure everything from intelligence quotient (IQ), to ability to learn in school, to likelihood of success in a given occupation. As with any test, be careful not to put too much weight on their interpretation. They are useful as general guides, but they hardly ever offer a complete picture of abilities. For instance, an aptitude test may be able to indicate if a student is underachieving (high aptitude scores, low achievement scores). However, a low aptitude score may simply indicate that the child had a bad day. We recommend using those tests that are normed with an achievement test for the best correlating information.

The **Otis Lennon School Ability Tests (OLSAT)** specifically measure skills that students need to succeed in school; it is meant to give a measure for determining if students are working up to their potential in school. The OLSAT seeks to provide an understanding of students' strengths and weaknesses in performing reasoning tasks. OLSAT assesses reasoning ability: verbal comprehension, verbal reasoning, pictorial reasoning, figural reasoning, and quantitative reasoning. This test is published by the Psychological Corporation and can be given in conjunction with the SAT achievement tests (see SAT listing for suppliers).

The **Cognitive Abilities Test (COGAT)** assesses reasoning and problem-solving skills and is normed and given in conjunction with Iowa tests. Results include scores for verbal, quantitative, and nonverbal reasoning abilities, as well as a composite score. Scores reveal an individual's ability to discover relationships and show flexibility in thinking. These are available for grades K-12 from suppliers of Iowa tests.

Intelligence Quotient (IQ) exams were all the rage in the 1950s and 60s, but have currently lost favor with many educators. It is unlikely that your homeschool student has ever had an IQ test. Actually, there are self-scoring (parent-scored) IQ tests available quite inexpensively from most book stores and especially easy to find online. If you are interested in your child's IQ, you can obtain and give these tests yourself. Just beware that IQ is by no means a final analysis of intelligence. IQ tests do not measure creativity or divergent thinking skills (finding unusual means for solving problems). They may also be very inconsistent, producing a wide variance of scores depending on when the test is given. IQ is also not necessarily a limitation of ability. It is possible to enhance the thinking skills tested by practice and exposure to new ideas. A low IQ score may indicate a learning disability and the need for special learning aids, but again, IQ scores alone should not be considered conclusive. Testing the IQ of your child may be harmful if it produces a label (even in your mind) that is limiting to the child. Remember, some of the most advanced thinkers and creative individuals in history (including Beethoven, Einstein, and Edison) were categorized by teachers as stupid and incapable of learning. Always be careful not to limit your child by any type of labeling.

Laurie majored in music in high school and intended to pursue a degree in teaching music until a test in high school revealed she had especially high mechanical aptitude. At the prompting of her guidance counselor, she applied to MIT and other technical institutions for their program in mechanical engineering. Unfortunately, though she had high mechanical aptitude, she hated the mechanical engineering program and ended up switching to a biology major at another school. In retrospect, she wishes she had stuck with the music program, since that represented her real interest.

Aptitude tests are given by employers to determine specific skills of potential employees. The **ASVAB (Armed Services Vocational Abilities Battery)** is an aptitude test used by the U.S. military to assess the technical and vocational aptitudes of those who apply for military service. A number of companies and schools use this test as well. The ASVAB consists of a battery of 10 tests that measure knowledge and skill in the following areas:

- General science.
- Arithmetic reasoning.
- Word knowledge.
- Paragraph comprehension.
- Numerical operations.
- Coding speed.
- Auto and shop information.
- Mathematics knowledge.
- Mechanical comprehension.
- Electronics information.

You can find some sample tests for the ASVAB and other aptitude tests online.

Special testing for special needs

Some achievement tests available to homeschool parents can help those who may have slight learning disabilities (check with test suppliers). Others have special forms or administration techniques that may accommodate a special need. College Board exams are also available in formats that limit discrimination due to a handicap. If you have a special-needs child, contact test distributors for more information.

If you want help with diagnosing a learning disability or accommodating a handicap, the best place to find help is with a private practice physician or psychologist. Most special-needs testing is performed by a licensed psychologist. Your school district may provide testing and services free of charge (except to the taxpayer), and you may want to take advantage of this. Beware, though, that many of these "free" services come with strings attached. In many states, using public services means giving the state authority to direct the student's education. We suggest that you contact the NATional cHallenged Homeschoolers Associated Network (NATHHAN), PO Box 39, Porthill, ID 83853; (208) 267-6246; Web site: *www.nathhan.com*; e-mail: *nathanews@aol.com*, for information on homeschooling a challenged child. Many states have separate homeschool organizations for families with challenged children. Check with your state homeschool organization or NATHHAN.

One more resource is The Essential Learning Institute. The institute offers home testing for learning disabilities, computer-based sensory integration therapy (SIT), academic evaluation and placement, and individually prescribed curricula. Contact: 334 Second Street Catasauqua, PA 18032; (800) 285-9089; Web site: *rsts.net/home/index2.html*; e-mail: *eli@fast.net*.

College boards

The first test used in the college admission process is the **Preliminary Scholastic Aptitude Test (PSAT-NMSQT)**. The PSAT is the practice version of the SAT and is usually taken in 10th or 11th grade. The exam has two puposes: It serves as a practice run for the SAT and is the National Merit Scholarships qualifier. Students who want to try to qualify for National Merit Scholarships must take this test in their junior year. The PSAT may be taken in other years, but only the junior year allows for NMS qualification. However, the PSAT is not identical to the SAT in form or content, and since the SAT can be taken more than once, it may not be of much importance. PSAT-NMSQT exams are given only once a year, in the fall, and only at schools. This will require that you contact the school district for information on how to sign up for the exam. The fee for taking the PSAT is currently less than $10.

There are two exams that may be used in college admissions: the **SAT (Scholastic Aptitude Test)** and the **ACT (American College Test)**. Students applying for freshman admission (not transfer) to a four-year college or university will certainly need to take one of these exams. Some very selective colleges will require scores from both. The SAT is most well known on the East and West coasts, while the ACT is popular in the South and Midwest. Most colleges, however, will accept either exam.

So what is the difference? The SAT focuses more on reasoning skills and only covers verbal (language) and math skills. The ACT also contains a science reasoning section. Both exams cover math skills from pre-algebra, algebra, geometry, and trigonometry. Both exams contain a reading comprehension section. Both exams are multiple choice in format and are timed. Both exams offer a qualitative analysis of readiness for college-level study. The SAT, however, deals more with logic, vocabulary, and reasoning skills, and the ACT focuses more on content.

It currently costs $22-$25 to take the ACT exam (in the United States). ACT exams are given throughout the year and may be taken more than once. You will find a schedule of testing dates and information about the ACT online at *www.act.org*, by calling (800) 525-6926 or (319) 337-1270, or by writing to the ACT National Office, 2201 North Dodge Street, P.O. Box 168, Iowa City, IA 52243-0168. You may also register for the ACT online, by phone, or in writing.

The SAT-I exam costs $23.50. The test is given throughout the year, and the student may test more than once. The College Board Web site at *www.collegeboard.com* posts information on fees, schedules, test help, and more. You may register for the SAT-I at the Web site or by contacting The College Board, 45 Columbus Avenue, New York, NY 10023-6992; (212) 713-8000.

Those homeschoolers who have taken standardized tests on a regular basis may be ahead of the game when the time comes to take the college boards. Having test experience is a definite advantage because it helps to minimize the test jitters that are common in traditional schools. There are many ways to practice for the SAT or ACT. There are several SAT preparatory book and software titles (see Appendix C). In many communities there are specific SAT or ACT prep courses offered outside the school. These typically meet once a week for six weeks and provide the interaction with a teacher that may be helpful to some learners. There is no problem making this preparatory training a part of your child's regular homeschool curriculum.

One advantage of taking the SAT or ACT is that they are often used to measure qualifications for academic scholarships available from the college your child wants to attend. If this is something you want to take advantage of, then preparation is very valuable. When we took the PSAT and SAT in the 1970s, students rarely prepared specifically for the tests. They relied on their general education. However, we would not suggest this as an option today.

SAT II exams are given to determine the knowledge and/or skill level of the student in a specific subject area. Each exam is one hour long, and, except for a 20-minute essay on the writing test, they are all multiple choice. Registration costs are $13 for each testing day plus $6-$12 for each subject test. Up to three subject tests may be taken on a given day. There are currently 22 subject tests.

Fees for ACT, SAT I, and SAT II exams include direct reporting to a limited number of colleges you choose. You may choose not to directly report the scores, as they can always be sent later. The easiest way to register for the ACT, SAT I, and SAT II exams is online (*www.act.org* or *www.collegeboard.com*). You may also register for the ACT by calling (319) 337-1270.

Avoiding the college boards

Students who have accumulated college credit during high school or who transfer from a community (junior) college will probably not be required to take SAT or ACT exams. The purpose of the college boards is to determine whether the student is ready for college-level work. If students have already accumulated college credits through CLEP exams, community college courses, or distance learning, these credits may allow them to transfer rather than applying as a freshman, therefore bypassing the college boards. Most community colleges have open enrollment—in other words, they do not turn away paying customers. Some require placement tests to be taken at the beginning of studies to determine which classes students are ready for. If the student scores low on a placement test, he may be required to take noncredit preparatory classes before beginning college-level work. Most homeschool students will place very well on these exams, sometimes qualifying them to begin earning college credit at age 14 or so.

To test or not to test

There are a growing number of parents (and educators) who do not believe testing is a valid measure of learning. Many are not willing to have their children tested at all. There are good reasons for concern. Standardized testing has several inherent weaknesses. The fact that almost all standardized exams are multiple choice means they are limited to showing whether a student can pick the best answer. They cannot tell whether students have the ability to come up with the answer on their own. Standardized tests are also limited to testing how well a student knows a certain curriculum. Many homeschool students use different curricula than do public schools (although they study the same subjects), so these tests are not an accurate representation of their learning. The fact that homeschool percentile scores are on average much higher than the norm is a testament to the fact that homeschool students quickly master the basics that comprise the total of public school curricula. A related problem is that while national achievement may actually be worsening, percentile scores may remain high, demonstrating that the tests are subjective in content and in scoring.

And finally, when standardized tests are used, the results are often falsified by the fact that teachers (and even homeschool parents) teach to the test. In other words, they specifically focus on material known to be on the test, and allow students to cram for them at the last minute. Material learned in this manner is poorly retained and applied. Therefore, a student who tests very well may actually have very little working knowledge of the subject.

In actuality, current standardized testing procedures and norms really favor homeschools. The limited content and norm referencing make homeschoolers look just fine. We are not trying to say that homeschoolers are deficient, but rather that because of the limitations of the tests, they are often easier for the homeschooled. Since the tutorial and discovery methods of learning are more efficient than classroom teaching, and homeschool students tend to be self-confident testers (on average), they score higher on the tests. In actuality, research indicates that scores for those who have been homeschooling longer (as opposed to those who have been in school, but are now homeschooling) are higher. (See *Homeschooling Works Pass it On!*, an independent study by Lawrence M. Rudner, Ph.D.)

For this reason, most homeschool parents find testing to be the lesser of evils in proving the competency of their homeschool program. Some states allow no option but to test for those who are following homeschool law. However, it is possible in many situations to use alternative assessments in place of testing. Keeping a narrative account of the student's progress is one option. Another is to keep a portfolio of the student's work. Ultimately, the student's ability to prosper in society and make a living will prove the ultimate test of your curriculum.

Tests not to take

Some states, like New York, give criterion-referenced achievement tests in the public schools at different grade levels. These tests are designed to provide specific information to educators and parents concerning the progress of the student in learning the state-mandated curriculum. Homeschool students are not required to take such tests and should not submit to them. These tests will provide false results (either high or low) unless the home school uses the exact same curriculum as the one mandated by the state, which is very unlikely.

One more note to those living in New York state. Regents exams are given for core high school subjects in the public schools and are being phased in as requirements for all graduates. Though it is possible in most cases to have your homeschool student take Regents exams, it is never necessary and seldom desirable. They are not necessary for getting into college. For proof of a student's ability in a specific subject area, have him take the SAT II exams.

For everything a season

The effectiveness of standardized testing is certainly arguable. However, at some point, nearly every student will need to take some form of standardized assessment. We encourage you to carefully consider your reasons for testing, the tests you will use, and the method you use to administer them. Treating testing as a normal part of the educational process will promote your student's confidence in test taking and allow him to attain his best scores.

CHAPTER 12

Providing a Mission Through Christian Training and Service

"I will say to the north, 'Give them up!' And to the south, 'Do not hold them back.' Bring My sons from afar, and My daughters from the ends of the earth, everyone who is called by My name, and whom I have created for My glory, whom I have formed, even whom I have made."
—Isaiah 43:6-7 (NASB)

Taking a year or two for special Christian training and service can have a profound impact on a young person's life. David spent a year after high school in Switzerland studying Bible and training as a missionary, and Laurie spent a year at a Bible institute before continuing her secular education. Both of us are thankful for that time that allowed us to develop Christian character and Bible understanding. It has been our goal to inspire each of our children to take on some sort of mission opportunity and/or Bible study as they begin their higher education. We believe it is important for them to know that a life career in missions is a viable and worthy choice among the options they may pursue.

Many homeschool graduates are still not sure what they should consider as a life vocation. If this is the case, it may be especially helpful for your student to take some time out and focus on Bible understanding and Christian character training.

The options available to high school students and graduates for training in missions and Bible are many and varied. We would encourage young people to explore the following options.

Attending a Bible institute can give young people an opportunity to be grounded in their faith, expand their understanding of the Bible, and practice Christian character in a setting outside the home. By a Bible institute (versus a Bible college) we are specifically referring to a school that focuses on teaching a curriculum around the Bible. It used to be that these were easily differentiated because of their shorter time frames. There are numerous Bible institute programs available throughout the United States and Canada, corresponding to nearly every evangelical denomination. Bible institute programs now range from one to four years in length, with courses in Bible, theology, missions, youth work, and pastoral training. Some institutes offer associate's, bachelor's, and even graduate degrees; others allow transfer of their credits to another institution for degree credit.

The focused Bible curriculum gives the student a chance to solidify his understanding. This is good preparation for any student, whether his goals lie in developing a career right away or in continuing his education.

You can find information about Bible institutes on the Internet (do a search for Bible institute), at homeschool convention booths, or from your local church.

Short-term mission opportunities abound these days, sponsored by a variety of churches and mission organizations. We have experienced the life-changing effects of such outreaches ourselves. Leading several groups on mission excursions has given us the opportunity to see first-hand how effective this sort of outreach is in changing the lives of those being ministered to as well as the missionaries themselves.

Youth With A Mission was one of the first organizations to send young people on short-term missions. YWAM is now a worldwide organization that provides all sorts of training opportunities, including discipleship training schools (usually about six months long), the School of the Bible in Tyler, Texas (a one-year training similar to a Bible institute), and the University of the Nations (offering a full-time college degree program). They also provide short-term mission opportunities all over the world. Check out the options at *www.ywam.org.*

Teen World Outreach is another short-term mission organization that works for young people. They provide mission training all over the world. Find information at *www.t-w-o.org.*

Operation Mobilization is another international mission organization that attracts young people from all over the world. They have a number of mission focuses, so there are innumerable opportunities for teenagers and homeschool families to participate, including ministries in Europe and India, teen street ministries, ships and mercy ministries, and short-term outreaches. Lots of information can be found at *www.om.org.*

Of course, we haven't done justice to the number of organizations that sponsor this sort of activity. Again, do an Internet search on "short-term missions" to find a multitude of options.

There are some good Web sites for teens to check out for information on Christian mission organizations for short-term mission trips.

One site that contains a list of a number of links to short-term opportunities is *christianteens.about.com/teens/msub5.htm*. Organizations like Adventure in Missions, Asian Minorities Outreach, the Center for Student Missions, Destination Summit, Fuel International, Group Source

---

In the spring of 1998, 14 teenagers and two adults gathered in a parking lot at their local Sunoco mini-mart for a car wash, getting wet, hot, and sweaty. They raised more than $400. The next week, they spent their Saturday running a multifamily yard sale, raising another $350. And for what? To go on a mission trip to a remote part of northern Wisconsin to minister to some 60 American Indian children for seven days. This mission trip changed the perspective of our eldest daughter, Rebekah, forever.

Laurie and Rebekah flew with the mission team to the nearest airport, then drove three hours to the reservation. For a week they lived without hot water, electricity, or many of the conveniences we take for granted. The times of worship, ministry, and fellowship became lasting memories of the value of Christian missions to Rebekah. The answered prayers that week were awe-inspiring. Young children responded to the Gospel for the first time and were made aware of God's love for them.

For our daughter, returning home was heartbreaking. Rebekah cried off and on for an entire week. Her heart was changed as a result of this experience. She has wanted to be a nurse since she was a child. Now she is dreaming of possibly returning as a missionary nurse to this remote village, to share the gospel message of the love of Jesus with these underprivileged children. This was an experience that was a supernatural intervention by the Holy Spirit in the life of a young Christian girl.

Bekah's commitment to these people has continued; she has returned to assist the mission staff during their winter discipleship training school. She took along four other friends to share her vision of ministering to those who have need for the love of God in practical ways. As you can see, it's contagious!

Travel, Jesus People USA, Mission Discover, Pioneers, Project Teamwork, Students International, Teen Mania, Youth Mission International, Teens in Missionary Service (TIMS), 30 Hour Famine, and Youth With A Mission (YWAM) are listed with links to their sites. Check them out!

Different families will find different areas of interest. You might relate to one particular idea for a mission trip over another. There's a lot there, so have fun as you select a mission trip that fits your preferences, burden, and other specifics. Interface with as many of the links that you can. E-mail the contacts and share your interest. You will be surprised at the response. These organizations are always willing to communicate with believers and share their stories. You will find that most of them, if not all, have a deep, burning desire to know and share Jesus Christ with anyone who will listen!

If you are concerned about sending your teens out "into the world" on their own, we understand. That's why we go too! Most short-term mission opportunities would love chaperoning help. Be adventurous and go with God!

Your biggest obstacle will probably be coming up with the costs for the trip. The prices can be high. But raising the cash can turn out to be fun. We have mentioned that our mission teams have done car washes and garage sales to raise money; you might also do auctions of household services to people in your church or community. Usually there are a few generous people who contribute more than the going rate to these kinds of events.

Note that different ministries have different policies on who can participate. For example, some have minimum age requirements of 18 and others 16. Some allow children to go with their parent(s), while others only accept young people over a certain age, even with parental supervision. It usually depends on the mission opportunity. Obviously, some will require a passport application, so give yourself enough time to apply (usually at least four to six weeks).

Make sure you scrutinize the group's mission statement to your level of comfort. (We probably don't need to tell you this.) Once you clarify the requirements, get ready. You're in for the time of your life!

Mission trips are available for virtually everybody. They can be local or in a remote part of the world. Some groups focus on a specific geographic area. Others focus on certain groups of people. Still others minister to a specific lifestyle. There are as many different offerings as there are varieties of human beings. All need Jesus Christ. We provide another means for the message to be heard.

As you can see, there is no limit to the opportunities for students to explore their understanding of God's mission for their lives. Short-term mission trips will affect your children's whole perspective of who they are and what they are called to accomplish. We know of many teenagers who have had their entire direction in life changed by a one-week mission. Just ask Rebekah!

These experiences are what we all hope and pray our children will have in their lives. We can help them participate by finding ways to work with other homeschoolers, either in a local support group or with their local church youth ministry. It's up to us as homeschool parents to give them these opportunities for spiritual growth.

A word of caution: Be ready for the consequences of sending your child on a mission. As we have noted, such a trip will change the course of your child's life forever. Even though you might expect that your child will become an engineer, doctor, or architect, he may return from a mission trip and announce that God has called him to the mission field. We suggest that you prepare for such a situation.

Our daughter Katie said for years that she wanted to be a veterinarian. Recently she informed her father that she decided that a career in animal medicine was no longer her desire and that attending college was not the next thing on her agenda (remember, she finished her homeschool requirements at age 14). She wants to go this fall to a discipleship training school, then a school of the Bible, and after that, we don't know. This is okay with us. We know she will succeed at whatever she puts her hands to, and, most of all, we want her to follow God. How can she go wrong with that?

We are convinced that we want to give our children that liberty. As a rather practical father, David wants to make sure that Katie thinks through the implications of not gaining career skills. He shares from personal experience. As a young man, he went to the mission field and spent three years in ghetto ministry in Newark, New Jersey. His computer operator job helped to pay many of the expenses of the mission during that time. That is not to say that Katie cannot take a different road, giving her life to a specific missionary calling. But we want to help her think through all of the issues so she is able to make an intelligent life decision.

There is no doubt that having your child announce a lifetime commitment to ministering will challenge you to your very core. Our advice is that you need to carefully weigh whether you are willing to give up your dreams for your child for the higher calling of God that may be unfolding.

This is not to say that you may not end up strongly advocating for your child to stay the course that was originally laid out. It may be the right thing to do. But we would encourage you to make sure you are fully convinced that it *is* the right thing to do. And the only way you can be anywhere near certain is by your own disciplined efforts to seek God and spend time in deep personal evaluation.

We caution you. Be very careful on this issue if it ever emerges. You could easily quench the Spirit in your child with a lack of delicacy in this situation. Remember, this young person has come to the conclusion that God has spoken. This is arguably one of the most profound experiences of life. If you ignore what your child has discovered or treat it as something that can be postponed, without carefully working through the dynamics, you could turn your child's heart forever. So walk circumspectly. Be humble in spirit as you ask the Lord to lead you.

Some of you may not see the relevance of these warnings. Don't worry about it. This caution is given for those who need it. For the rest, just know we have said it and remember where this page is if it ever applies to you.

What about "full-time missionary service?"

There is one other area of mission that we want to address. That's the situation where your son or daughter wants to go the conventional missionary route. The requirements for this type of work vary with the different missions, ministries, and denominations in the world working for the cause of Christ.

Most, but not all, of the long-term missionary organizations in the Christian world have educational and other requirements for deputation with their organization. Some require at least a bachelor's degree. Others require a theological degree from a specific seminary. Some want you to be a member of their denomination. Some, like YWAM or Christ for the Nations, want you to spend a year or two in their missionary schools. Some don't care what educational experience you have.

If you and your child agree that this is the right path for him, contact the mission and find out what they require for high school, college, and post-graduate work. Make sure you do your homework early so that your child has the best chance of pursuing that direction. Once again, the calling of God to the child is critical. Sometimes there are years of schooling involved in preparing to join particular mission boards. If your child has her heart set on a particular ministry with a specific organization that has such requirements, you would do well to get as much information as you can so that you can cover the basics early on.

Whether it is a week-long local mission, a summer of service in another state, a journey that takes your child to another continent for an extended period of time, or a lifetime missionary career, there is very little in this world that is more worthwhile.

In his book, *Four Trojan Horses*, our dear friend and mentor, Harry Conn, shares an interesting point:

> *A book was published,* Who's Who of America, *which was a study and analysis of the people listed in* Who's Who. *It was discovered that it took 25,000 laboring families to produce one child that would be listed in* Who's Who. *It required 10,000 families where the father was a skilled craftsman (electrician, tool and die maker, technician) to produce one child that would be listed in* Who's Who. *It showed that it took 5,000 lawyers, 6,000 Baptist preachers, 5,000 Presbyterian preachers to produce one listed in* Who's Who. *It showed 2,500 dentists and only 1,200 Episcopalian preachers or priests to produce a listee. It was found that for every seven Christian missionary families, one of their children would be listed in* Who's Who. *Surely this is a good example of Hebrews 6:10, "For God is not unrighteous to forget our work and labor of love."*

What about full-time Christian service?

We believe that every individual makes a commitment in life to love the Lord or not. All of us are commanded to do so with all of our heart, soul, mind, and strength. To us, full-time Christian service is daily life. True Christianity is living for Jesus Christ. The word Christian means "little Christ." We are all called to that standard; if we do not heed the call we break the commandment, "You shall not take the name of the Lord your God in vain. (Deuteronomy 5:11 [NKJB])"

But there is a high calling to missions. Do everything you can to encourage this kind of direction in your child. It will probably cost you something, as it will them. But it is undoubtedly the most rewarding calling in life. Make sure it is a part of your homeschooling experience. You will never regret it. It will have an eternal impact on you, your children, and the world.

Apprenticing in a Christian organization serves two purposes: developing the talents and interests of the young person and providing needed help to the organization. Many Christian radio stations and such organizations as the Home School Legal Defense Association (HSLDA) allow students to spend some time learning the ropes of their ministries. Many mission organizations offer the same opportunities.

Job opportunities with Christian organizations may also be an option for your homeschool graduate. InterChristo is a comprehensive Christian job referral network that allows Christians to access thousands of potential job openings at hundreds of ministries throughout the world. By accessing InterChristo's Web site, *www.jobleads.org*, you can fill out a personalized application, giving a specific listing of your homeschooler's work experiences, job interests, geographic area, and qualifications. The InterChristo database will then match any potential jobs to your child's background and interests. The cost is $59.95 for a three-month subscription.

Make sure that your homeschool effort includes time for ministry. Our children need to learn that life includes unselfishness, when you give for nothing in return. This is what "agape" is all about—the Christian type of love. It reflects on a person's choice to do the highest good for God and others simply because it is right, good, and holy, not for what the person will get out of it. As we provide chances for our children to practice this in their early years, it will become a regular part of their lifestyle when they leave home. The apostle John said that he found no greater joy than to see his children walking in the truth. We wholeheartedly agree.

CHAPTER 13

Taking on Advanced Studies

"Therefore be careful how you walk, not as unwise men, but as wise,
making the most of your time, because the days are evil."
—Ephesians 5:15-16 (NASB)

Many homeschool students are finding a multitude of opportunities for gaining advanced knowledge in specific areas before leaving the home school. In the home school, it is common to find that students complete their high school studies at an earlier age than in traditional schools. These students may not be ready to leave home yet, but are ready for higher-level studies. It is also possible for homeschool students who have not completed high school to begin college level work and receive credit for both high school and college. Advanced studies need not be limited to especially gifted students. The tutorial method of study in the home is more efficient than traditional schooling, and therefore often allows students to progress more quickly, whether or not they have special ability. Homeschooling may produce students prepared for at least some college work at 14, 15, or 16, and sometimes even earlier.

It will be necessary to decide together with the student which advanced studies to take on and when. Timing is important. We found that our children needed to experience taking a local community college course to give them the confidence that they could really do it. Taking a course in a real college setting (such as a community college) allows students who have not been exposed to classroom learning to be comfortable in that setting. There are also many opportunities to earn college credit by examination, on the Internet, and through advanced placement courses.

Advanced Placement (AP) courses, exams, and credit

AP courses, as they are called, are offered in most traditional high schools. They are available to homeschool students either through a local high school, online, or by self-study. We recommend either self-study or the online version, since this eliminates the need to deal with your local school district. The College Board currently offers 32 AP exams in 22 subject areas. Online preparation courses cost between $200 and $375, plus books. The cost for the exams is $76.

You may think these courses are a bit pricey, but the payoff is big. A passing score on an AP test will generally replace a three-credit college course (tuition for which is usually between $300 and $1200 or more, depending on the institution). If the student passes an AP course in his junior year of high school, it will provide evidence to college admissions offices that he can handle college coursework. This often results in academic scholarships. Some colleges will advance a student with an accumulation of AP credits to sophomore standing immediately upon entrance, saving a full year's tuition. AP examination grades are reported to colleges on a five-point scale as follows:

5   Extremely well qualified[a]
4   Well qualified[a]
3   Qualified[a]
2   Possibly qualified[a]
1   No recommendation[b]

[a]Qualified to receive college credit or advanced placement
[b]No recommendation to receive college credit or advanced placement
(Taken from the College Board Web site: *www.collegeboard.org/ap/students/exam/process.html*)

For more information on the AP program visit *www.collegeboard.org*. and go to the AP section, or contact them at: Advanced Placement Program/The College Board, 45 Columbus Avenue, New York, New York 10023-6992; (212) 713-8000. For online preparation courses visit *www.apex.netu.com* or *www.pahomeschoolers.com*.

College Level Exam Placement (CLEP)

We have to admit that "CLEPping" is our favorite way for students to accumulate college credit. The CLEP program is also administered by the College Board organization (*www.collegeboard.org/clep*). CLEP exams are administered in test centers located at local colleges. Some colleges only administer exams to students matriculated at their school; others are open test centers where anyone can test. The exams are accepted for credit at more than 2800 colleges and universities nationwide. There are two types of CLEP tests, general and subject. There are five general exams (social sciences and history, college mathematics, English composition, humanities, and natural sciences) covering courses usually taken in the first two years of college. Each is worth six college credits. The subject exams (generally worth three credits each) cover material found in individual undergraduate courses, ranging from foreign languages to science to business. There are 27 subject exams in five subject areas. Each exam (general or subject) costs $44 plus testing site fees (usually about $10).

CLEP exams are 90 minutes long and are multiple choice (except for an essay section on the English Composition general exam). The student may prepare for the exam with the CLEP preparation manual for that exam. The manuals contain all of the necessary information as well as practice tests and test-taking tips. The exams are scored on a scale similar to AP exams; however, when these credits are transferred they are generally done so in Pass/Fail format—no grades are entered.

A note of caution: Check with the college the student plans to attend to determine their policy on accepting CLEP credit. Each institution makes its own rules about how many CLEP credits they will accept, in which subjects, the scores necessary for transfer, and where the tests must be taken. However, most community colleges will award credit for CLEP exams, so if the student finishes the first two years at a community college, the sum of these credits will generally transfer (or constitute an associate's degree). In other words, there are usually ways to work within the system to obtain the desired end. Moreover, you may actually want to choose a college or university specifically because of their policy to grant credits for CLEP. You are in charge.

The only other caveat of this form of accruing college credits is that it does require a motivated self-study program. Generally, the student will not have taken specific courses in the subject area of the test. With CLEP, the student can take the test without having to sit through unnecessary classroom time. (Those who want to take a class to prepare might as well take an AP course or a regular college class for credit.) Instead, they will need to study the material on their own.

The preparation for CLEP exams is relatively simple, and for cost they can't be beat—$44 for three to six credits! The test centers are quite accessible and the exams are widely accepted. There is no minimum age requirement. So why have you not heard of CLEP exams? Obviously, colleges would rather charge you $300 to $1,800 to teach the same mate-

same material! In the true spirit of homeschooling, we strongly recommend that you investigate how CLEP can help your student(s). For more information, a list of colleges that accept CLEP credits, and a list of test centers, visit *www.collegeboard.org/clep*, call (609) 771-7865, write to CLEP at P.O. Box 6600, Princeton, New Jersey 08541-6000, e-mail *clep@ets.org*, or contact your local community college.

Community college

Many community colleges are beginning to offer special programs for homeschool students. Be careful, though. Many of these homeschool-friendly programs offer non-college credit courses for high school credit only. This may be useful if you want to supplement your home school in difficult areas such as chemistry or calculus. These courses will have a 0__ designation (i.e., Biology 001 or 091) rather than a 1__ designation (i.e., Biology 101). They generally cost the same as a college-level course. Often, your student should be able to take the freshman-level course instead, earning college and high school credit simultaneously.

In most cases, if your child has not completed high school, he will need to take a placement exam provided by the community college. Our three oldest children did this at ages 14, 15, and 16, respectively. Without any particular preparation, they all placed higher on the exam than the average applicant who was a high school graduate (according to the dean of academic affairs). However, they were asked to come in for a personal interview with the dean, because of their young ages. She was concerned (before she met them) about their lack of socialization, since they had always been home-schooled. Her doubts were erased when all three of them sat in her office and explained their reasons for wanting to pursue college work.

At your local community college, your child can take a full semester load or just one course at a time. Most community college courses are highly regarded by upper-level colleges and universities, especially if grades are good. These credits are much less expensive since they are government subsidized. Ttaking at least one course in this setting can also go a long way toward inspiring confidence in the home learner.

Beyond community college

Many other colleges offer classes to high school students in their area. In our region, these include Colgate University, Cornell University, and Syracuse University. Obviously, if a student succeeds in a course from one of these prestigious schools, it will be very impressive on his transcript.

Some universities offer summer programs especially designed for high school students who want to begin earning credit toward a college degree. These can be expensive, but are often good experience.

Distance learning

Where do we begin? There is truly a plethora of distance learning courses available via the Internet, satellite, or video. We cannot even begin to list them, so we suggest visiting *www.petersons.com* or searching the Internet for "distance learning." Nearly every institution of higher learning now offers classes online. Some also have classes available to special satellite dish subscribers or by video (though these are quickly becoming outmoded).

Within the next few years, we expect this trend to grow even stronger. We believe that soon college degrees earned from a distance will be the norm. What a great way to eliminate the huge costs of on-campus room and board!

Every distance program has its own criteria for accepting students, its own format, and its own costs. As a general rule, tuition for distance courses is not cheap. However, if you want your high school student to accrue credits from a well-recognized institution while staying right at home, this may be just the ticket. You will need to have fairly up-to-date computer equipment for Internet courses; the specifications are listed by each institution.

Keeping track of progress

Once your student begins to accumulate college credit, you will need to devise a way to keep track of his or her progress. If the student has taken a mix-and-match approach to earning credits (some from community college, some from Internet classes, some from CLEP exams, for example), it will be up to you (or the student) to carefully document when, where, and how these credits have been earned. You will also need to record any grades received. This can be done on the high school transcript or on a separate transcript of college work.

Ultimately, your records will serve as a summary. Official records are kept with the institution that has granted the credit and can be obtained by sending a transcript request to the registrar's office. You should document the addresses for obtaining official transcripts of credit in one place so that it will be easy to contact them all when needed. Obviously, if all the credits are earned at one place (such as a community college), all the records will be in one place as well.

It's up to you!

We recommend that most students in the home begin some advanced work before leaving high school. The experience, knowledge, and credits will be extremely valuable. When deciding whether to try CLEP, distance learning, community college, or AP, you should place a lot of emphasis on the student's learning style. Students who are self-motivated, interested in the subject matter, and able to study on their own will probably do well on a CLEP exam. Students who need more structure and personal interaction will more likely benefit from a local community college or AP course. Those who are self-motivated but want to take on a difficult subject they have had little experience in may do better with an AP course. There are plenty of options. Feel free to mix and match.

High school and college credit at the same time? Yes!

When college-level credits are being earned before the student has finished high school, you can double-credit these courses to both high school and college. Credits earned in this way count toward high school graduation and toward a college degree (when accepted through transfer). This is not cheating! In fact, this is a common practice in traditional schools. See the "Crossing Over" section in Chapter 7.

A final note

One more word about advanced studies: The more your children can accomplish while still in the home, the easier it is for you, the parent, to continue exerting your influence while they are learning. College-level courses, even though they are offered at Christian colleges and universities, can be challenging and controversial to a student's worldview. We homeschool our students, at least in part, because we want them to benefit from what we have learned along the way (rather than what some professor has learned). When your children can take courses while living in your home, they are more likely to be able to clearly think through issues that may be confusing to them. They can benefit from discussion with you and minimize the negative social influences that occur in dormitories and society houses.

Clearly, if you want to be a good steward of time, energy, and money, you will explore the many opportunities for getting a head start on college while your children are still at home.

CHAPTER 14

Keeping Records

*"Let this be a sign among you, so that when your children ask later, saying,
'What do these stones mean to you?' Then you shall say to them, 'Because
the waters of the Jordan were cut off before the ark of the covenant of the
Lord; when it crossed the Jordan, the waters of the Jordan were cut off.' So
these stones shall become a memorial to the sons of Israel forever."*
—Joshua 4:6-7 (NASB)

In almost every homeschool meeting we have led, we have been
probed by anxious parents who are concerned about how to keep
records. Many are daunted by the need to keep track of their child's
progress, while others are spending an inordinate amount of their
time recording every minute of their days. Many states require certain
forms of records to satisfy their homeschooling laws. In that case, it is
important to be aware of the laws that apply to your family and keep
records that will provide needed verification of your home school. Our
discussion of record-keeping will focus on how to retain the right information to ensure a smooth transition into adulthood.

It is essential that parents keep accurate records of all work completed, as well as an account of extracurricular activities. Many resources
are available to help with record-keeping. It is up to the parents to find the
system that works best in their family. Our goal is to address which records
need to be retained rather than how to retain them; however, we will
share ideas that have been especially helpful to us. Your goal is to keep
records that will enable your student to progress to the future of his choice.

You may want to review the material in Chapters 7 through 9 as it
relates to each child so that you can customize your material for him or
her. You must have a clear goal for each student in order to make sure that
you record the right information accurately.

Permanent records are definitely necessary for grades 9 through 12, but we recommend that you keep your junior high records as well.

Course grades and credits

In high school, it is important to record the credits or units that each class is worth. Traditional high schools usually report credits as Carnegie units. College admissions departments are accustomed to seeing transcripts that reflect Carnegie units. In a traditional setting, one Carnegie unit represents 120 hours of instruction in the classroom, plus assignments and study. In other words, one credit is awarded for each full-year class (40 minutes per day times 180 days). One-semester courses earn one half credit. Some classes only meet two to three times per week (like gym, or music lessons) and are awarded a fraction, such as one quarter credit.

We can hear you mothers mumbling now. We know; unless you use video curriculum, it is highly unlikely that you have 40 minutes of classroom instruction plus assignments for each high school class. Consider this, though. You also do not need to take attendance each period, deal with 30 students of varying levels of understanding and discipline at one time, hand out and collect papers, etc. As we have stated before, the home tutorial method of teaching is simply much more efficient. You can go quickly through material the student comprehends well, and spend more time on difficult areas. So, the Carnegie unit may not be a very accurate representation of class time for you. You simply will be able to complete more in a shorter (usually much shorter) amount of time.

The key is to translate the credits your child earns into a form that is understandable to you and to admissions departments. In that traditional class, a certain amount of material is covered in a year. Most courses, for instance, will strive to cover at least 80 percent of a high school-level textbook. Alternatively, they may need to pass midterm and final exams that cover the scope of the course. So, if your student studies through a textbook and can demonstrate (through tests, projects, contract work, essays, etc.) that he or she has grasped a majority of the material, you can feel confident in awarding one credit for that course.

Some schools simply award half a credit for each semester of work in a subject, disregarding the 120-hour rule. Whatever system you use should correspond to ones used by traditional schools and expected by college admissions offices. Be sure to explain your method of awarding credit in a note on the transcript. As a general rule, to graduate high school will require 20 units (some schools or states require slightly more or less).

Progress Report

Student: John Homeschool   **Age:** 14
Grade Level: 9 (Second Quarter, 2000-2001)

SUBJECT	MATERIAL COVERED	EVALUATION
Mathematics	Algebra I Chapters 8-11	B
English	Grammar Review	A
	Learning Language Arts through Literature - Gold Level, Lessons 3-5	
	Literature	
History	Economics Class - Group Lessons	A
	Unit Study on Civil War	
Science	Units on Cellular and Molecular Biology w/Labs	B
Spanish	Spanish I Chapters 9-12	A
Music	Piano Lessons	S
Physical Ed.	Bowling	S
Home Economics	Typing, Cooking and Meal Planning, Computer Basics, Child Care	S

S = Satisfactory

(Pass/Fail [P/F] or Satisfactory/Unsatisfactory [S/U] grades are permissible, but we recommend that you use letter grades [A-F] at least for the main subjects.)

After saying all that, we should warn you that some colleges will not even want your transcript. Many are now admitting homeschoolers with SAT or ACT scores alone, or on the basis of a portfolio. Make sure to check with the school for its specific requirements.

Progress reports

We suggest that you keep progress reports for your own information. Interim progress reports will facilitate maintaining a transcript, and will help you determine appropriate grades. In addition, they will serve as mile-markers to document progress and problem areas.

You may choose a quarterly, semiannual, or yearly report. Choose whatever frequency works best for you. Don't space them so far apart that you cannot remember what was done, or so close that you are doing unnecessary paperwork.

Some states require some form of progress report as part of their homeschool education laws. In that case, keep reports to the state simple, including only the information required. For instance, on quarterly reports we submitted to our school district in New York, we did not include Bible unless it was credited for an elective in high school. The state did not require Bible in its curriculum, so it was unnecessary information to them. We did keep record of Bible on our progress reports, however, since they were for our use only. Giving excess information on state-required reports does you no good, and may cause others to look bad.

Take a look at the sample progress report on page 149. The materials listed and evaluations are just examples. You will find a blank copy in Appendix F, which you may reproduce.

Grade point average

The grade point average is meant to be an objective measure of what the student has learned. In reality, it is not quite that easy. Grades are always subjective. Even when a grade reflects a simple multiple-choice test, it is still subjective, because someone wrote the test. For this reason, we downplayed grading and emphasized mastery of skills in our home school. However, for a transcript, you need grades. How you award a grade is up to you. You may require a student to complete a given list of assignments in order to obtain a particular grade (a contract course). You may require passing certain tests for a grade. You may have the student write papers or complete projects for a grade. You may even assign a grade by pure subjectivity (what you think the student deserves). All of these methods are used in traditional schools. A word of caution is in order, though. If you are awarding all A grades and your child does not do well on standardized tests or the college boards, your grades will be highly suspect. On the other hand, some students are just bad testers. In that case, it is wise to prepare a portfolio of the student's work that will substantiate the grades that were given. To figure a grade point average:

1. Assign a letter grade (A, B, C, D, F) for each class.
2. Convert the letter grade to a point value using this scale*:
   A = 4 points, B = 3, C = 2, D = 1, F = 0
3. Find the total number of units (for the period you want to average).
4. Divide the total number of points by the total number of units.

*(Some schools use other point scales such as A = 5, B = 4, but these are the exception. We suggest you stick with the more common 4-point scale.)

You can figure a grade point average for a semester or year, cumulatively (up to a given date), or at the end of studies. However, use the process above to figure each: Do not average semester grade point averages to find the cumulative GPA.

In our home school we did not accept less than a B; if the work was not B-quality it was redone. You are free to make your own grading judgments and rules; just be sure to explain your methods on your transcript. Remember that these records are kept as a form of communication with others. Be sure they are understandable.

Standardized test results

If standardized tests are part of your homeschool routine, be sure to keep copies of the results for the high school years. They may be requested by colleges instead of class rank or even a transcript.

SAT or ACT scores should be sent directly from the testing organization to the prospective college.

Documentation of extracurricular activities

In homeschooling, it is especially important to keep and document any awards or special notices your child receives. Simply keep a file folder of certificates, newspaper notices, prize ribbons, and photographs of trophies or ceremonies in a secure but accessible place. You will probably never need to show the actual awards to anyone, but keeping the file will allow you to make a list of awards and accomplishments for college or job applications.

Portfolios

Some homeschool parents start to sweat when they hear portfolios mentioned. It sounds like so much work! Actually, portfolios are not that hard to maintain if you have an overall plan. They can be very persuasive tools when put before a college admissions board (if it requests one).

Keeping a portfolio is a good habit to get into. Artists, writers, architects, designers, and even engineers keep portfolios of their accomplishments to show the overall scope of their work and abilities.

We suggest that you start collecting entries when your child begins high school studies. Put away samples of essays, artwork, math work, book reports, test scores, anything on paper (or floppy disk, or CD, or videotape, for that matter). We do mean samples, though. Do not try to keep everything—you will drown! Go through the portfolio yearly, choose representative pieces of work, and discard the rest. Take pictures of presentations given through the years, as well as dramatic and musical performances, and add those with some descriptions of the activities (written by the student). Include reference letters, your personal evaluations, and any outside evaluations you may have. We also suggest that the student write a yearly self-evaluation for the portfolio.

At the end of high school studies, finalize a permanent portfolio of the best samples from high school. You will be amazed how well it will come together. The student will also be able to use the portfolio as a gauge of his progress through the years. It will make apparent which areas are strong and which need more work.

The high school transcript

The high school transcript is the most important record of the student's work that you will need to maintain. The transcript is the real documentation of the student's accomplishments during high school. Remember, whenever your student begins high school-level work (no matter what grade he is in), you should begin keeping a high school transcript. In other words, if your student is in 5th grade but begins working on a high school Spanish text, begin recording progress on the transcript (even if he takes three years to finish the text). The one thing a transcript does not need to show is the date the work is done. It is simply a cumulative report of progress toward the goal of graduation.

We have provided a sample transcript for you on pages 153-154. (See Appendix F on pages 250-251 for a blank copy that you may reproduce.)

The transcript must contain the following information:

1. Name, parents' names, school name (home), date of birth, gender, social security number, address, phone number, and expected graduation date. (It is necessary to include the SSN if the student is applying for any kind of financial aid or for a job. If you do not want to publish the SSN on the transcript, just be prepared to supply it when asked by the recipient.)

Secondary school record/transcript

School: *Home*
Name: *John Homeschool*
Parents: *Mom & Dad Homeschool*
D.O.B.: *12-12-83* **Sex:** *M*
Date of Graduation: *5/22/2000*

Home Address: *9876 Your Street*
Hometown, TX
Home Phone: *(888) 555-5555*
SSN: *123-45-6789*

Grade Level	Course Description	Credit Hours	Grade	Points
9	English - Classic Literature	1	A	4
9	Math - Business & Consumer	1	A	4
9	Physical Science	1	B	3
9	American History	1	A	4
9	Physical Education	0.5	A	2
9	Music Appreciation	0.5	A	2
9	Personal Health & Growth	0.5	A	2
9	Bible Survey	0.5	A	2
9	Typing	0.5	A	2
9	**Total:** 6.5	(GPA 3.85)		25
10	English - Grammar & Comp	1	A	4
10	Algebra I	1	B	3
10	Biology w/Lab	1	B	3
10	World History	1	A	4
10	US Gov't & Constitution	0.5	A	2
10	Physical Education	0.5	A	2
10	Photography	0.25	A	1
10	CPR	0.25	A	1
10	**Total:** 5.5	(GPA 3.64)		20
11	Creative Writing	0.25	B	0.75
11	Novel	1	A	4
11	Journalism & Yearbook	0.25	A	1
11	Algebra II	1	B	3
11	Economics	1	A	4
11	Physical Education	0.5	A	2
11	French I	1	A	4
11	Home Economics	1	A	4
11	Computer Science	1	A	4
11	**Total:** 7	(GPA 3.82)		26.75
12	Bible History	1	A	4
12	Business Practices	1	A	4
12	Spanish I	1	A	4
12	Physical Education	0.5	A	2
12	Chemistry w/Lab	0.5	B	1.5
Comm College	English 101 - Composition	1*	B	3
12	**Total:** 5	(GPA 3.9)		18.5

(*Double Credit: high school 1 credit hour, college 3 credit hours)

Secondary school record/transcript (continued)

Total Credit Hours: *24*
Total Points: *91.25*
Cumulative GPA: *3.76*

Extracurricular Activities/Awards:

4-H Member, Journalist, County Fair Participant, Public Presenter
Homeschool Basketball Team, MVP, Student Coach, National Tournament
Homeschool Yearbook Staff
Basketball Camps: XYZ College, Christian Camp, 4 yrs., Director's Award
Bowling League
Church Youth Group—Leadership Team
AAU Basketball
Community Baseball (3 yrs.)
Work Experience:
Clerk—Family Business (1997)
Clerk—Bagel Shop (1998)
Regular Freelance Landscaping (1998-99)
Printing Apprentice—Lots of Graphics (1999-2000)
Hobbies:
Golf
Ice Skating
Model Building
Bird Study - Birds of Prey

Note: For the purpose of our homeschool, the following grading system was used:

A   4 pts. Excellent Work
B   3 pts. Good Work
C   2 pts. Average Work

Because our homeschool program was based on mastery of subjects, the passing grade was C and the honors grade A. Averages were computed based on number of course hours times grade points earned, divided by total number of units.

2. Course and credit information, including course description or name, grade level, units, letter grade, and points (see grade point averages on page 150).

3. The cumulative grade point average.

4. A list of extracurricular activities and all awards from high school years.

5. A description of any paid or volunteer work experience.

6. A list of hobbies and interests.

7. A note of explanation on how you awarded credits and grades. It is important to show that you actually did have a method,

and to highlight any unusual practices you may have used in your system.

Obviously, a homeschool transcript does not need to include class rank. Colleges may, however, request standardized test scores (Iowa, Stanford Achievement, etc.) or a portfolio in place of class rank.

Conclusion

Every prospective employer, college, university, or military organization will have its own specifications for the information it wants from the applicant. Even if you have done a good job of record keeping, the form your records are in may not exactly match what is requested. However, it should be easy for you to make changes in how the information is reported to conform to any request. You will not want to have to try to reconstruct four years of study at the end of the senior year—it will be very difficult. Keeping consistent records through the years is not difficult, or even time consuming, if you know what information is important and you have a method for keeping it.

CHAPTER 15

Preparing for Commencement

"Being confident of this, that he who began a good work in you will carry it on to completion until the day of Christ Jesus."
–Philippians 1:6 (NIV)

W e have found that many homeschooling families become very anxious as they near the end of their homeschooling years. Parents who were completely comfortable teaching their children all through their school years are too timid to announce they have accomplished their goal. Many families we know have actually placed their children, who were homeschooled throughout their lives, in a "real school" for the last quarter just so they could graduate and get a "real" diploma! Until now, we have just shaken our heads. But in this chapter, we offer specific help with that important milestone—high school graduation.

In our society, it has become a custom to signify the end of high school with a graduation ceremony. Many people prefer to call it a commencement, because it really signifies the beginning of a new stage of life. Whatever you call it, this celebration is a milestone that marks the completion of the basics and the beginning of continued learning in adult life. Don't ever let your children think that this is the end of learning. Even if they do not plan to go on to college, they should realize by this time in your home school that learning is a habit for life.

We want to encourage you, the parents who have diligently taught your students through the years, to embrace this occasion with confidence and faith. He who began this good work in your home will be faithful to empower you to complete it.

So, let's discuss some of the details of making your child's graduation the grand finale (and the grand beginning) it should be.

Closing off high school records and making a permanent transcript

You have probably already given some thought to the diploma issue, but the important final record for high school is the transcript. (We discuss diplomas later in this chapter.) We hope that you have been keeping good records throughout the high school years. Without them, making a transcript will be almost impossible. This will be the end of that transcript. No more entries for high school will be made.

The transcript is simply a written record (usually one page, though it may be double-sided) of what was accomplished in high school. A good transcript will include a listing of courses taken, grades, grade point average, extracurricular activities and awards, college board test scores if taken, and general student information (name, address, date of birth, social security number, etc.). You will find a full discussion of how to keep a transcript throughout high school in Chapter 14.

When it is time for graduation, you should finalize the transcript by checking that it is complete, then writing or stamping the word "final" on it. You may even want to use an embossing seal with your family name or the name of your home school (if you have one) to signify the official transcript. (Embossing seals, like those used by notaries, are available from several mail-order stationary companies. They can be personalized any way you like.) You should file at least two official copies: one in your files, and one in the student's personal files. When an employer or college admissions office asks for a copy, simply make a copy and send it. (Or save yourself some steps and make several copies in the first place, especially if the student hasn't applied to colleges yet.)

Preparing your own final evaluation and recommendations

We also recommend that you write out a final high school evaluation of the student and your parental recommendation letter. Though colleges and prospective employers will probably want recommendations from sources outside the family, you should compose one as well. After all, you were the faculty, advisor, and administrator for your children; no one knows their strengths and weaknesses better than you.

This evaluation should be a typed and signed paragraph (or two) summarizing the student's high school experience, strengths, and weaknesses. It can have contributions from both parents, if you like. You will find this a handy piece of paper to have in the file. It is very likely that sooner or later you will be asked for such a document. It will be much more accurate if you record the information while it is fresh in your mind.

Providing a diploma

What is a diploma anyway? Here is a dictionary definition:

diploma: a document certifying the successful completion of a course of study. (Source: *WordNet ®1.6,* ©1997 Princeton University*)*

A diploma is a piece of paper (unless you use real sheepskin) that designates or confers the completion of some line of study. We find it interesting that parents who confidently homeschool turn to jelly when it is time to award a diploma. If you have homeschooled your child and he has completed your designated course of study for high school, you may and should award a diploma.

So the issue is not whether you may award a diploma, but rather, what does that diploma mean to others. There are several considerations here. In many states, including New York, the state mandates that only the State Board of Education (board of Regents) is authorized to grant a diploma. That is their opinion. We do give our children diplomas; the fact that the state does not recognize them does not mean much to us. After all, we know plenty of people who hold accredited diplomas who could not pass the requirements to receive one of our diplomas!

Frankly, we both hold those accredited and coveted New York State Board of Regents high school diplomas, and neither of us has had to show them to anyone, ever. We have been hired by employers and accepted into prestigious colleges (MIT and the Air Force Academy) without ever being asked for them. What did matter were our transcripts and college board exam scores. The transcript is the official record of the student's course work and grades. The transcript will be validated by college board exams and sometimes with a portfolio of completed work.

It is true that in the past most colleges required accredited diplomas. However, the current climate is quickly changing in favor of the home school. Colleges and universities are beginning to recognize that homeschooled students are generally very well prepared for higher learning, regardless of their lack of accredited education. There are now research studies that indicate the academic success of homeschooling and the success of homeschooled students in institutions of higher learning.

In the past, some institutions required a GED or a state-accredited diploma for admission. The United States House of Representatives Committee on Education and the Workforce and the Senate Committee on Labor and Human Resources addressed these colleges and universities in a report accompanying Pub.L. No. 105-244 (Reauthorization of the Higher Education Act) with the following recommendation to those that accept federal funding:

> *The Committee is aware that many colleges and universities now require applicants from non-public, private, or nontraditional secondary programs (including homeschools) to submit scores from additional standardized tests...(GED or SAT-II) in lieu of a transcript/diploma from an accredited high school... Given that standardized test scores (SAT and ACT) and portfolio- or performance-based assessments may also provide a sound basis for an admission decision regarding these students, the Committee recommends that colleges and universities consider using these assessments for applicants educated in non-public, private, and nontraditional programs rather than requiring them to undergo additional types of standardized testing. Requiring additional testing only of students educated in these settings could reasonably be seen as discriminatory.... The Committee believes that college admissions should be determined on academic ability of the student and not the accreditation status of the school in which he or she received a secondary education.*

(For more information, read "Homeschool Students Excel in College," published by the Homeschool Legal Defense Association, PO Box 3000, Purcellville, VA 20134; [540] 338-5600; *www.hslda.org.*)

Clearly, our Congress recognizes the discriminatory practice of requiring homeschooled students to obtain a GED. Many homeschooling families find the GED requirements to be an insult to the fine education their children have received.

In another section of the amendments cited above, the committees changed the eligibility requirements for federal college financial aid. The law used to require an accredited high school diploma, GED, or a semester of college work to prove eligibility for aid. Now the requirement has been changed to include those students who have *"completed a secondary school education in a home school setting that is treated as a home school or private school under state law."*

These advances in the recognition of the effectiveness of homeschools are very promising. Two states have already enacted legislation to restrict discrimination against homeschooled students; others are sure to follow. The military has also changed its policies about requiring the GED for homeschooled students. For more information on the military and homeschooling, see Chapter 17.

Employers will accept a transcript or a homeschool diploma. Job applications will usually ask what school the applicant attended and whether he graduated. The homeschool student should just write in "homeschool" and that he did graduate.

Let's face it: When we decided to homeschool, we believed we were able to do a good job of educating our children. We believed that we would do better than the government-sponsored schools, and better than private schools. (If you do not believe this, don't homeschool!) So why wouldn't we believe that our homeschool diploma is better than a government diploma?

Homeschool coalitions in some states (Pennsylvania, for example) have worked with the state's department of education to provide a program for homeschooled students to obtain a state-accredited diploma. This may be of interest to you. To be honest, we find these efforts counterproductive. We do not recognize the state as the ultimate authority in determining what constitutes a good education. Therefore, we do not feel the state-accredited diploma is of real value. The essence of homeschooling is that it is totally parent-directed. It follows then that it should be parent-accredited. Colleges, universities, financial aid programs, and potential employers are quickly realizing the value of the homeschool diploma, and accreditation is becoming a non-issue.

So, where do you get this piece of paper? You print it yourself or order it from a printer. There, that was simple! Actually, there are organizations that sell diplomas that you can personalize, intended especially for homeschool use. Some of these come with very nice covers as well. For a list of suppliers, see Appendix C.

Commencement service options

Finally, we hope that you will finish this part of the homeschooling experience as it started—as a family endeavor. You will certainly want to have a family celebration of the accomplishments of the graduate. That does not mean that you won't want to take part in statewide, local, or church events as well. The completion of high school studies is certainly a worthy occasion to commemorate. And there are many different commencement options for the homeschool graduate. We encourage you to make preparations during the student's senior year to take part in one (or all) of the following:

Statewide commencement

These will most likely be sponsored by a state homeschooling organization. In New York, we have a commencement service for members of the statewide Loving Education at Home organization. It is held during the organization's annual convention in early June. One of the main convention speakers gives the address. The statewide homeschool band plays. The students wear caps and gowns and have a photographer available for pictures. Members of the organization's board serve as the masters of ceremony, but the parents give their students their diplomas. The fees for the ceremony, cap and gown, and printed diploma total only $40. Each student prepares a two- or three-sentence biography that is read and printed in the program. It is a simple, inexpensive, well-organized, short, and very moving ceremony. (Last year 41 homeschoolers took part.)

Since the commencement takes place during the convention, it is held in an auditorium with ample space. This makes it possible for all the graduates to invite as many guests as they like. (At traditional schools invitations are usually only sent to immediate family because space is very limited.) It is also very accessible to the general homeschooling community. We have really appreciated the opportunity for our children to take part in this graduation ceremony. It has been a wonderful time to share the joy of homeschooling and its accomplishments with friends and loved ones.

Our family then holds a party following the graduation, inviting friends, relatives, and church family to enjoy our personal celebration with some food and fun.

Check with your state organizations if you are interested in this option for your graduate.

Local commencement

It is also becoming a common practice for local homeschooling support groups to hold services for their graduates. Some are sponsored by a coalition of regional groups.

Church commencement

If you are active in a local church, it may be willing to support your homeschooling efforts by holding a graduation ceremony. Many churches have many homeschooling families who would greatly appreciate keeping commencement a church family affair.

▲ ▲ ▲

We hope you will make the effort to mark the end of high school with some sort of special event for the graduate. Whether you choose a church, local, or state ceremony, or choose to celebrate on your own, it is important to recognize the accomplishments of the graduate. Homeschooling is homespun. We have had years to develop our own creativity in how to teach our children—put some of that creativity to use in planning a special acknowledgment of the graduate's achievement.

For those of you who have been through this event, congratulations on a job well done! Welcome to the world of veteran homeschoolers!

CHAPTER 16

Finding Opportunities in the Military

"Suffer hardship with me, as a good soldier of Christ Jesus. No soldier in active service entangles himself in the affairs of everyday life, so that he may please the one who enlisted him as a soldier."
—II Timothy 2:3-4 (NASB)

Note: Because military regulations and requirements are constantly changing, some of the material in this chapter may not be up to date at the time of publication. We have made every effort to keep the material as general as possible to minimize inaccuracies. However, we strongly recommend that you contact a local armed forces recruiter or other suggested reference before acting on any of the information outlined in this chapter.

⋏⋏⋏

The military can provide outstanding opportunities to the young adult, but students should carefully evaluate the costs (financial and personal) before selecting their options. There are many possibilities in military service, each with its own benefits and drawbacks.

Many young people finish their high school education with no idea of what they want to do as a career. Don't worry! It is not a problem if your senior does not know what he wants to do in life. Perhaps we feel this way because, like many families, we have experienced the problems associated with changing careers later in life, when it seemed that there was a clear job path already in place. For those who have experienced the trauma of a layoff, or "downsizing," a college degree can be worth little more than the paper it is written on. So, do not get overly concerned if your high school graduate is not completely clear about the next step.

One of the options that makes sense for a student without future plans is military duty. It is not the scope of this book to argue the moral and Biblical positions regarding Christianity, war, and the military. Christians have many different positions regarding military service. We personally believe that military duty for the Christian is both honorable and worthy of consideration. For those who wish to study this subject more thoroughly, we would recommend *War and Conscience*, by Allen C. Isbell (Biblical Research Press). It may be out of print, but it is worth finding in a used bookstore, as it provides a good overview of the issues and gives answers to complicated questions. There are other resources as well for those struggling with this issue.

Before high school graduation

There is a lot you can do to prepare your homeschooler for the military as you plan his secondary school curriculum. One recruiter we spoke with told us that 7th grade is not too early to begin preparing a student for testing. We will also discuss in detail the extracurricular activities that can be particularly useful to prepare for military service.

In order to prepare your child for the clearly different lifestyle of military service, you may want to consider signing him up for membership in an organization recognized by the military as helpful in teaching the basics of military bearing and protocol.

One obvious choice for this would be the Boy Scouts or Girl Scouts of America (including the co-ed Explorer scouts), since they are arguably the most well-known. The general purpose of these organizations is to build character, teach life skills—including survival training—and develop leadership skills. There is a legitimate affinity by the military for scouts who wish to enter the service after high school. Both of us were scouts as teenagers. (Laurie was also an Explorer Scout.) Our experience was rewarding; perhaps it will be for your children as well.

Particularly significant is the opportunity for achievement in becoming an Eagle Scout (boys) or a USA Gold Scout (girls). All of the branches of the military give instant promotions in entry grades to those who have achieved this status in high school. The U.S. Army starts Eagle Scouts at grade E-2—an immediate $200 per month pay increase over the normal entry grade. That is not a bad deal when you consider the value of the award itself in developing character, knowledge, and skills.

Another option to prepare children for the military is to enroll them in a local drum and bugle corps or marching band. Again, the goal is to give your children the opportunity to participate in a group that teaches the military bearing, discipline, and protocol that will be needed once they enter the service. It is better for your children to be exposed to the military ethic before they experience it in a forced, "no turning back" environment.

The benefits of CAP

If you want your children to have an experience that is even more relevant to a military career, look into the U.S. Civil Air Patrol. It provides many good experiences contributing to the community while gaining leadership, technical, and moral training. The Civil Air Patrol, or CAP, as it is called by its members, is the official volunteer civilian auxiliary of the United States Air Force. On May 26, 1948, Civil Air Patrol was given a stated national purpose, chartered by the United States Congress, to provide emergency services, aerospace education, and cadet programs to and through its members. Its purpose is benevolent—it does not take up arms in times of war and does not encourage the use of military force within the organization. However, for the student who is considering a military career, it is a fantastic opportunity to learn and to experience the rigors of military conditions.

Civil Air Patrol is open to both boys and girls, though usually boys are most interested in participating. However, CAP encourages girls to join. The opportunities for either gender are equally valuable to the homeschooler. CAP policy forbids any form of discrimination on the basis of gender. Girls do very well and advance in rank just as quickly as boys do.

One of the things about CAP that appeals to us in particular is the emphasis they put on spiritual and moral leadership. Every CAP squadron (local chapter of the organization) is encouraged to have a chaplain. The chaplain is an ordained local pastor, minister, rabbi, or priest, whose responsibility is to teach "moral leadership" to the members on a monthly basis. In order for CAP members to attain new rankings, they must complete moral leadership training on this monthly cycle, along with their training in aerospace, personal leadership, and cadet materials. If no chaplain is available for a squadron, a moral leadership officer is appointed by the Squadron Commander, the senior CAP officer who oversees the training program at the local level.

To become a CAP cadet, a student can join at the age of 11 (if he is in the 6th grade) or 12, and remain active in the organization until age 21.

(The cadet may elect to become a senior member upon turning 18.) The cadet may work up through 16 ranks, from Cadet Basic Airman through Cadet Lieutenant Colonel, over the course of the program. Each promotion is based upon testing in knowledge, character evaluation, and physical fitness. Age is not a consideration for promotion, so a young child who is motivated can move up in the ranks just as quickly as an older one. Upon reaching the midpoint in rank, the cadet becomes eligible for academic scholarships, which can be quite substantial. Cadets may qualify to take up to 11 flight orientations in certified CAP aircraft during their CAP membership. Nationally, Civil Air Patrol owns more than 535 light aircraft, which are actively flown for more than 130,000 hours each year. Both of our youngest boys—Wesley, who was 11 when he had his first orientation flight, and Josiah, who was 13—were excited about this experience alone. They can learn to fly single-engine airplanes, gliders, and even hot-air balloons. All CAP training is free to the cadets, who will have the chance to learn such skills as amateur radio operation, rocketry, aerospace science, and emergency services.

According to a CAP brochure, "Cadets have the opportunity to take part in a wide range of activities, including encampments on military bases, orientation flights, and a variety of national and international activities. Through its National Scholarship Program, CAP provides scholarships to cadets to further their studies in such areas as engineering, science, aircraft mechanics, and aerospace medicine. Scholarships leading to solo flight training are also provided.

"The U.S. Air Force recognizes the high standards the cadets must meet. When CAP cadets enlist in the Air Force, they now enter as an E-3 (Airman First Class), instead of as an Airman Basic."

Your local homeschool organization may be able to organize a local squadron by working with the group commander for your area. We believe this is a great way for fathers to get involved in their children's lives. David joined our local squadron as a senior member when Josiah and Wesley wanted to participate. He became a leader and helped to build the local cadet squadron when there was a vacuum in parental leadership. We find this a great way for homeschooling fathers to work with their children in a balanced, productive organization that greatly benefits every child who participates.

Civil Air Patrol fits in very well with homeschoolers who want to provide their children with a solidly American experience that helps teach strong character, citizenship, and respect for all that our nation stands for.

To learn more about Civil Air Patrol, check them out on the Internet at *www.capnhq.gov*, or by doing an Internet search for Civil Air Patrol to find your closest squadron. You can also look up your local squadron in the phone book.

Junior Reserve Officer Training Corps

Another option, though it is not quite as accessible to homeschoolers, is Junior R.O.T.C. Each of the military branches has its own program. Most of these programs are organized by local high schools (public and private). Depending on where you live, you may be able to contact a school district office to see whether your children can participate in its program. Starting a Junior R.O.T.C. apart from a local school district is difficult because the program requires hiring at least one retired military officer, with a salary equivalent to those for active duty. This would be very difficult for a homeschool group to do on their own. The most realistic route is to find a local R.O.T.C. at a high school and see if you can join.

The Navy Sea Cadets (part of the Navy Reserve system) is another organization that may be of interest to homeschoolers. It is similar to Junior R.O.T.C. The Sea Cadets allow young people to prepare for a future in the Navy in the same way that Junior R.O.T.C. prepares young people for the Army, Air Force, or Navy R.O.T.C. programs in college. The Sea Cadets usually meet and work with the local Naval Reserve base, so anyone within range of one of these facilities may be able to take advantage of it.

These groups all have a place for those who wish to give their children a chance to taste what it means to serve "God and country." There are many options. Take advantage of them and help your homeschoolers prepare for the future.

The real deal

In preparing this book, David went to our local U.S. Military Recruiting offices and spoke with recruiters. He wanted to experience what many of you will if you drop in to get information for your homeschooler. It was a very revealing experience.

To understand David's experience, you need to realize what has happened recently with homeschoolers and recruitment. Up until October, 1998, homeschoolers were considered Tier II candidates for admission into the armed services. Essentially, they were relegated to the same status as high school dropouts or those who have had to take the GED for high school equivalency. Thus, because homeschoolers did not have accredited high school diplomas, they had a hard time entering the military.

To exacerbate the problem in 1998, the Marines and Air Force decided they would only accept Tier I candidates. Only 10 percent of all Navy and Army enlistees were Tier II candidates that year. Numerous homeschool candidates were scoring above the 90th percentile on the Armed Services Vocational Aptitude Battery (ASVAB) test, meeting all the eligibility requirements, and yet being rejected simply because they did not have an accredited diploma!

In an effort to rectify this situation, U.S. Senator Paul D. Coverdale of Georgia proposed an amendment to House Resolution 3616, the Defense Authorization Bill, to end this discrimination against homeschoolers. It created a five-year pilot program to automatically place homeschoolers in the Tier I status for recruitment eligibility. Each of the armed forces is now required to allow up to 1,250 homeschool diploma recipients to be considered under Tier I status, along with all other high school graduates. The bill was passed into law and is now in effect. Homeschoolers can no longer be rejected for military enlistment simply because they do not have a completed transcript from an accredited high school.

According to W.S. Sellman, Director of Accession Policy at the Pentagon, all that is necessary to demonstrate academic eligibility is for the homeschool graduate to produce a "letter from a parent with a list of completed coursework." But before you get too excited, we want to share David's experiences with you. As he learned, whether or not things go smoothly depends on which branch of the service you and your child are interested in.

Which branch?

When David walked into the Armed Forces Recruitment Center in Liverpool, New York, he immediately got an idea of the diversity within the Armed Forces simply from the center's environment. Although each of the service branches was represented in the same building, they all had their own entrance with their own brochure cases, office decor, and atmosphere. They also showed diverse approaches to David's questions.

One of the recruiters, whose branch will remain anonymous, told David, "I really don't think we can do anything for you," when he asked for information about options for homeschoolers. He then proceeded to call his commanding officer on the phone to find out what he should tell us specifically. After about 10 minutes, David was able to get some information. The long and short of it is that you should be prepared for recruiters to have to dig around a bit before they are able to get you the information you are asking for. You may even have to find another recruiting office, or get the name of someone else farther up the chain of command to help you. That's just the way it is.

Now, we don't think that these people do not want to help us. Remember: The more recruits they enlist, the more they get paid. But as homeschoolers, we are a definite anomaly to them. They are used to going to the local high school or community college guidance office and working their system. These recruiters really do want to help us. We just have to be willing to do some detective work because they are not experienced in dealing with homeschoolers.

David learned several lessons. These may help you navigate your own process with your local recruiter:

- ▲ Recruiters will have varying levels of experience and knowledge with the new law and how it relates to the admission policy for his or her branch of the armed forces.
- ▲ Each branch of the armed forces will have a different set of procedures to follow to apply for admission.
- ▲ The recruiter you speak with will probably have limited experience working with homeschoolers.
- ▲ You may have to be adamant with the recruiting officer about the fact that you know your child is qualified to apply for admission as a Tier I applicant (subject to passing the ASVAB test and meeting the moral, physical, and medical requirements for that branch of service).
- ▲ There are specific requirements for each branch. In general, recruits must be at least 17 years old with parental consent (otherwise 18 and up), cannot have asthma, cannot be allergic to bee stings, cannot normally be on medications like insulin or allergy shots, and cannot be drug abusers (although branches differ in their tolerance of drug infractions). Each branch has its own minimum test score requirements, particularly on the overall Armed Forces Qualification Test (AFQT).

There are other specific minimum requirements for each branch of the armed forces beyond the ones above:

Air Force

1. Minimum AFQT score of 40.
2. A notarized letter from the homeschool "principal" (you) with a list of the senior-level courses completed, and an associated final grade.

3. No pins, screws, plates, or "anything holding you together that God didn't put there."
4. Minimum height and weight requirements.
5. Use of any illegal drug, except minor marijuana use, is an automatic disqualification.

Army

1. Minimum AFQT score of 31.
2. Homeschoolers must present one of the following:

    (a) A diploma and transcript from the state department or local school district that indicates the applicant met all graduation requirements.

    (b) A diploma and transcript from a homeschool association (organization, sponsor, curriculum developer) that indicates the applicant met all graduation requirements.

    (c) A letter from the state department of education or local school district that verifies homeschool registration, and transcripts and a diploma issued by the parent(s) or guardian(s) certifying completion of secondary education.

3. Students who are instructed (homeschooled) by their parents during the compulsory age for education using correspondence schools approved by the Distance Education and Training Council (DETC) will also be considered Tier 1.

Marines

1. Minimum AFQT score of 31.
2. Provide homeschool transcripts to be submitted to Marine headquarters for an education waiver as a homeschooler.

Navy

1. Minimum AFQT score of 31.
2. Same qualifications as private or public high schooler; allowed to be placed on delayed entry program (up to 365 days), just like traditional schooler.
3. Can join at age 17 with parental permission; otherwise 18.
4. Uses the Department of Defense policies and looks at each recruit on a case-by-case basis.
5. Looks at records accumulated by parents, including attendance, transcripts, and state requirements.

Each branch of the armed forces is unique. Their testing guidelines are equally as unique. All of the branches provide the same "tangibles," though perhaps with slight variations like time periods for rank promotion, living quarters, military base locations, and so on. The following is a breakdown of some of the distinctives of each branch:

Air Force

- More than 150 specialties to select from.
- Written guarantees in the job you select only after basic training, if qualified based upon your ASVAB test results.
- Job training to the level of technical requirements through the Community College of the Air Force.
- No educational costs paid beyond GI Bill ($19,298).
- No student loan repayment program.
- Terms of Enlistment: 4- and 6-year enlistments available.
- Enlistment (cash) bonuses of up to $12,000.
- Additional aptitude and classification tests or counselor interviews to determine job assignments following basic training.
- No payments deducted for initial issue items.
- Air Force bases primarily in North America, Europe, and Middle East.

(Web site: *www.airforce.com*)

Army

- More than 240 jobs to select from (this is the largest branch of the service).
- Written guarantees in the job you select.
- Numerous bases throughout the world.
- Job training immediately following basic training.
- Educational costs paid beyond GI Bill ($19,298):
    2-year enlistment: $26,500.
    3-year enlistment: $33,000.
    4-year enlistment: $50,000.
- Student loan repayment program up to $65,000.
- Terms of enlistment: 2-, 3-, 4-, 5-, and 6-year enlistments available.
- Enlistment (cash) bonuses of up to $20,000.

⅄ No additional aptitude and classification tests or counselor interviews to determine job assignments following basic training.

⅄ No payments deducted for initial issue items.

(Web site: *www.army.mil*)

Coast Guard

⅄ Part of the Department of Transportation except in times of war, when it becomes a part of the Department of the Navy.

⅄ Predominately assigned to U.S. coastlands, borders, and territories.

⅄ The Coast Guard Academy is the only branch academy that does not require a congressional nomination for admission.

(Web site: *www.uscg.mil*)

Marines

⅄ 23 occupational fields.

⅄ Written guarantees in the field you select, but not the job, except for RECON (Special Forces) assignments.

⅄ Job training following basic training as required.

⅄ Educational costs paid beyond GI Bill ($19,298): 4-year enlistment: $50,000.

⅄ Student loan repayment program up to $65,000.

⅄ Terms of enlistment: 4- and 6-year enlistments available.

⅄ Enlistment (cash) bonuses of up to $5,000.

⅄ Additional aptitude and classification tests or counselor interviews to determine job assignments following basic training.

⅄ Additional payments ($800) deducted for initial issue items.

⅄ Part of the Department of the Navy; mainly assigned to naval bases throughout the world.

(Web site: *www.usmc.mil*)

Navy

⅄ More than 80 job skills available.

⅄ Written guarantees in the job you select, provided school quotas are not filled and are available.

⅄ Most jobs receive training immediately following basic training.

⋏ Educational costs paid beyond GI Bill ($19,298):
4-year enlistment: $50,000.

⋏ Student loan repayment program up to $10,000.

⋏ Terms of enlistment: 3-, 4-, 5-, and 6-year enlistments
available.

⋏ Enlistment (cash) bonuses of up to $12,000.

⋏ Additional aptitude and classification tests or counselor
interviews are required to determine job assignments
following basic training.

⋏ Additional payments ($800) deducted for initial issue items.

⋏ World travel possible through tours of duty by sea and
assignments on naval bases throughout the world.

(Web site: *www.navy.mil*)

⋏ ⋏ ⋏

Other options are the Armed Forces Reserves or the National Guard. Most of these units provide a more flexible and normal lifestyle, while still giving young people the benefit of military participation.

Our research indicates that the difference between Reserve units and National Guard units is not obvious in all cases. Discuss this with your local recruiters.

The new recruit's normal commitment starts with a regular boot camp of four weeks, followed by monthly meetings at the local reserve or guard center, and a tour of duty (usually two weeks) once a year. Additionally, there can be a six- or eight- year commitment.

The benefit of the tour of duty is a regular paycheck. Educational benefits are available as well. It is a pretty good deal, especially for those who have a particular area of vocational interest, as many soldiers get assignments in their civilian area of expertise.

Each of the service branches has its own reserve units, and the Army and Air National Guard have a presence in every state.

Reserve Officers Training Corps (R.O.T.C.) programs are available to high school graduates who want to be trained as commissioned officers in the Army, Navy, Air Force, and Marine Corps. Selected applicants for the individual branches of the armed forces' R.O.T.C. programs are awarded scholarships through an extremely competitive national selection process. The SAT is usually used as a criterion for awards. Most recipients receive full tuition and other financial benefits at many of the country's leading colleges and universities. Applications for these scholarships are available from the recruiting office of the selected service branch, or from the college that sponsors an R.O.T.C. program. Special courses associated with military subjects will be required, along with the regular academic courseload. Most programs require the R.O.T.C. cadet to abstain from outside work during the first year, so budgets must be considered seriously before committing to this program. Upon graduation from the four-year college degree program, the student will make an additional commitment to serve in his branch of service for a period of time agreed to in the scholarship requirements, usually eight years, with three to four years of active duty, depending on the program. Students who want to apply for an R.O.T.C. college scholarship will need to apply by the end of the junior homeschool year.

Military academies

Your child may want to attend a military academy, such as the United States Military Academy (West Point), the United States Naval Academy (Annapolis), the United States Air Force Academy, the United States Coast Guard Academy, or the United States Merchant Marine Academy. These schools rank academically as some of the finest in the country. They demand a serious commitment to the military, usually including a desire to serve as a career officer. Students are committed to seven or more years of military life after graduation.

Each of these schools is open to any student who is a U.S. citizen and meets the requirements for admission. However, most of the appointments are made through a recommendation by a U.S. Senator or Member of Congress or a military officer from one of the four branches of the service. Students who really want to attend a U.S. military academy (except for the U.S. Coast Guard Academy, which doesn't require a congressional appointment) should contact their elected federal officials, or other nominators, early in their junior year of high school to find out how that particular appointee screens candidates.

Each process is unique, according to the public official's preferences. Most require a written application, followed by an interview and screening process. It will challenge your child's communication and interpersonal skills. The completeness of your transcripts, including extracurricular activities and specialized experiences, will be essential to success in receiving an appointment. Grades and SAT and ACT scores will be reviewed seriously. The earlier you plan to prepare your child for this direction, the better his chance for success. The recruiters we spoke with say to have your homeschooler apply for the academy by December of the junior year at the very latest. Recruiters can provide you with information about the application process of each academy.

Here are the Web sites for each branch academy for further research:

- ⅄ West Point (U.S. Military Academy, U.S. Army): *www.westpoint.edu.*
- ⅄ Annapolis (U.S. Naval Academy, also U.S. Marines): *www.nadn.navy.mil.*
- ⅄ Air Force (U.S. Air Force Academy): *www.usafa.af.mil.*
- ⅄ U.S. Merchant Marine Academy (assigns all branches): *www.usmma.edu.*
- ⅄ U.S. Coast Guard Academy: *www.cga.edu.*

Finally, there may be a select few homeschoolers, though admittedly an extremely small percentage, who wish to consider post-college military enlistment for some reason. This is a possibility, so we include it here. This can benefit someone who has specialized skills (for example, as an engineer, doctor, or lawyer) that may be of particular interest to the military. Sometimes the government will pay the graduate's expenses or perhaps provide a graduate degree program as part of the enlistment contract. It might also provide an opportunity for the young person to see the world at the government's expense.

Usually, college graduates can qualify for Officer's Candidate School and enter the active service as commissioned officers. Upon graduation from the OCS, they will be commissioned as second lieutenants, or perhaps higher if they have a completed graduate degree. All of this will need to be negotiated at the time they are recruited.

If settling down and having a strong family life is important to your child, he should think hard before choosing the military. It is probably not a good idea to consider both marriage at a young age and joining the Navy, for example. In the 1980s, when we lived near San Diego, we had many friends whose spouses were stationed on tours of duty in the Pacific for months. This places incredible stress on a marriage. It can be particularly hard on those with young children because the service owns you and can tell you where to live and how long to be away from home on active duty.

We recommend that you spend a lot of time in prayer and thought about the consequences of a military career. It may be the right thing to do. Just make sure you weigh all the options and their ramifications before you make that decision. Remember, you are making a commitment to the machinery that makes war and defends our country. Soldiers die. Families are torn apart by these historical incidents. Make sure you have thought through all of this. It will have an impact on several generations.

Benefits

There are many benefits to military service. One of the most rewarding intangible benefits is the satisfaction of serving your country. Service to one's country is an honorable calling. Jesus Christ told us that "no greater love is there than this, that one lays down his life for his friends (John 15:13)." This is a risk that every soldier takes when he dons a uniform in the United States Armed Forces. To protect our freedom as Americans is a sacred trust and gives back to this country in ways that cannot be expressed materially.

A young person who wants to be able to tour the world and get paid to do it can hardly find a better way to do so. A young person who does not truly know what to do in life can take advantage of a military tour to see what options are out there.

With the Montgomery GI Bill and other tuition programs available in specific branches of the service, a homeschooler can get a lot of education paid for with just a minimal military commitment. Different branches offer up to $50,000 in college tuition costs after completion of a tour of duty. Several branches offer tuition payback programs, as outlined earlier in the chapter. The military academies and R.O.T.C. programs will pay for a college education in return for a commitment as a commissioned officer. Bonuses for enlistment can go as high as $25,000, depending on the area of specialty. Some of the best training in the world is found in the U.S. military. It is clearly not for everyone, but for the right young person, it can be a tremendous opportunity. Check out all the possibilities and then decide. The choices are up to the student.

Just keep in mind that in most cases, once you have made a commitment to the U.S. military, it is permanent (for the length of the contract). Once you sign on the dotted line, there is no turning back. The exceptions to this may be the military academies, who demand no commitment for the first 18 months of participation at their colleges, and some R.O.T.C. programs. When you join the military you give up your independence; someone else controls your life. Another concern is that there is a tendency for military life to lack moral norms. Much of today's military environment is crude and rough. Our military's new "don't ask, don't tell" policy may expose our children to homosexuality, and we may object to that. We suspect that in the years ahead, this policy will be expanded to be more accepting of homosexuality, so be prepared for it.

Entering the military can be a great career decision for the right person. Maybe your homeschooled child is such a person. Hopefully, with this material in hand, you can help make the right choice.

CHAPTER 17

Getting Your Student into the Right College

"And do not be conformed to this world, but be transformed by the renewing of your mind, that you may prove what the will of God is, that which is good and acceptable and perfect."
—Romans 12:2 (NASB)

When we speak of the right college for your child, we do not mean the most prestigious. The right college is the one that fits your student's abilities and plans for the future.

Take the time to decide how you want to approach the road to college admission. Institutional high schools use what we call the standard route. The standard route prepares the college bound by making sure they earn the proper credits in a four-year high school. As juniors, students are expected to start college testing (PSATs, aptitude tests), think about possible majors, and begin collecting information on schools of interest to them. In the fall of their senior year, students take the SAT or ACT, visit colleges, and collect applications. By the end of January, students have applied to the colleges of their choice, and are working on financial aid applications. By spring, seniors receive their acceptance letters and choose their college. In the fall following high school graduation, the new college student will move into a dorm at his four-year, live-in school and begin study. Four years later, he will graduate in the spring with a bachelor's degree and move on to his first job or to graduate school.

The standard route may be exactly what you and your student want. That's fine, and homeschool students should have no difficulty being successful with this plan. The only difference is that your child will not have access to the school guidance counselor to keep the process going and to gather all the necessary forms, tests, and information. (We wrote this book to help you act as your children's guidance counselor.)

We want to let you know, though, that the standard route to college and an eventual career is not the only way to go. We found this out for ourselves in our college experiences.

We both were groomed by our parents and high schools to take the standard route. We were both excellent students, involved in extracurricular activities, student government, and community service. However, what we did not know in high school was that God was about to enter our lives and change them forever.

David received an appointment to the Air Force Academy in 1973. He began his training there in the summer, but left the academy after several weeks. He now attributes his leaving to both "being a dumb kid" and to following God's leading. (That may seem odd to some of you, but if you think about it, you will realize that God often leads through our mistakes.) David spent a year working full time, and experienced some serious health problems during that period, requiring major surgery. He went on to study at the State University of New York at Geneseo, where he attended a Christian event that changed his life forever. At a concert by YWAM's music group, The Family, David answered a call by God on his life to become a missionary. He wasn't even a Christian at that time, but he recognized that God had first dibs on his life, and David agreed to follow Him. The summer of 1975 found David on his way to the Youth With A Mission School of Evangelism in Lausanne, Switzerland. On his way there, during a stop off at YWAM's mission in Amsterdam, Holland, David decided to give his life completely to Christ. He completed one year of training at the YWAM base in Lausanne, then returned to America and began working with an inner-city mission in Newark, New Jersey. He worked a full-time job, went to New Jersey Institute of Technology three nights a week, and worked with children at the ministry one or two nights a week and on weekends.

Meanwhile, Laurie was led to the Lord in April of her senior year of high school, right after receiving an invitation to join the MIT class of 1981 on full scholarship. Her senior year of high school consisted of racking up several credits at a community college an hour away, paid for by her public high school. By late summer of that year, she realized her need to become grounded in her new-found Christian faith and decided to attend Word of Life Bible Institute's one-year program. MIT graciously offered a one-year deferment and encouraged her spiritual endeavor (believe it or not)! A year later, she enrolled at MIT, a little older, and certainly more spiritually equipped to handle life. There was another wrench in the works, though.

David and Laurie met in the summer of 1978 (right before Laurie started MIT) at an Institute for Creation Research Conference in Clarks Summit, PA. They realized very quickly that the Lord was leading them to start a life together. So, after attending one semester at MIT, Laurie moved to New Jersey, got a full-time job, went to NJIT at night with David, and worked in the ministry alongside him. We were married in June, 1979.

You might be wondering at this point why Laurie left MIT—was David that irresistable? Well, yes...and no. Actually, by this time Laurie had changed in many ways. Her one-time dream of getting a degree from MIT and going on to be an advocate for women's rights had become hollow. She no longer had any desire to spend her entire life working as an engineer; she wanted a Christian home and family. And while she loved college, MIT was a bit much at that point. She has never regretted this decision.

After our wedding, we continued working, ministering, and going to night school, while praying for provision for both of us to go back to school full time. Our answer came in September as God (through a complicated set of events) provided the funds for us to move to California and pay our first semester tuition at Christian Heritage College. David worked nights full time until graduation. We both graduated from CHC in August 1982, after the birth of Jeremiah, and while awaiting Rebekah.

So, although we started out on the standard route to college education, the last few years of college were anything but! Our variety of college experiences qualifies us as experts in getting college credit in every way known to man. (And that was just our undergraduate work!)

So what is involved in a nonstandard education? We strongly urge you to think creatively about higher education. Unless you are independently wealthy, you may not have a choice. Know that, for the most part, a college degree is a college degree and there are many ways to get one.

We encourage you to check into getting advanced credit for your high school students (see Chapter 13) through the College Level Exam Placement (CLEP) program, Advanced Placement (AP) testing, transfer programs, and more. We would also encourage you to explore options available through community colleges, distance education, and night school.

We have presented the topics of this chapter in timeline order to facilitate successful navigation of the college admission process. In other words, we will start with what you must consider first, and end with the last things you need to accomplish in the process.

Is college the best option for my child?

We were both brought up in families that saw college as the only real road to success. We were encouraged to go to college from our earliest days, before anyone knew what we would be interested in or talented at. We did go to college, and found that getting a degree was not the key to success we were led to believe it would be. Actually, though we learned a great deal about life and some very useful information in our college experience (thanks to some wonderful professors), we have both done only limited work in our degree areas.

In our experience over the years, we have found that most homeschooling parents and children are quite a bit more practical than we were. Parents and children should carefully compare the costs of higher education (in money, time, and effort) with the prospective benefits. In many cases, students who want to pursue a career in business, a skilled trade, or self-employment (such as farming, carpentry, or another vocational skill) may do just as well to apprentice or go right to work. If they find later that college will benefit them, it is never too late to start. Programs abound these days for part-time classes, night school, distance learning, and even credit for experience. Tuition-assistance programs are also a common benefit of working for a corporation full-time.

If your students want to be doctors, lawyers, teachers, dentists, veterinarians, nurses, or journalists (to name a few), they will obviously need college educations. If they have yet to make up their mind, then the call is up to you. If you can afford it, college can be beneficial in helping guide the undecided. You should also be aware that those with bachelor's degrees have significantly higher salaries, on average, than those who don't.

If your child decides to pursue higher education, the options available are innumerable. In fact, many books published in the last few years about homeschooling have included a list of colleges and universities that have accepted homeschoolers. You will not find such a list in this book, because we do not know of any schools that do *not* accept homeschoolers (there may be some; we just don't know of them). The best route is not to look for a college that has already accepted homeschoolers, but to pick a college that your child wants to attend and pursue it. We doubt you will be turned away.

Searching for the right school and narrowing down choices

Once the decision is made to pursue a college education, you need to determine where to apply. There are many factors that should contribute to your decision-making process.

Christian or secular?

The first thing you should consider is whether to apply to a Christian or secular institution. Before you discuss secular options with your children, you may want to evaluate their ability to withstand opposing viewpoints and peer pressure. While any college experience will challenge the convictions and character of the student, a secular education is more likely to be a source of negative impact. How will your child hold up under pressure when his stance on creation and evolution, political issues, atheism, and materialism are confronted? If he needs more time to develop his Christian convictions, attending a Christian school might be best. Students at secular institutions will certainly encounter anti-Christian philosophies and possibly living arrangements that compromise their beliefs.

There are some instances when a secular education may be warranted. Christian schools are likely to be expensive. If you cannot afford a private education, it may be wise to postpone college until the young person has solid convictions. If he is already at that point, a secular education shouldn't shake him. It may also be difficult to find Christian colleges that offer majors in certain disciplines. Some disciplines, such as marine biology or criminal science, for example, may only be available at select schools. Again, we wouldn't advocate sacrificing the student's moral conscience in order to follow a particular career path, but if the student is strong in faith it may be fine. You are the only one who knows your children well enough to determine this.

Secular schools will usually be rougher environments for your homeschooler. The party lifestyle, loose cultural mores, profanity, innuendo, and anti-Christian professors will be much more common at a secular school. These are just the facts of life in twenty-first century American academia. Is your student ready for this harsh reality? Only you know.

If the choice is a Christian school, you should know that many different philosophies are taught at these institutions as well. For instance, there are relatively few schools that teach from a creationist perspective. You may obtain a list of creationist undergraduate schools from *www.ICR.org.* There are as many different theological differences between schools as there are between churches, so if this is a particular concern to you, be sure to do your homework. Also be aware that schools change over time. A college that was conservative when you were in school may now be quite liberal. (After all, Harvard and Yale were founded as Christian theological institutions.)

Academic concerns

You must also consider the academic level your student will be able to comfortably function in. By the time you begin looking at college options, you should have a good idea what kind of student you have. Although admissions boards use SAT or ACT scores to determine whether students can succeed academically at their colleges, you will want to take a broader view. It is possible for students to be accepted into schools that have academic standards that will mean the student must constantly focus on studying and grades. So what's wrong with that? Maybe nothing, but if the challenge is too great, the student may become frustrated and even give up when he gets lower grades than expected. It may be a better idea to go to a school with less stringent academic requirements.

Economic factors

You also need to consider the cost of prospective schools. (See Chapter 18 for ideas on cutting college costs.) However, you should not necessarily disqualify a school simply because of its cost. Many schools offer significant financial aid to students with need, depending on factors such as family assets and income and the students' abilities.

Intended majors

The majors offered by a given school should be investigated before your child applies. It obviously won't do any good to consider a college if it doesn't offer the right degree for your child. You can often find this information at the college's Web site, or you can order a catalog by mail or phone.

Campus visits

Once you have determined several potential schools, you must narrow your selection. The best way to do this is to visit campuses. Colleges have open-house days throughout the year for high school juniors and seniors. If you miss them, you can usually make an appointment for a personal tour. You will probably be able to attend a class, check out the living and academic facilities, and speak to an admissions officer. After visiting a few campuses, you and your child should narrow your choices down to three or four.

Distance from home

So what happens if you and your child don't agree on school choices? What if the student wants to attend a college on the other side of the country? If your children have reached the age of majority, you may actually not have a choice in the matter unless they give it to you. However, there is no reason that you need to support a decision (morally or financially) that you cannot sanction. This would be an unfortunate situation to encounter, but it does happen. Just remember that if you are paying the bill, you have control. Use that control prudently to help your maturing student understand the law of consequences. It may be the last chance you get to steer moral directions with your influence.

▲ ▲ ▲

There are a number of tools available now to help students in their search for the right college. These tools allow a student as early as the 9th grade to create a portfolio of potential colleges and universities from which to select and later apply. Following is a list of some of these tools:

ACT and CollegeNet have collaborated on a new Internet-based planning tool called C^3. This product combines the previous capabilities of ACT's College Connector Service with the industry-leading Web-based application service to allow students to plan for and apply to colleges and universities. The product includes: College Search, a search engine that helps students identify colleges that meet their needs; College Applications, the C^3 Apply Service, which allows students to apply to colleges electronically and eliminates redundant typing; and ACT's Financial Aid Need Estimator, which uses federal financial aid formulas and information provided by the student to estimate family contributions and financial aid. To access , log on to *www.act.org* and select the "Apply to College" icon, or type *www.act.org/cc/index.html*.

Peterson's *CollegeQuest*, a free online service, provides everything from college search tools to financial aid advice to help students get oriented. They can describe their career goals and find those colleges that will help them best meet those goals. It even has links to online courses and scholarships for such courses. *CollegeQuest* has links to more than 3,000 colleges and universities. It is a powerful, comprehensive research tool for college preparation. Check it out at *www.collegequest.com*.

The College Board, the company behind the SATs, has an excellent Web site with everything your students need to prepare for and complete their college searches. The Web address is *www.collegeboard.org/toc/html/tocstudents000.html*. There is a link to a page called "The Path from Homeschool to College—Guide for Homeschool Students." Need we say more?

▲ ▲ ▲

So how do you go about paring down your choices? We suggest using a method such as the following:

Once your child has completed the first half of the junior year, you have an idea of his grade point average. In the spring of the junior year, your child should take the SAT or ACT. Once these scores are available, you can begin compiling a list of potential colleges. Have your child write down in the middle of a sheet of paper these three pieces of information: cumulative SAT score, ACT score, and GPA. Add 50 points to the SAT score, 5 points to the ACT score, and .20 to the GPA. Then subtract the same from each. Write those numbers above and below the original, actual numbers. This gives you a numerical range to work within.

Next, write down next to your scores the names of three schools whose average students have scores similar to your child's and that meet your criteria for feasibility based on your requirements (e.g., location, educational philosophy, Christian or public education, degree options, etc.). You can find out the necessary test statistics from a college guidebook. Follow that by selecting three schools that are a little bit tougher to enter, based upon your scores. Then select three schools that should be a bit easier to get into. What you will have as a result of this exercise is a list of potential schools for your homeschooler. That way you can work toward obtainable college goals without worrying that there will be no options, while still shooting for the stars.

Gaining admission to the school of your choice

Now comes the moment you've all been waiting for...time to apply for college. It is normal to feel a bit intimidated by this process. Just think how your child feels! There are quite a few steps to this endeavor, and if you think filling out your tax forms is annoying, just wait till you get to the FAFSA financial aid form. But if you go through the following steps in order, you will make this passage as tolerable as it can be.

Admission testing

The first step in gaining college admission is to take the college board exams. The first test to take is the PSAT-NMSQ in the junior year if you want to try to qualify for National Merit Scholarships. In the fall of the senior year, you should have your student take the SAT and/or ACT. If you don't have them take the SAT or ACT at that time, don't fear, they are offered throughout the year. You just need to have the results in time to send with applications. You can find a full explanation of these tests in Chapter 11. Most colleges will require that the results be sent directly from the test organization to the admissions office. The testing service will notify up to five schools at no extra charge.

Transcript musts

Not every potential college will require a transcript from the home school, but we would suggest you provide one anyway. For those who do require it, you should make sure it contains a full accounting of all your high school student's courses and grades, as well as a listing of extracurricular activities, awards, and test scores where available. You will find more information about transcripts, as well as sample forms, in Chapter 14.

The application process

Finally, a break for Mom and Dad. The application form itself must be filled out by the student. The institution will then require additional documents. It will ask for letters of recommendation and it will specify who can submit these. The school will probably ask to have them submitted directly to the admissions office. If there is a question concerning these forms, call the admissions office. For instance, if they ask for recommendations from a guidance counselor or teacher, you should ask if they will accept forms filled out by you.

The student will be asked to write essays. These essays are very important. Not only do they demonstrate writing skills, but they give the college its only glimpse into the applicant as a person. Many colleges read the essay first. They believe essays give the best overall impression of the student's potential. Essays show things that test scores and extracurricular activities only imply, things like character and intellectual passion. They help differentiate the applicant from every other application on the reader's desk. Since some schools get thousands of applications a year, it can be very competitive. This is one tool that helps sift out the more desirable.

Urge your students to write what they really believe in the essay. There is no reason to hold back. Colleges want to know how strongly students hold their convictions and whether or not they have thought through issues. It doesn't matter whether they are writing about their experience working as a bagger at the grocery store or as the editor of the homeschool newsletter, or what their opinion is on abortion. So have your students do their very best on the essay. It will give them a step up on the competition. You can get more information on essay writing at *www.petersons.com/ugrad/evaluate.html*. Make sure to also read Peterson's "Writing a Winning College Application Essay," which appears on that site.

Some schools will ask that you attach a recent picture of the applicant. This will personalize your application, which is always a good idea.

College admissions officers are usually looking for something different to pop out at them when they sift through piles of applications. Try to provide this stand-out appeal by including a list of extracurricular activities and awards, and any personal information that will set the applicant apart. In many cases, being homeschooled may provide this advantage.

Interviews

Some schools will ask the student to come to the campus for a personal interview or to meet with an alumnus/alumna in your area. Students should treat this interview as they would a job interview. They should dress with care and be prepared to answer questions about their interests, accomplishments, and why they have chosen that particular college.

Once you are accepted

Now that those acceptance letters are pouring in, it is decision-making time.

Choosing between options

Once your child has been accepted at more than one school, you will have to choose. Unless you are paying cash, once your financial aid forms are filed, each school will send a letter with a plan for financing. Every school has a different cost and different amount of aid available, so this may influence the final choice.

Beyond financial considerations, you should go back through your original choice factors (academics, economics, spiritual factors, majors, and information gleaned from visits). In the end, it may just be a matter of personal preference, and that is fine.

Finding financial aid

See Chapter 18.

Choosing living arrangements

Where to live is an important decision. If it's possible, we love the option of living at home. Not only will you save a great deal of money, but you will also maintain a safe and moral environment for the student. We find it unfortunate that many young people want to go away to college so they can leave home. Our culture treats college as a long-term summer camp—a chance for students to get away from parents and authority and live with a bunch of people their own age. While this may be necessary in many cases, it is certainly not the wonderful arrangement for social development our society would like us to think it is. For many young people, it is downright dangerous. (Don't be fooled, this is true even at Christian schools, though stricter rules may calm things down a bit.) Age segregation is always a bad idea.

In our experience, the only place worse than a dorm is a fraternity or sorority house. These "homes" have become a hotbed of all sorts of evil—certainly not havens for the studious. We obviously reject the idea of going to college for the "experience." A young person has no business spending money on a college education only to have an extended adolescence.

If dorms are the only option, be sure your student is ready. If it is a Christian school, they should be able to use the rules as a protection for their moral lifestyle. In a secular institution, anything goes and choices are limited. Most schools still have limited single-sex housing, and that should be your first choice. Beyond that, pray— a lot. Of course, good kids go to school too; we don't mean to make it sound hopeless. But the reality is that a majority of dorm students — in most cases a vast majority—will be more interested in parties than in grades.

Preparing to encounter opposing philosophies

We have one last suggestion for you. No matter whether you have chosen a Christian or secular school, your student will certainly encounter philosophies contrary to those they were brought up with. It is very valuable to give the student a "booster shot" through programs designed to help them strengthen convictions. Summit programs, sponsored by Summit Ministries and WorldView Academy can help students strengthen their thinking skills and clarify their positions. The Institute for Creation

Research (ICR) holds Back to Genesis Seminars and other creation science seminars (like Summer Institutes) that can prepare students to understand creation/evolution issues.

Bon voyage

Hopefully, your careful exploration of options and prayerful choices will set the stage for a successful trip through the college experience. The more prepared your student is for this endeavor, the more he will benefit from the opportunity. Start preparations early, in the junior year of high school at the latest, and take every opportunity to study all the options. It is a great deal of work, but your effort will pay off by allowing your student to have a seamless transition to higher education.

CHAPTER 18

Paying for College

*"And my God shall supply all your needs
according to His riches in glory in Christ Jesus."*
–Philippians 4:19 (NASB)

Your homeschool student is nearing graduation and you are realizing (probably not for the first time) that living on one income has annihilated any hope of saving for college. Don't give up yet. In almost all cases, you can make college financing work if you are willing to diligently check out your options and be a little creative.

Strategies for cutting costs

Taking a nontraditional route

Homeschooling families are used to bucking the trend, and when it comes to getting a college degree, taking a nontraditional route can mean big savings. Community colleges offer several advantages. Tuition is always low, and students can live at home so you do not have to pay room and board. Living at home also provides the advantage of staying away from the college party scene. A student who accumulates two years of community college credit with a good grade point average is usually able to transfer into the four-year school of his choice. (If your student is planning this route, and knows where he would like to eventually study for a degree, check with the admissions office of that school ahead of time to determine its community college transfer policy and which courses should be taken.) Students who transfer for their final two years of degree work get the same college diploma as those who spent four years at an institution, and the monetary savings can be substantial.

As explained in Chapter 13, the College Level Exam Placement (CLEP) program allows students to take tests for college credit. Each test costs $44 and is worth three to six credits. In a traditional setting, obtaining three to six credits can cost $300 to $1800! Some institutions may charge a fee for transferring CLEP credits, so check ahead of time. Most community colleges will accept CLEP credit toward an associate's degree, and the credit is then transferred to a four-year college toward a bachelor's degree. This program can save thousands of dollars per student. Read the section on CLEP in Chapter 13 for more information.

Distance education courses vary greatly in price. Some cost as much as on-campus study, but there are some programs with much lower costs. Ultimately, you will need to research the options for the degree your student wants. Note that distance education programs allow students to live at home, which by itself can drastically reduce the total cost of education.

Living at home

Any college program that allows your student to live at home will save money. Room and board costs at most schools will be vastly greater than what you would pay to house, feed, and transport the student yourself. Four-year colleges may have residency requirements, but these can often be waived for students who live in their parents' homes.

Buying a house near campus

We once heard about a father of several teens who decided to provide for his children's college education by buying a house near campus. He required the children to all attend the same school, and they had to choose from state colleges (to lower costs). Once they chose the school, he bought a large house near campus. The children lived in the home during their years at school, renting out spare rooms to other students. When all the children had graduated, the father sold the house, which had appreciated in value, recouping much of his tuition costs. He also gained a tax advantage for owning a second home. Quite ingenious! Of course, this approach requires having the means to buy a house near a college campus.

Going to state schools

Tuition at state universities and colleges is often half that of private institutions for residents of that state, since the schools are supported by government funds (your tax dollars). The quality of education at these schools is usually excellent and the variety of degrees available in state university systems is vast. While they may not be as prestigious as private schools, a diploma from a state school will almost always meet the goal of higher education (going on to graduate school or getting a job).

Financial aid programs

If you cannot pay cash for your child's education, read on. When you apply for financial aid, your child's need for aid is determined according to a governmentally developed formula that calculates what portion of the total school costs your family is expected to pay. Your expected family contribution (EFC) is the amount you are required to pay beyond any offered financial aid. The forms from which your EFC is calculated take into account your income, dependents, liabilities, assets, and number of other children you have in college.

Forms to file

As soon as you have filed your college application(s), it is time to file a Free Application for Federal Student Aid (FAFSA). All colleges that accept any form of federal financing will use this form (Patrick Henry College is an example of a college that does not receive any federal loans or grants). You can get a copy of the FAFSA from the financial aid office of the prospective college, or you can download a copy or file one online at *www.fafsa.ed.gov*. Filing this form will require your previous year's income and tax information and cannot be filed before January 1 of the year the student plans to enter college.

While nearly all schools require the FAFSA, some also require the PROFILE form. The PROFILE requires additional information, including demographic facts about your family. If this form is required by the prospective college, you will need to file both forms earlier, as it will take longer to receive results.

Once these forms are filed, results will be sent to the colleges that have offered admission to the student. Each college will then send you a financial award letter outlining how much money your family will be required to contribute and what forms of aid the student is eligible to receive.

Scholarships

Academic scholarships

We mentioned the National Merit Scholarship program in Chapter 11. Taking the PSAT in the fall of the junior year automatically enters students in the National Merit Scholarship contest program. Those deemed semifinalists based on PSAT scores may then go on to compete for a finalist position, based on standards set by the National Merit Scholarship Corporation. Those who qualify as semifinalists often are eligible for academic scholarships from schools of their choice. Finalists are offered sizable awards for study at their predetermined school choice.

There are also some national scholarships that have designed an application process especially for homeschoolers. One example is the Easley National Scholarship. If you are a homeschool senior, go to the National Academy of American Scholars Web site: *www.naas.org/faql.html* for an online application. Scholarships are offered based on SAT or ACT scores, as follows:

- ▲ 1120 SAT / 25 ACT: ($8,000 to $10,000)
- ▲ 1100 SAT / 22 ACT: ($6,000)
- ▲ 859 SAT / 15 ACT: ($4,000)

Applications must be completed by February 15 for the following school year. The scholarship is based on performance on the above tests, letters of recommendation based on the student's character, and community service.

The National Endowment for the Humanities (*www.neh.fed.us*) supports scholarships on the state level. For example, the New York Council for the Humanities sponsors the annual Young Scholars Contest, now in its eighth year. New York high school students compete in an essay contest with judging "in a blind competition by a panel of humanities scholars familiar with the work of high school students." The essays are evaluated according to specific criteria. The NEH Web site has links to state scholarship Web sites.

Another program worth considering for students interested in working with computers is the international ThinkQuest $1,000,000 Scholarship competition. The program:

"...encourages students to use the Internet to create Web-based educational tools and materials that make learning fun and contagious. Structured as a contest, the ThinkQuest program encourages students on different levels of the information technology ladder to form teams to build their educational materials. Along the way, it provides significant help to participants. Teams, typically coached by teachers, collaborate in the 'Internet Style' and develop innovative, high-quality educational tools that take advantage of the strengths of the Internet."

Students must be between the ages of 12 and 19 by February 28 and may not be registered as full-time students in an institution of higher education. Students from homeschools are eligible if "the situation fulfills all the requirements of the jurisdiction having authority over the student's education." Register at *www.thinkquest.org/tquic/tqic-student-steps-shtml*.

Individual universities and colleges usually provide their own academic scholarships with their own qualification processes. Some rely on SAT or ACT scores or grade point averages from high school. For specific information on academic scholarships from your child's chosen school, contact the financial aid or admissions office directly.

Athletic scholarships

If your child is gifted in athletics, be prepared for some challenges in acquiring athletic scholarships. We have dealt with this because of our son's desire to play basketball. Jeremiah is 18, he recently graduated from high school, and he is very interested in playing college ball. He has played on teams throughout his junior high and high school years, including church leagues, amateur clubs, and homeschool leagues, and has attended summer basketball camps sponsored by colleges throughout the northeastern United States. He wants very much to play at the next level. This is a particular challenge for homeschoolers.

Obviously, if your child is not athletically gifted, this section will not be relevant. Competition for funds is fierce, and homeschooled students may need to prove more exceptional abilities than others, as it is harder for them to get noticed. As always in preparing your child for college or career, it is wise to plan ahead.

Jeremiah first became interested in basketball at the age of 13, playing with his friends on a single hoop at the mission we attended in the early 1990s. We saw his intense desire to play and signed him up in an organized league at the local YMCA. We just wanted him to have fun and enjoy the game. He developed his skills and found out that he wanted to go on.

When Jeremiah outgrew the YMCA league, we did not know how to get him into junior high athletics without going to a traditional school. David started researching the community options and found a CYO league where Jeremiah could play. After his first year of CYO basketball, Jeremiah was named to the Greater Utica CYO All-Star team, representing our church at the annual all-star game. The hard work and effort was paying off. But by the next year he was too old to play CYO anymore.

Jeremiah already had a basketball college scholarship in mind, so playing in CYO alone would not cut it. Once again, David checked out the options and he decided to organize a homeschool basketball program. There were many details to work out. We needed to find and pay for a court and find other interested homeschooled boys. With David's help and exhaustive effort, the homeschool basketball team was organized and playing. Jeremiah became one of the star players. We played teams all over New York state, from Binghamton to Syracuse to Albany. We played Christian schools and the team from Utica's Jewish Community Center (where we practiced twice a week.) The team played in city tournaments and in the state homeschool tournament.

The first two years of high school basketball were fine for Jeremiah to hone his skills. Then we met another obstacle. Four of the boys on the team were going back to private school the next year, leaving too few players to continue. Additionally, the quality of play was such that it would be hard for Jeremiah to be noticed by any college coaches. We needed another level for Jeremiah to continue preparation for college.

At this point we learned about the Amateur Athletic Union (AAU). The AAU is an organization of amateur sports teams in virtually every sport known to man. We saw an ad in our local paper in the spring of 1998 announcing tryouts for boys 16 and younger to join the Adirondack Spirit AAU Men's Basketball Squad. Dad and Jeremiah went.

It was immediately clear that this was where boys who wanted to play college basketball went to polish their skills during the off-season. Many of the boys who were there were stars on their local high school teams. Now Jeremiah had a real challenge. But first he had to make the cut. David introduced himself to the coaches and made them aware of Miah's homeschool experience. Needless to say, Jeremiah was the first and only homeschool tryout on the roster. By the time the two-day tryouts were over, he had made the team. He worked on his skills again that season and throughout the summer, attending basketball camps. He even won an MVP trophy at one of them. But then came the problem of organized play for the 1998-1999 season.

Jeremiah and his best friend were able to try out for the Syracuse homeschool team, an hour away. The Syracuse Eagles had the ambitious goal of winning the New York State Homeschool title, and going to the National Homeschool Basketball Tournament in Wichita, Kansas. The Eagles put together a 24-4 record in 1999, won the regional Christian high school basketball championship and the state homeschool championship, and finished fifth in the national tournament! All of this gave Jeremiah great material for his high school transcript in the basketball section.

In his final year of high school eligibility, Jeremiah has continued to work hard on getting onto a college team. His dad went to bat for him one more time and wrote to the head basketball coaches at five schools Jeremiah selected to consider in the fall of 2000. Now he is being offered the chance to visit schools. One coach came to a game to see Miah play. Although the process is tougher for him as a homeschooler, it is not impossible. It has taken tenacity and work by David to see that our homeschool athlete gets the chance to qualify. The rest is up to the student—stay tuned.

There are many opportunities to improve your child's skills through traditional means; however, when you are homeschooling you have to pave your own way. You need to find out what is available and plug your children in where it makes the most sense for their interests.

You have to be prepared to work hard to get your child hooked up to the right school after high school. Success will depend on a number of factors, including academic performance, athletic ability, experience, and qualifications. Your child is probably already ahead of the academic curve. This is an advantage because colleges are always looking for academically superior students for their athletic programs. Your years of preparation will pay off here if you simply keep good records.

Athletic ability is going to mostly be a result of the child's gifts and training. If it is an individual sport like gymnastics, tennis, golf, or swimming, you will need to put together a portfolio of accomplishments. Everything you can do to demonstrate your child's achievements should be included. Nothing is too insignificant here. It is your one chance to market your child's abilities. We highly recommend that you make a video of your child's performance for the colleges to which he wants to apply.

Try to find every way you can to provide experience through common and uncommon channels. Take advantage of AAU teams. Provide private lessons if you can afford it. Play with your child if that is all you can do. (That experience itself was worth it to David, even though Jeremiah can pretty much cream him now on the court.) You may have to travel to find the experience your son or daughter needs to succeed. It is up to you to decide how much you want to devote to the effort.

When you have put all of your "marketing" material together, it will be up to the college to determine if your child is qualified for an athletic scholarship. If you do your work right, you should have a shot at it, if for no other reason than the novelty of being a homeschooler. It works both against you and for you. It is up to you to do what you can to present it in the positive light. The outcome remains in the Lord's hands.

Your activity is critical. You will have to become your child's personal agent! Normally, no one is going to scout out your student-athlete. You will have to make contact with the schools you are hoping will consider your child. You will need to market each child's experience to the proper athletic director or coach. Just face up to the fact that this will be your job. That's just the way it is for most parents who want to help their children gain recognition. Roll up your sleeves and do what it takes to give your child a fighting chance.

Many schools have private scholarships available. Write to or call the schools you want your child to attend and learn about their athletic scholarship programs. Do your research. It may save you hundreds or even thousands of dollars in education costs. The work may well be worth the effort.

Can my child play in the NCAA?

As we have already stated, many students will have a chance to play in organized sports as homeschoolers. Some will play in college on the intramural level. Others will be able to play in an organized college sports team or as an individual participant. But homeschooled or not, it is the rare child who gets a scholarship for athletics.

How can you qualify your child for National Collegiate Athletic Association (NCAA) scholarships if you are homeschooling? Some states allow for your children to participate in high school sports, others do not. If your child is able to play for a high school, you probably will be able to qualify him through the school district. However, the NCAA process for determining Division I and II eligibility is different for homeschoolers than for traditionally schooled students. It is good for parents to know what to do if the student-athlete is capable of participating on this level in college.

The NCAA has a staff that works with homeschoolers to prepare the information for qualifying at their chosen colleges. Keep in mind that the standards for qualification *athletically* are no different for a homeschooler than for a traditionally schooled student. However, the certification process (NCAA terminology) for homeschool athletes is different. You need to pay close attention to this or your child will not be eligible!

For your convenience, we have included a copy of the current NCAA Eligibility Standards for Division I and II schools in Appendix E. The NCAA will undoubtedly change regulations for eligibility from time to time. For the most updated information check the web site, *www.ncaa.org*, contact them by phone at (317) 917-6222, or write to them at: Membership Services, Attention: Homeschooling Requirements, P.O. Box 6222, Indianapolis, IN 46206.

The risks of college athletics

It goes without saying that athletics are secondary to academics. Even if your child is good enough to receive an athletic scholarship, you need to make sure he understands that academics are primary and sports are secondary. Playing on the college level is extremely intensive. Balancing classwork with training will demand extreme discipline. Make sure your child is well aware of the sacrifices necessary to succeed.

Teach and prepare your student-athlete about the many challenges he will face:

- ▲ Dealing with a lot of pressure and stress, both on and off the team.
- ▲ Maintaining relationships and activities outside of the locker room.
- ▲ Keeping on top of grades and coursework.
- ▲ Developing a disciplined lifestyle in training and study; maintaining self-control (no one is going to be there to keep Johnny or Suzie organized like Mom did).
- ▲ Be ready for issues like homesickness, fatigue, and failure.
- ▲ Watch out for the inevitable pressures to experiment with sex, drugs, and alcohol. (Of course, this will be more prevalent on certain campuses than others.) Exhort your student to "guard your heart" as the only sure way to prepare for the negative pressures of college life.

Remember, chances of making a college sports team are extremely slim compared to high school opportunities. Playing in college sports is very competitive. Being the best in one's senior year of high school may be followed by a benchwarming season on the freshman squad in college.

Consider the following information from *Counseling Today's Secondary Student*:

 ▲ Of 400,000 high school seniors playing football or basketball, only about 20,000 will be signed by the 800 NCAA member schools.

 ▲ An additional 5000 students will play for the 400 colleges affiliated with the NAIA (National Association of Intercollegiate Athletics).

 ▲ 3,000 will take the field for the 500 members of NJCAA (National Junior College Athletic Association).

 ▲ Only some 300 colleges and universities award full athletic scholarships.

Make sure your student visits the prospective school, particularly to check out the sports program, meet the coach, and get a handle on whether the school meets his expectations. Remember, a good academic program may not necessarily accompany a strong sports program.

For further reading:

 ▲ *The Athlete's Game Plan for College and Career*, by Howard Figler. (Peterson's Guides, Princeton, N.J., 1984)

 ▲ *Winning an Athletic Scholarship*, by Dennis K. Reischl. (FPMI Communications, Huntsville, Ala., 1994)

Military scholarships

In Chapter 17, we discussed military career options for homeschoolers. College-bound students may be interested in offsetting the cost of their education with military service, and there are many opportunities to do just that. Those who sign up for full-time military service may sometimes be awarded scholarships to college. Or, after their active duty is over, they will be eligible to benefit from the Montgomery GI bill. This program allows military personnel on active duty to put away $100 per month in an educational fund and it gives them $10,500 for college at the end of a two-year enlistment (a four-year tour will bring $13,200). Enlisting in a part-time military program, such as the National Guard, often yields significant scholarship opportunities, as well as pay for time on duty. There are also college tuition programs available through R.O.T.C. for students who want to commit to military service upon completion of their four-year baccalaureate degree. Additionally, your child may wish to apply for an appointment to a military academy (West Point, Annapolis, the Air

Force Academy, the Coast Guard Academy, or the Merchant Marine Academy). Each of these options demands a serious commitment after graduation. Your child will have to decide if the funds are worth it to him or her.

Grants

Grant money is simply money given for a specified purpose. Grants do not have to be repaid. All 50 states have grant programs for residents who attend school in their home state. Most of these grants are need-based, but a few are merit-based. Contact the college's financial aid office for information on applying for a state grant.

The federal government offers Federal Pell Grants and Federal Supplemental Educational Opportunity Grants. If these are a possibility for your child, they will be listed in your financial aid award letter from the college.

Loans

Consider carefully whether taking out college loans is wise for your family. This is a personal decision that should be made with prayer. The financial aid award letter will include any loan possibilities that are suggested by the college. College loans come in many forms, including federally guaranteed loans, loans from private institutions, and personal bank loans. Again, if these are part of your financial aid picture, your financial aid award letter will include them.

Working

Holding a job while going to college can offset some expenses. Many colleges offer work-study programs, allowing students to get on-campus work that pays a portion of their tuition or room and board. Part-time work will certainly not pay all expenses for full-time study. Working during school vacations allows students to put away money for living expenses or for a portion of their tuition. Some students prefer to work full-time and go to school part-time in order to avoid accruing debt.

Fear not!

Basically, the adage, "where there's a will there's a way," is true when it comes to paying for college. There are so many options available for financial aid and nontraditional enrollment these days (distance education, CLEP, part-time programs, night classes), that if you are creative and determined, you will find a way to get a degree. Remember: Although tuition and room and board have never been more expensive, opportunities to get college degrees through alternative means have never been more common.

For more information about financial aid for college, check out the following Web sites:

▲ *www.ed.gov/offices/OSFAP/Students.*

▲ *www.petersons.com.*

▲ *www.collegeboard.com.*

▲ *www.freschinfo.com.*

▲ *www.4scholarships.com.*

▲ *www.free-4u.com.*

▲ *www.collegescholarships.com.*

CHAPTER 19

Evaluating All Options

"'For I know the plans that I have for you,' declares the Lord, 'plans for welfare and not for calamity to give you a future and a hope.'"
—Jeremiah 29:11 (NASB)

We are coming to the end of our journey through the secondary homeschooling process. We have presented the options, and now you must evaluate what is right for your children. In order to do this you must focus on their desires, gifts, and possibilities as you pray for God's direction.

Finding God's will

If you are part of the modern evangelical community, you have undoubtedly heard that "God loves you and has a wonderful plan for your life." We all hope our children will seek God's plan early and often as they are growing, and especially when they venture out on their own. In Jeremiah 29:11, we see God's plan in the broad sense: "'I know what I have planned for you,' says the Lord. 'I have good plans for you. I don't plan to hurt you. I plan to give you hope and a good future (NCV).'" What encouragement!

As parents, we should always be concerned that our children know what God requires of them. We should encourage them to seek and do the will of God. Your understanding of the will of God will affect how you and your children evaluate options. Some believers promote the idea that God's will consists of one narrowly defined target. They believe that to be in the will of God you must find and hit that dead-center target; if you miss this one road, you have missed the ultimate will of God for you.

In our study of Scripture, we have not been able to substantiate that idea. Our view is that God's requirement for our children, and for us as parents, is that we live in accordance with His revealed Word, allow the principles of Scripture to rule our lives, and seek Him for wisdom, understanding, and knowledge of the truth. God's will is not a predetermined narrow path that we must find and follow. Rather, the will of God is defined by His commandments and bound by them. God gives us the ability to choose and promises us wisdom (if we ask for it) to choose our paths wisely. He wants to lead us into truth and grace. He promises to guide us as we trust in Him (Proverbs 3:5-6); He provides a way of escape if we make a bad choice (Psalm 37:23-24); but He does not limit us.

Obviously, we believe that doing God's will is required of every Christian. We must make sure our children know they are commanded by the Lord to discern and do His will. This will is revealed in Scripture, is knowable by every child of God, and is not limiting. God's will is a liberating spectrum of options. These options fall within God's moral requirements for each child, allowing for a true sense of liberty and freedom. To choose among options is the right, privilege, and responsibility of every Christian. That is the essence of loving God with all your heart, soul, mind, and strength.

In Psalm 119:96 it says, "There is an end to all perfection; Thy commandment is exceedingly broad. (NASB)" We believe this verse tells us that God, in his wisdom, has given us His commandments to be obeyed. If we challenge our children to live within God's defined moral standard, the Scriptures tell us they will live a long, prosperous, satisfying and secure life. If they refuse and disobey, they will suffer negative consequences. The choice is up to them, as it is for all of us.

John tells us in his first epistle that "We know that we know Him, if we keep His commandments. (I John 1:3)" Jesus told us, "If you love Me, you will keep My commandments. (John 14:15)" He then said, "He that has My commandments, and keeps them, he it is who loves Me. And He that loves Me will be loved of My Father" (John 14:21). And again, "If you keep My commandments, you will abide in My love, even as I have kept my Father's commandments and abide in His love" (John 15:10). The point here is clear. Jesus calls us to obey the commands of God as revealed in His Word as an act of love.

When we teach our children that they can live within God's commandments, we are also giving them an opportunity to live with a great deal of liberty.

In other words, God's "commandment is exceedingly broad" because outside of God's requirements to keep away from evil practices (that is, murder, stealing, adultery, etc.), there is a tremendous amount of freedom and liberty to do many good and decent things while trusting in Jesus. There is an "exceedingly broad" range of options out there to choose from. Each homeschooled Christian is free to choose to be an athlete, or a nurse, or an engineer, or a missionary, or an actor, or anything else that he may desire that is within God's will. This is Christian liberty. This is doing the "perfect will of God" (Romans 12:1-2).

Our children's responsibility is to understand the Bible, and to study its pages to clarify God's requirements for each of them. Then, as they grow in grace and knowledge of God the Father and the Lord Jesus, through the attainment of saving faith in Jesus through the new birth, God gives them the gift of the Holy Spirit, who "leads them into all truth" (John 16:13).

The Holy Spirit comes alongside young believers and supports them in their walk of faith so they can do the will of God in Christian love. When children want to follow God, they must think practically about what they want to do with their lives. Thinking through God's will for their lives is crucial, as it makes them much more responsible in pursuit of college or career. God compels them to use the minds that He has given them, to think through what they want to become, and to know they must seek his wisdom and direction for the future.

Since it is not within the scope of this book to expound this position fully, we refer you to an excellent resource for further evaluation, *Decision Making and the Will of God: A Biblical Alternative to the Traditional View*, by Garry Friesen, Th.D., and J. Robin Maxson, Th.M.

The undecided

In many cases, it will be clear from an early age what a child wants to do after high school. For some, it will take much prayer and consideration. In cases where plans are not clear from the start, parents will need to help guide the student.

There are some resources available to help you direct those who don't know what they want to do when they grow up. Recognize that this is natural, particularly if your children don't have a family business to go into, or aren't planning to follow in Dad or Mom's footsteps.

For those who need a little extra decision-making help, the ACT Web site, *www.act.org*, provides DISCOVER software, which helps with career planning. It creates a personal profile, assessing interests, abilities, and job values. This helps the student clarify whether college, immediate employment, vocational training, or military service will be the best step after high school. *Career Direct*, a program developed by Larry Burkett, is a career counseling tool that helps "Christians make Biblically based vocational and educational decisions." We discuss this product more fully in Chapter 6.

If your children need a little more time and experience after high school before setting their future goals in stone, we suggest a short-term option. Consider one of the following:

1. Giving a portion of their next few years to mission work.
2. Attending a Bible college or discipleship training school.
3. Considering whether the military may be a reasonable option, even as a reservist.
4. Going to the local community college to experience college life while still in the home environment.
5. Spending a couple of years working while living at home to see if something "clicks" in terms of a career direction, while saving up for college or to buy a home or car.
6. Taking concerted time for prayer and reading to gain insight into God's will and to clarify what the best next steps may be.

Where is the boundary of parental input?

So what if your teen is not as interested in your opinion as you would like him to be? At some point, you need to be willing to "let go and let God." Ultimately, if you have been faithful in your parenting (we are not saying perfect), you can have confidence that the Lord can take it from here. You can certainly place some practical boundaries, though. For instance, we never promised to financially support our children's college or career directions if we don't feel they are taking a wise route. Our financial and moral support do not amount to a carte blanche—we cannot in good conscience support immoral activities, or even foolish ones. God offered "blessings and curses" to His children according to the decisions they made. We parents are justified in doing the same, and are even responsible to do so. Some young people will need their own wilderness experiences before they value your opinion. It would be nice if they let us guide them away from the potholes that we can clearly see, but sometimes they don't. Have faith. God is able to do what we cannot.

Purity for a purpose

A critical issue for many homeschooling parents is how to make their children understand why purity is important. We know that the best way to insure they get off to a healthy start in beginning their own family is to begin in purity. It is not an easy road in this society, where the problem is exacerbated by the American post-sexual-revolution culture that surrounds us. Many of us paid dearly for the permissiveness of our parents. How do we protect our children from going down a similar road? How do we prepare them for life in a modern college dormitory? What can we do to help them avoid the temptations and pressures that they will certainly encounter as they leave our protective home environments?

There are many books that can help our children think through the issue of purity. The ones that we know of include: *Of Knights and Fair Maidens* and *The Courtship Revolution*, by Jeff Myers; *His Perfect Faithfulness*, by Eric and Leslie Ludy; *Passion and Purity*, by Elisabeth Elliott; *Best Friends for Life*, by Michael and Judy Phillips; and *I Kissed Dating Goodbye*, by Joshua Harris. We also suggest the *Someday a Marriage Without Regrets* Bible study by Precept Ministries. Have your child do a Bible study on sexual immorality. Make sure to schedule the one-on-one adolescent trip we described in Chapter 5.

Establish a clear policy on dating. Communicate it unequivocally to your teenager. Try to work with your child to agree with your position. Have your homeschooler attend seminars on courtship and dating at homeschool conventions and conferences. Begin this training before the hormones kick in (age 12 or so). Enroll them in a Summit or Worldview workshop. The goal is to give your children the ammunition they need to guard their hearts during an incredibly volatile period of their lives.

The very best safeguard for preserving your teens' sexual purity is to make sure they have a strong relationship with God. Pray for the Lord to work deeply in their lives. Do everything you can to guide them into a love for God that will protect their hearts. You will need to make this a priority if you expect your children to do the same. Make sure their closest friends are strongly committed to Jesus Christ. Disciple them to follow Jesus first. Your support, guidance, and discipline will help them choose the right road.

Walk in faith

When Abraham left Ur of the Chaldees, he headed out into a vast desert, not knowing where he was going to end up. God spoke to him and told him what He wanted him to do. He said that he was to go to a strange land, that he would become a great nation and his name would become great. Abraham had no reason to believe this was true except that God told him it was so, and he believed God. In the same way, you have obeyed God and stepped out into homeschooling believing God has led you, without knowing where it will ultimately lead. But you can step out knowing that the Lord will keep His promises through the years as you walk in the obedience of faith like Father Abraham.

If you read the 11th chapter of the book of Hebrews, you will read many examples of people who had faith that the Lord had told them to do certain things, which they did. You also read that God rewarded their faith. It wasn't always rewarded in the way they wanted, but many saw their loved ones brought back to life, and some had even better rewards. But in every case, they trusted God.

It is our faith in God that gives us hope. It's not just hope that we will be successful in some earthly endeavor, but ultimate hope that one day we will see Him who is our hope, Jesus Christ, face to face. Ultimately, that is why we homeschool our children. We want to give them a Christian education. We want them to learn from us how to love Jesus Christ. Everything else is secondary to that. Everything.

As we close, we want to focus on a few other thoughts from the Holy Scriptures. First, Proverbs 16:9 says that "a man's heart devises his way, but the Lord directs his steps." We need to realize that ultimately we may put together our plans and ways, but in the end it will be up to God to get us through to the destination He directs. We need to put our trust in Him. "In all our ways, acknowledge Him, and He will make our path straight" (Proverbs 3:6). It may be that you and your child agree on a career pathway, move toward that goal throughout the school years, and then find God calling in another direction. Be thankful that you have trained a child who listens to God above all.

As we trust the Lord and fear Him for the awesome loving Being that He is, we will see our children follow our example and become the strong individuals we desire. They will be safe from harm as we teach them in the confines of a loving, caring home. "The fear of the Lord is a strong confidence, and his children will have a safe refuge" (Proverbs 14:26). That is what our home is to our children, a safe refuge. They need this in our day more than ever. Our strong family is a refuge of love, care, and protection for our young ones.

Finally, we can have confidence that we are doing the right thing as we train our children because the Word says that "without faith, it is impossible to please Him, for he who comes to God must believe that He is, and that He is a rewarder of those who diligently seek Him" (Hebrews 11:6). We can be confident in God, because we have this promise: If we trust Him for our children as we teach them what we are capable of teaching, and if we believe that He is there for us, seeking Him constantly for His guidance, help, and direction, He will reward us. Our children will become all that we desire and we will be able to complete our task, confident that we have done the job God has called us to do.

Do justly, love mercy, and walk humbly with your God

Our goal is to raise our children to love the Lord, to be intelligent members of their communities, and to be prepared for life. We hope they will not only follow our example, but will do an even better job with their children than we have done with them. As it says in II Timothy 2:2, "The things which you have heard...in the presence of many witnesses, these entrust to faithful men, who will be able to teach others also." Most of us were not homeschooled. Our children have the chance to build upon our instruction to impact succeeding generations, including their children and their children's children. May the Lord give you His strength as you participate in this wonderful calling for you and your children—to homeschool through to college or career. In the final judgment, may you and your children be found to have done the "good, and acceptable, and perfect will of God."

Parents and Education: the Biblical Mandate

by Dr. K. Alan Snyder

We live in a "new age," so to speak. Americans today, and even many evangelical Christians, have lost a basic principle that was not debatable in our nation's early years: namely, that *parents* are the ones given the responsibility by God for the education of their own children. Early Americans, most of whom subscribed to biblical thinking about the nature of education and the family's role in that education, would be astounded by the wholesale abdication of that responsibility today. Many Christians still say they are responsible for their children's education, yet their decision to turn their children over to state indoctrination opposed to biblical teaching contradicts their stated belief. How much of this is ignorance as opposed to irresponsibility? It is not my intent to imply that all Christian parents who place their children in government schools are being irresponsible. Perhaps they simply need to pay closer attention to what the Bible says about parental responsibility. Parents need to understand that allowing the state to be the educator of our children, more often than not, undermines biblical principles.

Children are a gift from God, the work of his hands

Let's begin with the premise stated above. All too often, modern parents see children as a drain on their resources or as a heavy burden they cannot wait to lay aside once their children are grown. I am not going to try to convince anyone that having children is always a joyful experience. There will be battles of the will and, at times, parents—even good Christian parents—may wonder why they voluntarily entered into this thicket, filled with thorns and thistles, called childraising.

Yet God tells each of us to walk in love, setting aside our own desires, denying our self-will, and grasping hold of the high calling of being a parent. There are joys on this path; selfish attitudes are what keep us from seeing the joys. We should remember the admonition in Hebrews 12:2, which reminds us: "Let us fix our eyes on Jesus, the author and perfecter of our faith, who *for the joy* set before Him endured the cross, scorning its shame, and sat down at the right hand of the throne of God." Whenever we begin to question whether parenting is worth all the trouble, we should be humbled when we realize that Jesus thought we were worth all the trouble He had to endure.

Our children *are* a gift from God and they deserve to be seen in that light. When the patriarch Jacob met his brother Esau again after many years, and Esau inquired about all the people with Jacob, Jacob responded, "They are the children God has graciously given your servant. (Genesis 33:5)" Later, when Jacob was reunited with his son, Joseph, in Egypt, and he saw all the young men accompanying him, Jacob asked who they were. "They are the sons God has given me here, (Genesis 48:9)" was Joseph's answer.

The testimony continues. Hannah was distraught because she had no children. She cried to God over her situation and when she finally gave birth to a son, she called him Samuel, which meant, "heard of God. (I Samuel 1:20)" Her son was a direct answer to prayer. King David commented in I Chronicles 28:5: "Of all my sons—*and the Lord has given me many*—He has chosen my son Solomon to sit on the throne of the kingdom of the Lord over Israel." Although David may not have been the best of parents at all times, he still believed that his sons were gifts from God.

We are told in Psalm 113:9 that "He [God] settles the barren woman in her home as a happy mother of children." This is another indication that the Lord is pleased to provide children to those who want them. Then in Psalm 127:3 comes this straightforward declaration: "Sons are a heritage from the Lord, children a reward from Him." This one Scripture by itself should be enough to melt any wrong attitude in those who claim the name of Christ.

When Isaiah prophesies the judgment of God on the Israelites, he ends his prophecy with this promise: "Therefore this is what the Lord, who redeemed Abraham, says to the house of Jacob: 'No longer will Jacob be ashamed; no longer will their faces grow pale. When they see among them their children, *the work of My hands*, they will keep My Name holy; they will acknowledge the holiness of the Holy One of Jacob, and will stand in awe of the God of Israel. (Isaiah 29:22-23)'" The Scripture is quite clear: Children are a blessing from the Lord!

Parents are responsible for educating their children

Having established biblically that God is the One who blesses us with children, the next step is to see from the Scripture that God gives responsibilities along with that blessing. The education of one's children is a key responsibility.

The first Scriptural indication that parents are to teach their children is found in Genesis 18:19. God, referring to Abraham, says, "For I have chosen him, so that *he will direct his children and his household after him to keep the way of the Lord* by doing what is right and just, so that the Lord will bring about for Abraham what He has promised him." It is significant to note the condition in this passage. God wants to bless Abraham, but it seems to depend on his faithfulness in teaching his household the ways of God.

In the book of Deuteronomy, Moses recounts all that the Lord has taught the people. He then gives a warning: "Only be careful, and watch yourselves closely so that you do not forget the things your eyes have seen or let them slip from your heart as long as you live. *Teach them to your children and to their children after them.* (Deuteronomy 4:9)"

Later, Moses is even more explicit: "These commandments that I give you today are to be upon your hearts. *Impress them on your children.... Teach them to your children, talking about them when you sit at home and when you walk along the road, when you lie down and when you get up.* Write them on the doorframes of your houses and on your gates, so that your days and the days of your children may be many in the land that the Lord swore to give your forefathers. (Deuteronomy 6:6-7; 11:19-21)" In other words, we are to teach our children at all times. This obviously does not mean that every minute of the day is to be filled with formal instruction, but the clear implication is that our lives are not segmented, but whole: The Lord is not omitted from any area. When we send children to an institution that does not teach the truths of the Lord, we are filling many hours of their days with instruction that is ungodly. Clearly, that is in opposition to the spirit of this passage.

We are not done with Moses yet. Near the end of Deuteronomy, we are told: "When Moses finished reciting all these words to all Israel, he said to them, 'Take to heart all the words I have solemnly declared to you this day, *so that you may command your children to obey carefully all the words of this law*. They are not just idle words for you—*they are your life.* (Deuteronomy 32:45-47)" Note the linkage between taking to heart the words of God and the transferring of those words to the children. It's as if the main reason for knowing God's law is that it be passed along to the next generation. Also note the strength of those final words: "*They are your life.*" Moses was not giving them mere advice; without these truths, people will be spiritually dead.

Some people may object at this point, perhaps observing that these instructions all deal with the laws of God. Of course we do that, they might say, because we have family devotions and our children go to church and Sunday school. Surely this does not apply to math, grammar, or science. Those subjects have nothing to do with the laws of God.

Such a response is indicative of the state of our society at this time. We have become so accustomed to believing in a dichotomy between the spiritual and the secular that we no longer see the connection. It is not my purpose to focus on how each subject can be taught according to God's laws and from His perspective, but it is important to recognize that there is no purely secular subject. Math comes from the mind of God. He is the one who gave us numbers and all the concepts of algebra, geometry, and trigonometry. Language is a gift directly from the hand of God. If we do not teach it as such, we give ourselves over to an evolutionary interpretation of the origin of language, which teaches that language slowly developed over centuries with man "graduating" from grunts to fully structured sentences. God gave us language because He is a communicator and desires His people to communicate also. Science is primarily the discovery of how the Lord has made His universe. Most of the early scientists, men

men such as Kepler, Boyle, and Newton, who gave flesh to the scientific revolution, believed they were merely explaining the works of God.

It is imperative that we realize the spiritual/secular dichotomy is false and all subjects not only *can*, but *should*, be taught through the prism of God's Word. If we neglect to do this, our children may be led into false teachings and turn away from His truth. Thus, we will be responsible for allowing them to develop a worldview hostile to the laws of God.

The Lord's instructions on this parental responsibility do not end with the Pentateuch. Psalm 78:5-8 declares: "He [God] decreed statutes for Jacob and established the law in Israel, which *He commanded our forefathers to teach their children, so the next generation would know them, even the children yet to be born, and they in turn would tell their children*. Then they would put their trust in God and would not forget His deeds but would keep His commands. They would not be like their forefathers—a stubborn and rebellious generation, whose hearts were not loyal to God, whose spirits were not faithful to Him."

This Psalm reiterates the command to teach the succeeding generations, but it also focuses on the idea that faithfulness in doing so will manifest itself in a righteous generation, even if previous generations were not righteous. Obviously, the Word of God does not lend credence to the belief that we are in a downward spiral that cannot be reversed. If parents once again take seriously their responsibility to educate their children, the degeneration can be halted.

The book of Proverbs offers a number of insights on parental teaching. "The fear of the Lord is the beginning of knowledge, but fools despise wisdom and discipline. Listen, my son, to your father's instruction and do not forsake your mother's teaching. They will be a garland to grace your head and a chain to adorn your neck. (Proverbs 1:7-9)"

The first point to be made from this passage is that reverence for the Lord is the *beginning* of knowledge. If we place our children in an educational setting that has no reverence for God, will they even receive the "beginning" of real knowledge? They may learn some facts and skills, but in what context? What will they do with these attainments? As Proverbs 9:10 reminds us, "The fear of the Lord is the beginning of wisdom, and knowledge of the Holy One is understanding." Consequently, if our children receive an "education" that ignores God, they will be missing the basis for all true knowledge, understanding, and wisdom. Contrasted with that bleak vision is the promise that a child who listens to the teaching of his father and mother (assuming it is biblical teaching, of course) will be blessed.

Proverbs 4 is filled with exhortations showing the need for parental instruction. "Listen, my sons, to a father's instruction; pay attention and gain understanding. *I give you sound learning,* so do not forsake my teaching. *When I was a boy in my father's house...he taught me* and said, 'Lay hold of my words with all your heart; keep my commands and you will live.'" Later in the same chapter, we read: "Listen, my son, accept what I say, and the years of your life will be many. *I guide you in the way of wisdom* and lead you along straight paths.... *Hold on to instruction,* do not let it go; guard it well, *for it is your life.* (1-4, 10-11, 13)" It is clear that this father is taking his responsibility seriously, and he remembers that his father had taught him—a linkage through the generations.

Proverbs 22:6 is a classic Scripture commanding parental responsibility for a child's education: "Train a child in the way he should go, and when he is old he will not turn from it." Often this Scripture is used as a sort of proof-text, providing comfort to those who have wayward children. We are to believe, this interpretation goes, that because we trained them properly, they certainly will return to the faith. While I believe proper biblical training gives the Holy Spirit more leverage to use on a non-Christian child, I cannot endorse the idea that it is an absolute promise of a return to the fold. Notice that the verse says, "when he is old he will not turn from it." One can only turn "from" something if one "has" something to turn "from." I believe this verse is actually a promise that *if* your parental teaching takes hold in your child's life, you can be assured that he or she will *remain* faithful to the end of his or her days. That is still an awesome promise and provides an even greater impetus for the importance of teaching our children in God's ways.

All of these Scriptures have been taken from the Old Testament. I have no problem with that; it is just as much the Word of God as the New Testament. But it is good to see that the same concepts carry over into the writings of the Apostle Paul. In Ephesians 6:4, Paul directs: "Fathers, do not exasperate your children; instead, bring them up in the training and instruction of the Lord." Paul, before he was saved, was a Jewish scholar of what we now call the Old Testament. As a Christian, he did not turn aside from Old Testament commands. His doctrine here is simply the Old Testament repeated.

We also get some insight on how the teaching of a mother made all the difference in the life of a young convert who became an apostle himself. When Paul wrote to Timothy, he said, "I have been reminded of your sincere faith, which first lived in your grandmother Lois and in your mother Eunice and, I am persuaded, now lives in you also. (II Timothy 1:5)"

Timothy's grandmother and mother were instrumental in his conversion, as Paul notes later in the same book: "But as for you, continue in what you have learned and have become convinced of, because you know those from whom you learned it, and how from infancy you have known the holy Scriptures, which are able to make you wise for salvation through faith in Christ Jesus. (II Timothy 3:14-15)"

Creatures of the state?

The biblical passages already examined establish the stewardship responsibility God has given to parents over their children in the realm of education. Yet that is no longer a secure position in our society. As we have abdicated parental responsibility, we have allowed the civil government to become the new parent.

There is not sufficient space here to provide a comprehensive history of the development of civil government's authority over education. It is enough to know that state control of education had grown sufficiently by the early 1920s that the Supreme Court had to weigh in on the issue. The state of Oregon had passed a law requiring all children to attend public schools. A Catholic religious school took the law all the way to the Supreme Court. In 1925, the Court ruled on this case, Pierce v. Society of Sisters. In its ruling, the Court did reaffirm the educational rights of parents, but the wording was ambiguous. The Court declared: "The child is not the mere creature of the State; those who nurture him and direct his destiny have the right, coupled with the high duty, to recognize and prepare him for additional obligations."

In one sense, it is comforting to know the Supreme Court says the child is not the mere creature of the state, but why the use of the word "mere"? This leaves the door open for the idea that all children *are indeed creatures of the state*, just not "merely" creatures of the state. And what does it mean that parents "prepare him for *additional* obligations"? Is it the state's right to take care of training children for basic obligations, while the parents handle anything "additional"? Again, this is unclear.

The last half of the 20th Century saw a multitude of Supreme Court cases in which the Court tried to figure out where to draw the line respecting the so-called "separation of church and state." In every case, education was the issue. These are the problems we invite when we bow to the state's presumed authority over the education of our children. Why does the state believe it has such authority? We have allowed it to believe so by acquiescing to its demands. Parents who take their biblical authority over

I am aware of only one biblical passage that deals with government-controlled education. It is found in the book of Daniel, where the king of Babylon, Nebuchadnezzar, took some of the captives from Judah and taught them "the language and literature of the Babylonians.... They were to be trained for three years, and after that they were to enter the king's service. (Daniel 1:4-5)" Babylon was a totalitarian regime and the "students" were educated to serve the government. That is hardly a model Christians should follow.

As Christians, we must reject the claims of the civil government regarding its control of our children's education. We must reassert the biblical mandate that parents have both the distinct privilege of and the responsibility for the education of the children given to them by God.

Reasserting the biblical mandate

How can Christian parents best fulfill the biblical mandate? One option is to send their children to Christian schools. That is the option my wife and I chose for our children. Although I am cognizant that I am writing primarily to homeschoolers, I do not want to minimize the value of a good Christian school. The best of these seek to work actively with the parents to offer an education consistent with the biblical mandate. Yet there are potential drawbacks to Christian schools. Consider the following:

1. It is hard to find a Christian school that is Christian in more than name only. Too often, schools started by churches are primarily reacting to the bad discipline and wrong teachings of the public schools, but offer little in the way of positive course development based on biblical principles. Chapel services and stronger discipline are great, but are not the essence of real biblical education.

2. The cost can be prohibitive for many parents. This drawback could be reduced significantly if those who choose Christian education could be exempted from paying taxes for the government system, but that is a public policy debate that will have to be waged at the national and state levels over a number of years.

Consequently, homeschooling has become for many parents the most viable option for ensuring that their children are brought up in the "training and instruction of the Lord." I believe it is also noteworthy that the Bible

we know today are not present in the Scripture. It was assumed that children would get what they needed from their parents or from the community of believers. One of the most interesting developments in homeschooling has been the informal bonding together of homeschooling parents to help one another with specialized subjects. This is particularly important when we face the very real problem of higher-level subjects that not all parents are capable of teaching.

We embark on the homeschooling endeavor principally because God wants our children brought up in His ways, but it is encouraging to be able to show the world that those who are homeschooled actually perform better than their counterparts in the government system, and even better than those who are in private schools. In March 1999, the Home School Legal Defense Association (HSLDA) released the results of a report it commissioned to study the effectiveness of homeschooling. The study was conducted by Dr. Lawrence M. Rudner, Director of the ERIC Clearinghouse on Assessment and Evaluation, an organization that maintains no affiliation with the HSLDA. Dr. Rudner examined 20,760 homeschoolers and their families.

Overall, the study showed that homeschoolers do exceptionally well when compared with students nationwide. As the HSLDA Web site (*www.hslda.org*) notes, "In every subject and at every grade level of the ITBS and TAP batteries, home school students scored significantly higher than their public and private school counterparts." Most astonishingly, the study reports, "On average, home school students in grades 1-4 perform one grade level higher than their public and private school counterparts. The achievement gap begins to widen in grade 5; by 8th grade the average home school student performs *four grade levels above the national average*." God's wisdom is confirmed by man's research!

I feel constrained to end this brief article with another warning from God's Word. In Hosea 4:1, 6, we are told:

"Hear the word of the Lord, you Israelites, because the Lord has a charge to bring against you who live in the land: 'There is no faithfulness, no love, no acknowledgment of God in the land.... My people are destroyed from lack of knowledge. Because you have rejected knowledge, I also reject you as my priests; because you have ignored the law of your God, I also will ignore your children.'"

According to this Scripture, if the knowledge of God is lost, if it is not transmitted to our children, we will be destroyed as a nation. Approximately 85 percent of our nation's children are in an educational system that has no knowledge of God. For this nation to survive, we who believe

that has no knowledge of God. For this nation to survive, we who believe the Word of God must take seriously the biblical mandate to educate our children in His truth. We take this challenge not for our own children exclusively, but for the sake of an entire people.

One final charge: "When the Son of Man comes, will He find faith on the earth? (Luke 18:8)" One of the real tests of our faith is whether we will be true to our responsibilities to our children. May He find that faith at work when He returns.

Dr. K. Alan Snyder is Associate Professor of Government at Regent University's Robertson School of Government, Virginia Beach, Virginia (www.regent.edu/ acad/schgov/asnyder/home.html).

Science Projects and the Homeschooler

by Laurie Callihan

Completing science projects as part of your homeschooling experience can be a great way for students of any age to enhance their understanding of this important subject area. A project can relate textbook work or a unit study to real-life situations. If done well, projects can also help a student gain mastery of a topic he enjoys. I have even found that doing a series of science projects is a great full-scale science curriculum for an entire year. Whether you children are experienced with doing science projects or not, I hope you will find the following ideas helpful.

My experience in conventional school teaching, as well as in my home school, have made me a believer in the value of science projects. However, I must admit that as a mother, I approach science-project season with much of the same (dare I say) dread that I'm sure many of you have experienced. Thoughts of the living room being overtaken by a genetics experiment involving lots of cages and small mammals can strike fear into the heart of the most devoted educator/parent. Then you have to provide endless trips to the variety store in search of poster board, magnets, pipe cleaners, and electrical tape (this is my children's favorite), and hours of helping (without, of course, actually doing the project yourself). It can be quite an undertaking.

So, in the interest of science-project sanity, let me suggest some tips:

1. Let your children own the project. By this I mean let them choose a topic that they are personally interested in, whether or not it fits into your scope and sequence for the year.

2. Provide lots of reference materials for ideas. Take a trip to the library. Let the children learn how to ask the librarian directly if they need help finding something. There are many, many books available that have hundreds of project ideas. Seek and ye shall find.

3. Have your student make a list of needed supplies, then shop once. Or you can provide a variety of household objects and have the child work from what you have.

4. Plan ahead for ample time to complete the project. Help the student make a timetable to maintain steady progress toward the goal.

5. Encourage, encourage, encourage!

6. Make sure the project is one the student can do with little help. Be sure it is age appropriate.

7. If the project doesn't work, don't give up! One of the most important aspects of real science is accounting for why something went wrong. If it can be redone, try again, but include an explanation of "trials gone wrong and why" with your finished project. Failing is part of learning, and malfunction is part of science! Use it to your learning benefit.

8. Include a written explanation (an explanatory paragraph, a poster, a notebook, etc.) with the finished working project. (You can even design an entire cross-curricular unit study to accompany your project if you like.)

9. Make sure the finished project is neat, but don't obsess over looks. The best projects I've seen have not been art masterpieces but rather have shown mastery of a topic.

The most important step in the science project is choosing the right project for the student. Allow lots of time for this. You might help generate ideas for project topics through brainstorming, wandering in the library, or family discussion. Of course your current course of study in your home school will probably provide ample opportunities to expand upon a subject. A parent's help is quite necessary and appropriate in helping to determine whether a given project is right for the student. Don't hesitate to help at this step, but try to resist the temptation to push the student into a project beyond his skill level. Remember: It is not appropriate for the parent to end up *doing* the project for the child. I have judged many science fairs and I am always more inclined to appreciate a simpler project that I know the student conquered on his own than a project in which the parent obviously did most of the work.

Learning about science can also be a great way to enhance your child's relationship with the Lord. A study in any area of science reveals God as a creator, sustainer, redeemer, and judge of the physical world. All science projects can have spiritual implications, so be sure to help the student make the connection between his study of science and his knowledge of the character of God.

I also encourage students to display their projects in some way to others. Your local support group may want to organize a science fair. Our Loving Education At Home chapter (Sauquoit LEAH) has sponsored a science/history fair for the last two years. Children of all ages (K-12) have contributed their projects and have been evaluated by a team of parent judges. We have chosen to include history projects in our fair to give students a broad range of options. This year some of our students also competed in a science fair sponsored by a local TV station. Three homeschoolers won second-place awards in their categories and gained the experience and confidence that comes with participating in a public event.

Finally, have fun! Science can be very exciting as you learn to discover, invent, explore, and explain. Whether you are an avid science buff or you barely get by with your science curriculum, I hope your family will make science projects a part of your homeschooling and that you will learn to enjoy this creative experience in learning!

(This article was originally published in the New York State Loving Education At Home Newsletter, Homeschool Report 8 (June 1997): 16-17.)

Our Personal Favorites

W e are often asked what curriculum we use or what books and games we have found helpful. We have compiled this list of our favorite things for homeschooling, but it is obviously not exhaustive. However, we have personally used—and liked—everything on this list at some time or another in our homeschooling adventure. We have not given sources for finding most of these items; they are usually sold in bookstores or homeschool supply catalogs. They are listed in no particular order.

Audiocassettes

Preparing for Adolescence, by James Dobson, Ph.D. Book and cassette series that helps parents deal with sexuality, peer pressure, self-esteem, and other issues.

Home and Family Business Workshop cassette tape set, by Gregg Harris. Seven cassettes help sort out the issues in starting a family business. Noble Publishing Associates, P.O. Box 2250, Gresham, OR 97080; (501) 667-3942. ISBN# 0-923463-87-9, $40.

Books

(See bibliography for complete publication information.)

Chronicles of Narnia, by C.S. Lewis. We love these books for all ages. The allegorical representation of the atonement is unparalleled.

For Dummies series (*Computer Programming for Dummies*, *Guitar Playing for Dummies*, *Creating Web Pages for Dummies*, and more) from IDG Books worldwide, Foster City, Calif. Great books for self-motivated learners, which we all are!

Children's books from the Institute for Creation Research, www.icr.org, on topics ranging from dinosaurs to Noah's Ark, have been excellent additions to our elementary library.

AlphaPhonics, by Samuel Blumenfeld. The basic reading primer that our children used to learn to read.

If the Foundations Are Destroyed, by K. Alan Snyder, Ph.D. The best single discourse on the origins of our republic in a single, readable volume, by the author of the Afterword to this book. A must-read for every homeschooling parent.

Teaching and Learning America's Christian History, The Christian History of the American Revolution, The Christian History of the Civil War, The Christian History of the Constitution of the United States of America, Rudiments of America's Christian History and Government, and *Webster's 1828 English Dictionary*. These reference books are published by the Foundation for Christian Education (FACE), 2946 25th Avenue, San Francisco, CA 94132.

History of Our United States, from A Beka Book. This 4th-grade textbook is Laurie's all-time favorite for teaching American history.

Economics in One Lesson, by Henry Hazlitt (New York: Crown, 1979). A terrific one-volume course for high schoolers, though we used it in college.

A Short History of the United States, by John Garraty. Another college text that our children studied in high school.

The American Adventure Series. Historical fiction for the elementary grades.

Peace Child and *Eternity in Their Hearts*, by Don Richardson. Inspiring books on missions.

Writer's Inc. and *Write Source 2000*. Absolute necessities for our homeschool writers.

Evidence That Demands a Verdict, by Josh McDowell. Essential material for defending Christian faith against secular arguments.

Curricula

Learning Language Arts Through Literature. This is one of the few curriculum systems that we actually stuck with from 3rd to 12th grades. It takes only a few minutes a day, yet covers the basics of language arts. We did lots of extra reading and writing, so we felt this was just enough to keep up with grammar and vocabulary. (Common Sense Press, Melrose, Fla.)

Great Editing Adventure. We found this a fun addition to our daily routine. It kept everyone up on spelling, vocabulary, and grammar in just about five minutes a day. We also were able to use this across a wide range of grades. (Common Sense Press, Melrose, Fla.)

Coloring the Classics. Our kids would all sit and listen to the musical selections while learning about the composers by coloring pictures in the books. Believe it or not, they ranged in age from eight to 14 when we used these, and we didn't get much complaining. (Color the Classics, Athens, Tenn.)

Videos

Nest Videos. These are animated videos of Bible stories and biographies of historical figures. They are very well produced.

Standard Deviants Review Videos. We found these tapes originally in an educational bookstore and then at Amazon.com. We have used the chemistry, geometry, French, and astronomy tapes and loved them. Most are about two hours long and provide very thorough reviews of the subjects, presented in an entertaining and memorable format. They are produced for college students, but we have used them for ages 10 and up. Also, they are produced secularly, so there are a few words and situations that are not appropriate, and they are evolution based; however, our children pointed out the problems to us (discernment pays).

Organizations

Summit Ministries. Jeremiah attended the two-week summer seminar for teens and loved it. It was well worth the time, money, and effort.

Institute for Creation Research. *Acts and Facts*, the free monthly newsletter, is a great resource for understanding issues in science. ICR also sponsors seminars and publishes numerous books.

Walk Through the Bible Ministries. We all participated in a Bible Walk-Through program on a Saturday at a local church a couple of years ago. This system for understanding the sequence and events of the Bible is incredibly useful.

Youth With A Mission. International missionary organization focusing on sending short-term and long-term missionaries without the need for years of higher education and theological degrees; one of the pioneers of the short-term mission movement. David was saved because he joined YWAM when he was 20. He knew that if he became a missionary, he would find God. It worked. All of our children have joined us on short-term mission trips to Mexico and Wisconsin with YWAM.

Christian Businessmen's Committee USA. We used the *Operation Timothy* series of discipleship books with our children.

Precept Ministries. We were blessed to be a part of a couple of Precept Bible studies taught by a dear friend when we lived in Iowa briefly last year. The Marriage Without Regrets (for married couples) and Someday a Marriage Without Regrets (for teens) studies were very valuable to our family.

The American Red Cross. Their first aid, CPR, and babysitting courses can't be beat.

Word of Life Camps. Our children have attended summer, basketball, and snow camps every year and have been challenged in their faith while having a great time.

Magazines

Highlights. Lots of good, clean fun.

Nature Friend. Great creation information and fun stuff for kids.

Creation Ex Nihilo. An excellent full-color magazine that proclaims the wonders of God's creation.

World. A current-events magazine with a Christian perspective.

Software

Dorling Kindersly Software. These CD-ROMs are very well produced and great to use for references.

Pro One Software. Good basic software in all sorts of subjects and levels, for review, for supplemental work or practice, or for main curriculum in some subjects from math to grammar.

PC Study Bible. Very easy to use.

SAT/ACT prep software from various sources.

Syracuse Language Systems Language Software. For learning foreign languages.

Math Blaster. Has all levels of math.

Games

Authors. A card game with names of literary figures and their books. Also, they now have historical figures, sports figures, etc.

Hail to the Chief. Teaches the presidential election process and U.S. geography.

Money Matters. This game from Larry Burkett teaches budgeting and financial concepts.

Geografacts. Teaches many geography facts.

Masterpiece. Teaches art appreciation.

Where in the World is Carmen Sandiego? Geography fun.

Jeopardy! Lots of facts in a fun format.

(Plus all the standard classics like Scrabble, Monopoly, Life, and jigsaw puzzles.)

Trips

Washington, D.C. We visited our nation's capital several times, visiting all the historical attractions. We also trooped all five children (at various ages, but starting very young) through the Capitol to visit our congressmen.

Philadelphia. We love walking on the floors of Independence Hall, the very same ones the United States' founding fathers walked on. The Franklin Institute is an incredible hands-on museum.

Boston. The Old North Church, Paul Revere's home, Fanueil Hall, The New England Aquarium, and so much more!

The Henry Doorly Zoo, Omaha. During our brief residence in the Omaha area, we visited this zoo several times. We have been to the spectacular San Diego Zoo many times (though our children have not), and we think the Omaha zoo is just as impressive. They have a great three-story indoor rain forest and a huge aquarium.

State capitals. We love to visit museums and our state legislators.

Florida. We live in upstate New York, where the winters get very long! We also love the Kennedy Space Center and the surrounding wildlife park.

Resources

Note: You can get educational games from Christian Book Distributors, diplomas from HSLDA, and graduation supplies from National Quality Products.

A Beka Book
P.O. Box 19100
Pensacola, FL 32523-9160
www.abeka.com
(800) 874-2352

Association on Higher Education and Disability (AHEAD)
Univ. of Massachusetts Boston
100 Morrissey Blvd.
Boston, MA 02125-3393
www.ahead.org
(617) 287-3880

Affordable Christian Textbooks and Supply
Suite 321, 262 Hawthorne Village
Vernon Hills, IL 60061
(847) 546-8028
(800) 889-2287

Alpha Omega Publishing
300 N. McKerny Ave.
Chandler, AZ 85226
www.homeschooling.com
(602) 438-2717
(800) 523-0988

American Adventure Book Club
P.O. Box 721
Uhrichsville, OH 44683
(740) 922-6045

Answers in Genesis
P.O. Box 6330
Florence, KY 410226330
www.AnswersInGenesis.org
(606) 727-2405
(800) 350-2405

Christian Book Distributors
P.O. Box 7000
Peabody, MA 01961-7000
www.Christianbook.com
(978) 977-5000

Christian Financial Concepts
P.O. Box 2377
Gainesville, GA 30503-2377
www.cfcministry.org
(770) 534-1000

Christian Liberty Academy Satellite Schools
502 W. Euclid Avenue
Arlington Heights, IL 60004-5402
www.homeschools.org
(708) 259-4403

Christian Light Education
P.O. Box 1212
Harrisonburg, VA 22801
(540) 434-0768

Color the Classics/Around N.Y.
in 80 Days
2611 Highway 39 W
Athens, TN 37303-6125
(423) 745–5788

Cornerstone Curriculum Project
2006 Flat Creek Place
Richardson, TX 75080
(972) 235-5149

Dorling Kindersley Family
Learning
4230 Fireside Dr.
Liverpool, NY 13090
(315) 652-8744

Elisabeth Elliot
10 Strawberry Cove,
Magnolia, MA 01930
(978) 525-3653

Focus on the Family
Colorado Springs, CO 80995
www.family.org
(800) A-FAMILY (800-232-6459)

Hewitt Homeschooling Resources
P.O. Box 9, 2103 B St.
Washougal, WA 98671-0009
(360) 835-8708
(800) 348-1750

Homeschool Dad Magazine
609 Starlight Dr.
Grand Junction, CO 81504
www.acsol.net/hsd/index.html
(970) 434-6946

Home School Legal Defense
Association (HSLDA)
P.O. Box 3000
Purcellville, VA 20134
www.hslda.org
(540) 338-5600

Institute for Creation Research (ICR)
10946 Woodside Ave. North
Santee, CA 92071
www.icr.org
(619) 448-0900

KONOS Character Curriculum
P.O. BOX 250
Anna, TX 75409
www.konos.com
(972) 924-2712

National Academy for Child
Development (NACD)
National Headquarters
P.O. Box 380
Huntsville, UT 84317
www.nacd.org
(801) 621-8606

NATHHAN (NATional
cHallenged Homeschoolers
Associated Network)
P.O. Box 39
Porthill, ID 83853
www.nathhan.org
(208) 267-6246

National Quality Products
10855 Lee Highway, Suite 300
Fairfax, VA 22030
www.nationalqp.com
(703) 691-8783

National Writing Institute
7946 Wright Road
Niles, MI 49120
(616) 684-5375

NEST/Family Media Resources
P.O. Box 734
Boylston, MA 01505
(508) 869-0174
(800) 988-6378

PowerGlide Language Courses
988 Cedar Ave.
Provo, UT 84604
www.power-glide.com
(801) 373-3973
(800) 596-0910

Precept Ministries
P.O. Box 182218
Chattanooga, TN 37422
www.precept.org
(423) 892-6814
(800) 763-8280

School of Tomorrow
P.O. Box 299000
Lewisville, TX 75029-9000
www.schooloftomorrow.com
(972) 315-1776
(800) 925-7777

Simplified Learning Products
P.O. Box 45387
Rio Rancho, NM 871745387
www.joyceherzog.com
(800) 745-8212

Sing 'N Learn
2626 Club Meadow
Garland, TX 75043
(214) 278-1973

Summit Ministries
P.O. Box 207
Manitou Springs, CO 80829
www.summit.org
(719) 685-9103

Teaching Home Magazine
P.O. Box 20219
Portland, OR 972940219
www.teleport.com/~tth
(800) 395-7760

The Book Peddler
P.O. Box 1960
Elyria, OH 44035-1960
(216) 323-9494
(800) 928-1760

Total Language Plus
P.O. Box 12622
Olympia, WA 98508
(360) 754-3660

Understanding Writing
1176 W. Satsop
Montesano, WA 98563-9328
(360) 249-2471

**University of Nebraska
Dept of Distance Education**
336 NCCE, P.O. Box 839800
Lincoln, NE 68583-9800
www.unl.edu/conted/disted/index.html
(402) 472-4321

**Usborne Books at Home/EDC
Publishing**
28 East Front St.
Marietta, PA 17547
www.usborne-usa.com
(717) 426-1437
(800) 705-8661

Walk Through the Bible Ministries
4201 North Peachtree Rd.
Atlanta, GA 30341
www.walkthru.org
(800) 868-9300

Weaver Curriculum
300 N McKemy Ave.
Chandler, AZ 85226
(888) 367-9871

Word of Life Fellowship, Inc.
P.O. Box 600
Schroon Lake, NY 12870
www.wol.org
(518) 532-7111

WorldView Academy
P.O. Box 310106
New Braunfels, TX 78131
(830) 620-5203

**Youth With A Mission—
Publishing**
P.O. Box 55787
Seattle, WA 98155
(425) 771-1153
(800) 922-2143

Web Sites

Following is a list of the Web sites we have referred to in the course of the book:

Chapter 1

www.britannica.com: *Encyclopaedia Britannica.*

Chapter 3

www.ywam.org: Youth With A Mission International.
www.wol.org: Word of Life International.
www.icr.org: the Institute for Creation Research.
www.masterbooks.org: creationist materials.
www.answersingenesis.org: creationist organization.
www.humanist.net/documents: Humanist Manifesto I and II.
www.creationresearch.org: the Creation Research Society.
www.christiananswers.net/summit: Summit Ministries.
www.worldview.org: WorldView Academy Leadership Camps.
www.walkthru.org: Walk Through The Bible Ministries.

Chapter 6

www.cfcministry.org: Christian Financial Concepts.
www.ansir.com and **www.keirsey.com:** free online personality tests.
www.maidinnz.com: GiftMaid Spiritual Gifts Software (shareware).
www.lhbc.com: Spiritual Gifts assessment from Lake Highland Baptist Church.
www.act.org: for DISCOVER and Realizing the Dream.
www.4-h.org: national 4-H.
www.jaintl.com: International Junior Achievement.

Chapter 9

www.nacd.org/articles/parexprt.html: article by the National Academy for Child Development stating that the home is the best educational environment for the special-needs child.
www.ets.org/disability.html: eligibility requirements for special accommodations when taking the college boards.
ww.collegeboard.com: official SAT Web site.
www.act.org: official ACT Web site.

www.teleport.com/nawca: employment for the physically disabled.

www.familyvillage.wisc.edu: disability-related resources.

www.disserv.stu.umn.edu/TC/Grants/COL/listing/disemp: employment resources for people with disabilities.

www.ablelink.org/public/default.htm: Ability Online, an electronic mail system that connects young people with disabilities or chronic illness to disabled and non-disabled peers and mentors.

www.ahead.org: Association on Higher Education and Disability.

www.familyvillage.com: a global community of disability-related resources.

www.acenet.edu/about/programs/access&equity/health/home.html: a national clearinghouse on higher education for people with disabilities.

www.nathhan.org: dealing with physically and mentally disabled children.

www.donjohnston.com: curricula, software, and solutions for students with disabilities.

www.rjcopper.com: computer resources for disabled children.

www.joyceherzog.com: resources for the learning disabled, gifted, and those who learn differently.

Chapter 11

www.familylearning.org: offers standardized tests.

Chapter 12

www.t-w-o.org: Third World Outreach, a short-term missions organization.

www.jobleads.org: InterChristo's Christian job referral site.

Chapter 13

www.collegeboard.org/ap/students/exam/process.html: reference site for scaling of Advanced Placement grading and other AP information.

www.apex.netu.com and www.pahomeschoolers.com: online Advanced Placement preparatory courses.

www.collegeboard.com/clep: College Level Exam Placement (CLEP) information.

www.petersons.com: distance learning opportunities.

Chapter 15

www.hslda.org: Web site of the Home School Legal Defense Association, featuring, "Home School Students Excel in College" and other articles.

Chapter 16

www.capnhq.gov: the Civil Air Patrol's national headquarters.

www.army.mil: United States Army.

www.navy.mil: Unites States Navy.

www.airforce.com: United States Air Force.
www.usmc.mil: United States Marine Corps.
www.uscg.mil: United States Coast Guard.

Chapter 17

www.icr.org: The Institute for Creation Research's site lists colleges that officially teach creationism in their undergraduate curriculum.
www.act.org: ACT web site.
www.act.org/cc/index.html: ACT's C³ Apply Service.
www.collegeboard.org/cc/toc/html/tocstudents000.html: helps students prepare and complete their college quests; includes a link to "The Path from Home School to College."
www.petersons.com/ugrad/evaluate.html: help writing college application essays.

Chapter 18

www.fafsa.ed.gov: offers free applications for federal student aid.
www.naas.org/faql.html: offers online applications for the Easley National Scholarship for homeschooled students.
www.neh.fed.us: the National Endowment for the Humanities.
www.thinkquest.org/tquic/tqic-student-steps-shtml: register here to compete for ThinkQuest's scholarship competition.
www.ncaa.org: National Collegiate Athletic Association; contains the requirements for homeschool athletic eligibility through the NCAA Eligibility Clearinghouse.
www.ed.gov/offices/OSFAP/students: college financial aid information.
www.petersons.com : college financial aid information.
www.collegeboard.com: college financial aid information.
www.freeschinfo.com: college financial aid information.
www.4scholarships.com: college financial aid information.
www.free-4u.com: college financial aid information.
www.collegescholarships.com: college financial aid information.

Chapter 19

www.act.org: DISCOVER software for career planning.
www.careers.crosswalk.com: a Christian-oriented site that we highly endorse (particularly because we have a weekly column on their homeschool page! Check it out at **homeschool.crosswalk.com**).

Afterword

www.regent.edu/acad/schgov/asnyder/home.html: The official Web site of our friend and contributor of the excellent afterword: "Parents and Education: The Biblical Mandate." Dr. Snyder has lots of great stuff to review including resources, links, and other writings of his own.

NCAA Eligibility Rules

Traditionally schooled students must be certified by the NCAA's Initial-Eligibility Clearinghouse as having met the initial eligibility requirements. Homeschooled student-athletes must be certified as having met initial-eligibility requirements through the initial-eligibility waiver process administered by the NCAA national office. These qualifications are required for student-athletes who wish to attend a Division I or Division II school. These are the ones who have the majority of NCAA scholarships available. Division III NCAA schools, as well as NCCAA (National Christian College Athletic Association) and NAIA (National Association of Intercollegiate Athletics) will have limited scholarships available directly through the college financial aid programs at the college. Parents should contact each school to learn how to qualify and apply for these resources for their child.

For Division I and Division II NCAA programs:

The initial-eligibility waiver process

A homeschooled student-athlete who attends an NCAA Division I or Division II institution has their eligibility status determined by having the college or university they attend submit to the national office an initial-eligibility waiver application. The waiver application must include the following items:

- ⮭ Homeschool transcript.
- ⮭ ACT/SAT test scores.
- ⮭ If available, evidence of outside assessment (tutors, tests graded by an outside agency, etc.).
- ⮭ Evidence that homeschooling was conducted in accordance with applicable state laws.

- ▲ Copies of the table of contents for books utilized in core courses (a sampling).
- ▲ Samples of work completed (tests, papers) by the student.
- ▲ NCAA Initial-Eligibility Clearinghouse form 48C (only if student attended some traditional schooling).

The initial-eligibility waiver application and the above information must be sent to the NCAA national office for processing by the member college or university. The member institution submitting the waiver application should receive a reply within three weeks of submission.

Whom to contact

The following NCAA office can answer questions about homeschooling as it relates to NCAA legislation and academic eligibility:

Membership Services, NCAA, P.O. Box 6222, Indianapolis, IN 46206; (317) 917-6222. Mention that you need help with homeschooling requirements.

Frequently asked questions by homeschooled student-athletes

Question: I attended one year of public schooling in grade 9 before I started being homeschooled in grades 10-12. Do I do anything different?

Answer: YES. You must register with the NCAA Initial-Eligibility Clearinghouse. Also, you will need to have your grade 9 high school submit your grade 9 transcripts to the NCAA Initial-Eligibility Clearinghouse for review. Additionally, you need to send the Clearinghouse a copy of your ACT/SAT test score(s). The Clearinghouse will determine the number of core courses and your grade-point average for grade 9 and return to you a form 48C. The NCAA member institution you attend will need a copy of this 48C to submit with your initial-eligibility waiver application.

Question: I did not keep good records from my homeschooled years, so I do not have copies of papers I wrote or exams I took. Can I still obtain a waiver?

Answer: YES. The process is made easier if you have samples of your homeschool work for grades 9-12. Do the best that you can to accumulate information which will assist the committee in determining the validity of your homeschool work as core courses. The committee will make its best judgment based on the available information.

Question: Is there any way I can get approved as a qualifier myself before I graduate from high school?

Answer: NO. High school graduation is one of the NCAA's initial-eligibility requirements. Therefore, no student-athlete is certified prior to graduation.

Question: Some coaches who are recruiting me are afraid that I won't get approved as a qualifier. What can I do to assure them I am taking all the right courses?

Answer: You will want to work with your parents or homeschool instructor to ensure that you are indeed taking the required number of core courses in the appropriate subject matters. You may want to consider providing the coach a copy of your homeschool transcript and ACT/SAT test score. Ultimately though, there is not a way for you as a homeschooled student-athlete to receive a "preliminary" certification of your high school credentials.

Question: Some of the materials the NCAA asks for, like evidence of outside assessment, I do not have. I did not have any outside assessment during my homeschooling. Will this hurt my chances of obtaining a waiver?

Answer: NO. The committee recognizes that each homeschool experience is unique, and would not expect a student-athlete to produce supporting documentation that was not part of your home school program. You should provide the materials that are applicable to your homeschool experience.

Question: What are some of the key elements the NCAA will look at to make my certification decision?

Answer: The primary factors that will be considered in determining whether you are a qualifier are: the required number of core courses successfully completed; ACT/SAT test score results; evidence of following state laws governing homeschooling; and outside assessment results (if available).

NCAA Division I freshman-eligibility standards, college entrants 1996-97 and thereafter

All student-athletes must register with the NCAA Initial-Eligibility Clearinghouse.

Qualifier

Can practice, compete, and receive athletic scholarship as a freshman.

Requirements:

- ⅄ Graduation from high school.
- ⅄ Can convert and combine subscores from an SAT taken before April 1, 1995, and an SAT taken April 1, 1995, or later to achieve the standard.

- The highest scores achieved on the verbal and mathematics section of the SAT or highest scores achieved on the four individual tests of the ACT may be combined to achieve the highest scores.
- The following GPA in 13 courses meeting the NCAA core course definition with the corresponding ACT sum or SAT total score is needed.

Core GPA	ACT (sum[1])	SAT (old)	SAT (new)
2.500 & above	68	700	820
2.475	69	710	830
2.450	70	720	840-850
2.425	70	730	860
2.375	72	740	860
2.350	73	750	870
2.325	74	760	880
2.300	75	770	900
2.275	76	790	910
2.250	77	800	920
2.225	78	810	930
2.200	79	820	940
2.175	80	830	950
2.150	80	840	960
2.125	81	850	960
2.100	82	860	970
2.075	83	870	980
2.050	84	880	990
2.025	85	890	1000
2.000	86	900	1010

[1]Previously, ACT score was calculated by averaging four scores. New standards are based on sum of scores.

High school core courses:
- At least 4 years English.
- At least 2 years math (one year algebra and one year geometry [or one year of a higher-level mathematics course for which geometry is a prerequisite]).

⅄ At least 2 years social science.

⅄ At least 2 years natural or physical science (including 1 lab course, if offered by any high school you attended).

⅄ At least 1 year of additional courses in English, math, or natural or physical science.

⅄ 2 additional academic courses in any of the above areas or foreign language, computer science, philosophy, or comparative religion.

Partial Qualifier

Does not meet standards for qualifier. Eligible to practice at institution's home facility freshman year. No competition during freshman year. Three seasons of competition. May receive institutional financial aid during freshman year, including athletics scholarship. Partial qualifiers may earn the fourth season of competition back if the student graduates prior to the start of the fifth academic year.

Requirements:

⅄ Graduation from high school.

⅄ The following core GPA in 13 core courses with the corresponding ACT sum or SAT total score is needed:

Core GPA	ACT (sum[1])	SAT (old)	SAT (new)
2.750 & above	59	600	720
2.725	59	610	730
2.700	60	620	730
2.675	61	630	740-750
2.650	62	640	760
2.625	63	650	770
2.600	64	660	780
2.575	65	670	790
2.550	66	680	800
2.525	67	690	810

[1]Previously, ACT score was calculated by averaging four scores. New standards are based on sum of scores.

Non-qualifier

No practice or competition during freshman year. Three seasons of competition. May receive institutional need-based aid only during the freshman year, which may not be from an athletics source.

Does not meet standards for qualifier or partial qualifier.

NCAA Division II freshman-eligibility standards, college entrants in the fall of 1997 and thereafter:

All student-athletes must register with the NCAA Initial-Eligibility Clearinghouse.

Qualifier

Can practice, compete, and receive athletic scholarship as a freshman.

Requirements:
- ▲ Graduate from high school.
- ▲ Have a GPA of 2.000 in 13 core academic courses.
- ▲ Must achieve a 68 (sum of scores on the four individual sets) on the ACT or a 700 on the SAT if taken before April 1, 1995, or an 820 on the SAT taken April 1, 1995, or later. Those entering in the fall of 1997 must achieve a 68 on the ACT.
- ▲ Can convert and combine scores from an SAT taken before April 1, 1995, and an SAT taken April 1, 1995, or later, to achieve the standard.
- ▲ The highest scores achieved on the verbal and mathematics section of the SAT or highest scores achieved on the four individual tests of the ACT may be combined to achieve the highest scores.

High school core courses:
- ▲ At least 3 years English.
- ▲ At least 2 years math.
- ▲ At least 2 years social science.
- ▲ At least 2 years natural or physical science (including 1 lab course, if offered by any high school you attended).
- ▲ At least 2 years additional courses in English, math, or natural or physical science.

⮞ 2 additional academic courses in any of the above areas or foreign language, computer science, philosophy, or comparative religion.

Partial qualifier

Eligible to practice at institution's home facility freshman year. No competition during freshman year. Will have four years of eligibility during college career. Can receive institutional financial aid, including athletics scholarship, during freshman year.

Requirements:

⮞ Does not meet requirements for qualifier.

⮞ Graduate from high school.

⮞ Successfully completed the 13 core courses with a minimum 2.000 core grade-point average or

⮞ Attained a minimum 68 ACT (sum of scores) or 700 SAT (if taken before April 1, 1995) or 820 SAT (if taken April 1, 1995 or later). Scores of 66 or 67 will be accepted for spring 1996 high school graduates who achieve their scores on a national test date prior to August 1996.

Nonqualifier

Cannot practice or compete during freshman year. Will have four years of eligibility during college career. May not receive athletics scholarship freshman year but can receive regular need-based financial aid if the school certifies that aid was granted without regard to athletic ability.

Has not graduated from high school or did not receive the core-curriculum grade-point average and SAT/ACT score required for a qualifier or partial qualifier.

Reprinted with permission of NCAA Documents.

Forms You May Reproduce

Summer Reading Contest

1. Make a list of five books to be read by _____ (date). You must include one biography (or autobiography), one non-fiction, one classic, one fiction, and another of your choice. You will get 25 points for turning in your reading list by _____ (date).

2. Each book read will earn 25 points.

3. Every page over 250 total pages will count for 1 point.

4. A written book report will earn up to 100 points (these will be graded on a 100-point scale and you will receive the amount of points of the grade). You may do book reports on all five books if you wish.

5. All points will be canceled if all five books are not completed.

6. Contestants who earn 500 points will receive a prize of _____ (list prize).

7. The contestant with the most accrued points as of _____ (date) will earn _____ (list grand prize).

High School Plan

Subject	Level	Credits	Course Requirements	Date Completed	Grade
English		Min. 4			
	I	1			
	II	1			
	III	1			
	IV	1			
Social Studies		Min. 4			
	I	1			
	II	1			
	III	1			
	IV	1			
Math		Min. 2			
	I	1			
	II	1			
	III	1			
	IV	1			
Science		Min. 2			
	I	1			
	II	1			
	III	1			
	IV	1			

High School Plan (continued)

Subject	Level	Credits	Course Requirements	Date Completed	Grade
Foreign Lang.		No Min.			
	I	1			
	II	1			
	III	1			
	IV	1			
Fine/Prac. Arts		Min. 1			
	I	1			
	II	1			
	III	1			
	IV	1			
Phys. Ed./ Health		Min. 2			
	I	1			
	II	1			
	III	1			
	IV	1			

High School Plan (continued)

Subject	Level	Credits	Course Requirements	Date Completed	Grade
Electives					
–	I	1			
–	II	1			
–	III	1			
–	IV	1			

➤ This form is for planning use and represents basic requirements. See chapters on college or career prep for specific course requirements for those routes.

➤ One credit in high school is traditionally accepted to be one year of a subject working 40 minutes per day for 180 days (or 120 hours).

➤ Levels (I – IV) are used rather then grade levels (9-12) to allow for freedom in when subjects are studied.

➤ At least 20 credits are recommended for graduation.

Progress Report

Student: _____   Age: _____

Grade Level: _____

Date: _____

Grading Period: _____

SUBJECT	MATERIAL COVERED	EVALUATION

Secondary school record/transcript

School: _____   Home Address: _____

Name: _____   _____

Parents: _____   Home Phone: _____

D.O.B.: _____   Sex: ___   SSN: _____

Date of Graduation: _____

Grade Level	Course Description	Credit Hours	Grade	Points

Grade Level 9   Total: GPA:

Grade Level 10   Total: GPA:

Grade Level 11   Total: GPA:

Grade Level 10   Total: GPA:

Total Credit Hours =   Total Points =   Cumulative GPA =

Secondary school record/transcript (continued)

Extracurricular Activities/Awards

_____
_____
_____
_____
_____
_____
_____
_____

Work Experience

_____
_____
_____
_____
_____
_____
_____
_____
_____

Hobbies:

_____
_____
_____
_____
_____
_____
_____
_____
_____

Tests/Scores:

_____
_____
_____
_____
_____
_____
_____
_____

Note: For the purpose of our home school the following grading system was used:

Bibliography

Books

Arthur, Kay. *Spiritual Gifts*. Chattanooga, Tenn.: Precept Ministries, 1999.

Blumenfeld, Samuel L., *Alpha-phonics: A Primer for Beginning Readers*, Old Greenwich, CT: Devin-Adair, 1983.

Bunyan, John. *The Pilgrim's Progress*, Chicago: Moody Press, 1985.

Burkett, Larry, and Lee Ellis. *Your Career in Changing Times*. Chicago: Moody Press, 1993.

———. *Finding the Career That Fits You,* Chicago: Moody Press, 1998.

Conn, Harry. *The Four Trojan Horses of Humanism*, Milford, MI: Mott Media, 1982.

Cruden, Alexander. *Cruden's Complete Concordance*. Peabody, Mass.: Hendrickson, 1988.

Elliott, Elisabeth. *Passion and Purity*, Old Tappan, NJ: Fleming H. Revell, 1984.

Ellis and McNeilly. *Guide to College Majors and Career Choices*. Gainesville, Ga.: Christian Financial Concepts, 1999.

Friesen, Gary, and J. Robin Maxson. *Decision Making and the Will of God: A Biblical Alternative to the Traditional View*. Portland, Ore.: Multinomah Press, 1981.

Garraty, John Arthur. *A Short History of the American Nation*. New York: Harper and Row, 1973.

Good News for Modern Man. New York: American Bible Society, 1985.

Hall, Verna M. *Christian History of the Constitution of the United States of America*. San Francisco: Foundation for American Christian Education, 1966.

———. *The Christian History of the American Revolution*. San Francisco: Foundation for American Christian Education, 1976.

Halley, Henry G. *Halley's Bible Handbook*. Grand Rapids, Mich.: Zondervan, 1979.

Harris, Joshua. *I Kissed Dating Goodbye*. Sisters, Ore.: Multinomah, 1995.

Hazlitt, Henry. *Economics in One Lesson*. New York: Pocket Books, 1948.

Hitchner, Kenneth, and Anne Tifft-Hitchner. *Counseling Today's Secondary Student*. Englewood Cliffs, N.J.: Prentice Hall, 1996.

Isbell, Allen C. *War and Conscience*. Abilene, Tex.: Biblical Research Press, 1966.

Klicka, Christopher, *Homeschool Students Excel in College*, Purcellville, VA: NHERI Publications, 1999.

Lewis, C.S., *Mere Christianity*. New York: MacMillan Publishing Company, Inc., 1960.

———. *The Chronicles of Narnia*. New York: Harper Mass Market Paperbacks, 1994.

———. *The Screwtape Letters*. New York: Simon & Schuster, 1996.

The Living Bible. Wheaton, Ill.: Tyndale House Publishing, 1976.

Lore, Nicholas. *The Pathfinder: How To Choose or Change Your Career for a Lifetime of Satisfaction or Success*. New York: Fireside, 1998.

Ludy, Eric, and Leslie Ludy. *His Perfect Faithfulness*. Littleton, Colo.: Harvest Books, 1996.

Mangrum, Charles T., ed. *Peterson's Colleges with Programs for the Learning Disabled*. Princeton, N.J.: Peterson's Guides, 1985.

McDowell, Josh. *Evidence That Demands a Verdict*. San Bernadino: Here's Life, 1979.

———. *More Than a Carpenter*. Wheaton, Ill.: Tyndale House, 1987.

McDowell, Josh, and Bob Hostetler. *Don't Check Your Brains at the Door*. Dallas: Word Publishing, 1992.

Moore, Judy Hull. *The History of Our United States*. Pensacola : A Beka Book, 1998.

Morris, Henry and John Whitcomb. *The Genesis Flood*, Phillipsburg, N.J.: Presbyterian and Reformed Publishing Company, 1989.

Morris, Henry. *Scientific Creationism*. Green Forest, Ark.: Master Books, 1996.

———.*The Genesis Record*. Grand Rapids, Mich.: Baker Book House, 1981.

———.*Many Infallible Proofs*. Green Forest, Ark.: Master Books/New Leaf Press, 1996.

Myers, Jeff. *Of Knights and Fair Maidens*, Dayton, Tenn.: Heartland Educational Consultants: 1996.

———. *The Courtship Revolution*, Dayton, Tenn.: Heartland Educational Consultants: 1996.

Nave, Orville J. *Nave's Topical Bible*. McLean, Va.: MacDonald, 1983.

New American Standard Bible. La Habra, Calif.: Lockman Foundation, 1971.

New Century Version Bible. Nashville: Word Books, 1991.

New International Version Bible. Grand Rapids, Mich.: Zondervan Publishing, 1994.

New King James Version Bible. Nashville: Word Books, 1990.

Phillips, Michael, and Judy Phillips. *Best Friends for Life*. Minneapolis: Bethany House, 1997.

Ray, Brian. *Homeschooling on the Threshold*. Salem, Ore.: NHERI Publications, 1999.

Reece, Colleen L.. *The American Adventure Series*. Urhicksville, Ohio: Barbour and Co., 1998.

Richardson, Don. *Peace Child*. Glendale, Calif.: G/L Regal Books, 1974.

———. *Eternity in Their Hearts*. Glendale, Calif.: G/L Regal Books, 1981.

Rudner, Lawrence. *Homeschooling Works Pass it On!*. Purcellville, Va.: Home School Legal Defense Association, 1999.

Schaeffer, Francis A.. *How Should We Then Live*. Old Tappan, N.J.: Fleming H. Revell, 1976.

Sclafani, Annette Joy, and Michael J. Lynch. *The College Guide for Students with Learning Disabilities*. Miller Place, N.Y.: Laurel Publications, 1998.

Snyder, K. Alan. *If The Foundations are Destroyed*. Marion, Ind.: Principle Press, 1994.

Strong, James, and Stephen L. Nelson. *The New Strong's Concise Concordance of the Bible*. Nashville: Thomas Nelson, 1985.

Sebranek, Patrick, *Write Source 2000: A Guide to Writing, Thinking, and Learning*. Burlington, Wis.: Write Source Educational Publications, 1995.

Sebranek, Patrick, et al. *Writers Inc.: A Student Handbook for Writing and Learning*. Lexington, Mass.: Write Source, 1996.

Slater, Rosalie J. *Rudiments of America's Christian History and Government*. San Francisco: Foundation for American Christian Education, 1994.

———. *Teaching and Learning America's Christian History*. San Francisco: Foundation for American Christian Education, 1965.

Straughn, Charles T. II, ed. *Lovejoy's College Guide for the Learning Disabled*. New York: Monarch Press, 1985.

Thompson Chain Reference Bible. Indianapolis: Kirkbride Bible and Technology, 1990.

Vine, William E., William White, Jr., and Merrill F. Unger. *Vine's Complete Expository Dictionary of Old and New Testament Words*. Chattanooga, Tenn.: AMG Publishers, 1995.

Wagner, C. Peter. *Your Spiritual Gifts Can Help Your Church Grow*. Ventura, Calif.: Gospel Light/Regal Books, 1997.

Webster, Noah. *Noah Webster's 1828 Dictionary*. San Francisco: Foundation for American Christian Education, 1967.

Young, Robert. *Young's Analytical Concordance to the Bible*. Peabody, Mass.: Hendrickson, 1993.

Journals

Journal of the National Academy for Child Development. National Academy for Child Development. Ogden, Utah.

Summit Journal. Summit Ministries. Manitou Springs, Colo.

C

D